Aidan Higgins was born in Celbridge, County Kildare, in 1927, and educated at James Joyce's College, Clongowes Wood.

He came to London to work as an assembly-line hand in factories, working by day and night in the early 1950s. He later joined a marionette company, touring in Germany, Yugoslavia and Holland, then in Africa from the Cape to the Congo. He now lives in London.

AIDAN HIGGINS

Langrishe, Go Down

PALADIN
GRAFTON BOOKS
A Division of the Collins Publishing Group

LONDON GLASGOW
TORONTO SYDNEY AUCKLAND

Paladin
Grafton Books
A Division of the Collins Publishing Group
8 Grafton Street, London W1X 3LA

Published in Paladin 1987

First published in Great Britain by
Calder & Boyars Ltd 1966

ISBN 0-586-08566-1

Printed and bound in Great Britain by
Collins, Glasgow

Set in Ehrhardt

To Jill Damaris

Contents

III
1938

I
1937

'If I fhould set downe the fluttifh and uncleanly obfervations of the Irifh, as well as of the men, as the Women, but efpecially of thofe manners & Conditions whereunto they invre themfelves in the remote Places of the Countrey, I might fet downe fuch unreverent & loathfome Matter, as were unfit for every queafie stomacke to understand of.'

Barnaby Rich
A New Description of Ireland
1610.

1

The lights in the bus burned dim, orange-hued behind opaque bevelled glass; ranged below the luggage racks they lit up the advertisement panels with repeated circles of bilious light. A white face that never seemed to turn away was watching her in the glass. She sat by the window midway down the bus, feeling her stomach beginning to turn over already. The hot engine fumes mingled with the smell of strong shag tobacco, with the cigarette smoke which she detested most of all, and with other poisons breathed out by two-score labouring lungs. In a great stench of perspiring and unwashed bodies, they were there, all about her. In the stuffy, smoke-laden atmosphere others more robust than she experienced no discomfort, giving off their warm bands of heat and well-being. Then the glass blurred once more; drops of moisture began to condense, wet lanes of it trickled down; the face broke up and vanished.

Her hands were open on her lap, one upon the other in buttoned kid grey gloves that spoke of better times, the return half ticket issued by the Irish Omnibus Company tucked in the vee of her left glove. The windows were shut fast and the passengers, saying little, well contented, smoking, sat shoulder to shoulder, exhaling carbon dioxide fumes. The temperature within the bus, toiling and moiling along, was of a stifling collective human warmth that she found distasteful, and in that malodorous place she sat alone. Crowded places did not suit her, did not agree with her claustrophobia; bus-travel in particular made her ill.

She took off her gloves. When she brought the palms of her hands together they were damp; she parted them, touched her forehead and found it damp too. She felt definitely queasy. The evening newspapers ran war headlines: Venta Deldiablo and

Portalrubio had fallen; Madrid had been bombed again by insurgent artillery.

The conductor came slowly, collecting the fares. When her turn came she surrendered up her ticket without a word, not lifting her eyes, seeing only the worn leather satchel and the clipping apparatus. His blunt nicotine-stained fingers took it; examining it he went away, saying something civil to her. She did not reply.

Well muffled up against the elements, the passengers read that the Italians were arming, that Herr von Ribbentrop had made a provocative speech at the Leipzig Fair, that the Pope had graciously given audience to Monsignor Pisani, Archbishop of Tomi. General Franco had spoken on the destined march of free Spain. At Melbourne, in cool summer weather, Australia had retained the Ashes. Repeated circles of bilious light, warm gusts of sweetish nauseous air.

The *Evening Herald* was spread out on her lap over the travelling rug. The pages were turned, for all the world to see that Venta Deldiablo and Portalrubio had fallen, that the city of Madrid had been bombed again. She read that a Kildare farmer named Furness had lost thirteen head of cattle in the snow blizzards (sheltering from the storms they had eaten yew and died). The Dublin welder who had killed his girl friend was pleading insanity.

The world was in a bad way. Full of calamities, real or imaginary, impending or completed. The heavy wheels ran on. Let it, she thought, let it be. Let it all happen, and as violently as possible – with the utmost ferocity. Let it snow, too. She would not live to see another war.

The warmth of the crowded saloon, its incessant motion, the smell of sweat and long-lain-in clothes, all this made her uneasy in the stomach. She sought to control it by sucking peppermints. For the distressed, she thought, life is just a scourge. I'll have to get off at the next stop.

She took another quick gulp of foul air. The warmth of the narrow and enclosed saloon with its advertisements for sausages and shoes, its smells of sweat and stout, of long-lain-in clothes, its humid bodily odours, its incessant motion, all this made her very uneasy in the stomach.

She kept sucking a spearmint, hoping it would pass, her mouth dried-up. Dejected, in the closeness she swallowed – swallowed again. Something began to throb inside her, perspiration broke out on her forehead. She swallowed hard. The moist convolutions of her insides seemed to rise into her throat. This was dreadful. Clenching her fists she hung on, staring before her, striving with all her will to master the rising nausea. It would be shameful, in public here like this, shameful.

Leaning forward she pressed her fingers to her closed eyes, inhaling slowly. The babble of voices reached her ears in weary pulsations – an oncoming and departing roar of sound. Slow and shallow (her life depended on it) she breathed in the faint scent of herself, her clothes: a fading odour of mountain fern. After a while the nausea began to pass away. She felt less constricted; now she could go on. With the heel of her glove she cleared the glass again, looked out. The night was clear, with the moon travelling fast over the trees. As she watched it fled into powdery white alps of cloud over the river, appeared to be land then, low hills, which disappeared as they passed along.

Close to her ear a man's voice said:

– You'll be the right ram when you get started, it breathed hotly. Oh ho the right ram, I'm telling you, it said with insufferable familiarity.

A strong male fist struck the back of her seat, sending her heart pounding up into her chest. A second voice said weakly:

– Ah now I'd be too shy. I'd be mortified, I'm that shy.

– *Shy!* the masterful voice said. Do you know *I* was shy ... desperate shy. But I got over it, and so will you.

The big thick lug of a fellow who sat before her wearing a soiled gaberdine raincoat very greasy about the collar now opened his mouth to its utmost capacity in a noiseless yawn. The bossy bones of his so cruelly barbered skull moved in recoil.

– Ah now I don't know, the voice said, doubtful.

– Amn't I telling you? the other said with the vigour of a man who had driven his bull through many a gap. You get over it, and (low innuendo) you'll feel the better for it after. And begob so will she. Tip her a sup of the blood while it's warm. In like a lion and out like a lamb.

Both voices joined in a low laugh. The upholstery at her back shook as the men, transported with merriment, drove their knees into it. The shy one tittered, unable to quell it, embarrassed yet taken with the notion of a willing and submissive womankind at his disposal. She felt herself getting hot in the face and under her clothes. This was too much. Her ears were burning. Beneath her feet the floor was vibrating; the thrust and crude power of it went up through her, the double beat of the big rear wheels.

– Oh the right ram!

The weak reflection of her face gave no indication that she had heard or understood. Do not stare back at me with those haggard, squinting eyes.

Snow had fallen on the outskirts of Madrid during the previous night. All was quiet on the Jarama front. The Italians were arming. At home, the Rosary of the Men's Sodality at the Pro-Cathedral of St Nicholas, Galway, were offering up their prayers for the success of the forces of Christ in Spain.

Voices. A hubbub from the world of sound; world of crush and sunder.

The dirty unequivocal sounds of strife, of explanation and of counter-explanation. Counsel said that the slashing of the girl was the act of a maniac. He had almost severed the head from her body with a cut-throat razor. A witness produced a section of the bloody wallpaper from the passage of the house along which she had run. Dr Cromie of Jervois Street Hospital gave evidence of the injuries. The accused was pleading insanity. He had known Ellen Boland for about nine months before her death; she was his sweetheart and he was very fond of her. Or had been.

A mute face watched her; Helen Langrishe turned away. The stocky one sitting in front of her folded his *Evening Mail* once, then again, stowing it away in his bulging pocket. Without the aid of hand or handkerchief he cleared his head, snorting back loose phlegm into his nasal passage in an unrestrained manner and swallowed it down. He lay back at his ease then, staring at the notice which said Spitting Prohibited, *Seiliú toirmiscthe*, in flowering grot.

Cattle-jobber; the man in the gap. A life given to bullocks and heifers, stringers. Bone and gristle. Stewing fat. Helen Langrishe looked away. The heavy wheels ran on. She cleared the glass once more with the heel of her glove and stared out through the port-hole at the countryside now coming into sight on the left hand.

The conductor, worn leather satchel hanging down, was talking to another passenger, his hand outstretched for a fare. She regretted not answering him. The way it was at Springfield, they had got out of the way of exchanging common civilities.

Voices began an argument behind her, quarrelling over prices, livestock and feed, taking the Holy Name in vain. Natives of Kildare (she recognized the grudging inflections and flattened vowels). I fukken well did dis, I fukken well did dat . . . I fukken well nivver.

The bombardment of Madrid (she read) had been, as previously, valueless from a military standpoint. The Italians were arming. Air-bases were under construction in Sardinia, in Sicily, in Southern Italy, as well as on the fortified island of (she screwed up her eyes, read with difficulty) Pantelleria, in an attempt to control the narrows between Sicily and Italy.

They were travelling out by Inchicore and the Phoenix Park on an icy and treacherous road. The People's Gardens, Clancy Barracks, Islandbridge Gate, they had all been passed unnoticed. Now a dingy mountain of refuse hove into sight; on the bluff beyond lights shone from a skyline cluster of mean cottages. Beyond that, what? Inchicore railway sidings?

Slag pits; good trains in a siding. The stench of sulphur, shadows of carriage windows sliding alongside dust-grimed walls, drawing in towards Kingsbridge Station.

Greyish vapours clung to the side of the dump. Long strings of whitish, smoking matter had been tipped down the sides. A frozen black field stretched away, its potato drills stiffened with hoar frost; then a glass house shining in Mount Street Market Gardens. A tattered scarecrow with straw for hair and hat awry stood with outstretched arms. The river beyond wound calm and shallow between the fields. Moonlight glittered on the water, pure and austere, cold, far away, with a second moon down in the river. Why was it considered unlucky to see the new moon through glass? She would have seen it anyway, no escaping it, its cold unearthly light would have pierced her eyeballs.

In the turning head-lights a small white church came on, framed

15

in glass; now going by; she saw chill statues of Christ the King and the Virgin enthroned in a grotto, staring with petrified stone faces over the gate; then the dog-track. The bus veered left, crossing a narrow bridge by the stadium. Lucan lay ahead.

Beyond the dead man Murray's low pub she saw, some way ahead, moving tram lights flickering on the wall. They were overtaking an outward-bound tram on her side, barging along on its swaying head-rail. As the distance narrowed she could hear its wheels grinding fiercely on the tracks. It looked odd and topheavy, quite weird, so far out in the country.

Soon they had drawn abreast and the passengers on the lower deck had an opportunity of staring at her. She shrank back, averting her head. It was three-quarters empty. They ran level, the driver standing exposed on his platform saluting them. Then it was left behind. Its lights, advertisements and white human faces fled back into the dark.

She herself had only to travel a short distance in a tram to feel sick, what with the lateral swaying and shaking and the uncertainty of it all.

Now they were going by the Ball Alley pub and Sarsfield's demesne, taking the hill out of Lucan village. Other voices, female voices, more subdued, whispered across from her. Whispering about nothing.

– Aye, a grand woman . . .
– There's a bit of grey in her hair . . .
– Aye, a bit of grey . . .

The road, forking left again, became narrower as it ran between the golf links and the embankments of the Spa Hotel. It followed the boundary of the course rising on the left in hilly fairways and shadowed bunkers. In the daytime she had seen poor ragged women down on their knees weeding the greens. The bus was running below the Crescent. High above it the Spa dome, lit from the hotel yard, glided by. Dr Broadbent lived there, and Miss Perry. The sulphurous waters of the Spa were reputed to rival those of Aix-la-Chapelle, or Bruges. The road turned right. Now they were travelling directly towards Back Weston. Donycomper lay beyond; and beyond that again the decline would take them into Celbridge village. A signpost pointed towards it.

At Donycomper cross-roads the bus stopped and five passengers alighted. The two from behind went tramping out. She avoided looking at them. Cold night air poured in when the conductor threw open the concertina doors at the back, and the pall of tobacco smoke, dense as fog by now, broke up before it and was swept away in the outdraught. Then the concertina door rattled shut and they drove on.

Presently they were crossing the bridge at Celbridge. The lights of the village again. Broken mill windows and a date on stone; hardly seen, now gone. They turned onto the Clane road. The noise of their passing volleyed off deserted mill walls. Travelling out between Oakley Park and the abbey. A high pebbledashed wall surmounted by battlements, crowned with ivy, broken glass, overhung by yew boughs. Behind the wall the lawns sloped down to the river, towards a plantation of old trees, gravelled walks by the river, shrubberies of rhododendron, laurel, a giant cedar from Japan, Vanessa's bower.

The bus went into low gear at the foot of the hill. A change before death. The wind moaned through the yews beyond the wall. No sign of a living soul. Brief life, she thought, brief life, breathed on for a while, allowed to live, then blotted out. Paisley's corner now . . .

They rounded it, ascending the hill. The wall gave way to open space, then began again. The Gaelic football field, the gate-lodge and wooded grounds of the Charter School for young Protestant ladies. Brady's corner, another glass-topped wall. Helen Langrishe rose up.

She had the rug folded and ready. Struggling to her feet she said Excuse me to the woman sitting beside her, turned, confused, raising her hand in a nervous signal. The conductor caught her eye, nodded, waited.

When she was clear of the seat, he struck the bell twice with the flat of his hand. As she made her way along the aisle, the bus began to slow down, coming to a halt directly opposite the white front gates of Springfield. Leaning out the conductor helped her down, his hand at her elbow. With relief she felt under her feet again solid ground. His hand released her arm.

– Good night, lady . . . And safe home.

– Good night, Helen said.

The door shuttled to. She saw curious faces pressed to the glass; then it and they were gone in a hot backwash of petrol fumes. Safe home. She stood there in the cold by the postbox in the wall, watching the ruby-red tail-light receding out of sight. Did it pass through Straffan or Clane or Prosperous or Naas, on its way to Edenderry? She didn't know. She had lived in the county all her life but didn't know the bus-route on this by-road. Single-decker omnibuses started at specific hours, as per timetable, from Aston Quay and stopped, on request, at Springfield gate. That was sufficient for her.

She waited a little longer, holding the handbag to her chest, waiting for her breathing to slow down. The white bars of the gate stood out of the darkness across the road. She crossed slowly.

Other noises began, timidly at first, then with increasing volume. The plantation stretched away between the gate lodges. Branches were swaying and causing a commotion overhead, the telegraph wires adding their *miserere* above the ditch; pushing open the side gate she passed through onto the avenue. She stopped to listen. The tall pine tree by the gate-lodge creaked and groaned down all its length. A breeze surged through its upper boughs, abating only to return with increasing force, then the murmuring and groaning began all over again. She closed the side-gate behind her.

She saw firelight dancing on the kitchen walls and over the ceiling, and heard the nearer murmur of prayers. The Keegan family were reciting the Holy Rosary before retiring for the night. The old couple, their three sons and two gormless daughters were kneeling on the bare flagstones before the turf fire. She heard the old man's rusty voice give out the invocation. The family took up the response, their different voices mingling together, the mother's highest of all, sweet-toned, pathetic; they were creating it link by link, Paternoster by Paternoster, Ave Maria by Ave Maria, Gloria Patri by Gloria Patri, a decade at a time, an oratorio for the voices of the humble, the good in heart. She stood listening. It moved her deeply; it always had. What she was listening to, said in secret, had

18

held the people together, the faith of poor and oppressed Catholic Ireland in the penal times.

She moved on into the darkness under the trees. The wind sighed through the uppermost branches; all the tall pines swaying and lamenting. As a young girl she had listened to it, as a young woman, and later; it made no difference. Over Donycomper the same wind was stirring the leaves. Emily was there, hidden from them. She went on, and all about her heard the sighing – the prayers becoming fainter, the stirrings in the plantation louder, sounds that evoked in her feelings difficult to express, more difficult still to dispel. The dank smell of mould, of fallen leaves now rotting on the drive, decayed in the sharp night air. She went forward slowly, putting one foot before the other in the direction she imagined the avenue inclined, but had not gone fifteen paces when she stumbled against the grass verge, lost her balance and fell, clutching at nothing.

She lay on the ground with her face pressed to the earth which had begun to freeze again, not offering to stir. The grip of her handbag was over her wrist; she had held onto it for dear life.

She began to struggle to her feet again, collecting her gear together, and went on. The avenue lay ahead, paler than the surrounding darkness, going in an arc towards the back lodge. At the apex of the curve stood the house; it showed up against a pale sky, but lay itself in darkness. Soon she was clear of the trees. She went on slowly between the palings, thinking of Imogen and Lily; they would be sitting over the fire in the study waiting for her. They would have to talk – Lily too – talk together, discuss what was best to be done, and make some arrangements to change their ways, for the old impossible life was ending. They would have to sell the house, that was all there was to it. Solicitors, land-agents, undertakers – as they came tramping in, the Langrishe world was falling down. No matter, she told herself, holding onto the paling, resting, no great matter now.

Then she was walking over gravel: she felt it bite into her rubber soles, and sensed more than saw the side shrubbery ending as she came out before the house. The front avenue had ended where the paling curved away from her. She walked through the shadows of the house as though she had no head, no eyes to see, passing unlighted windows, impenetrable darkness. The front porch and niches on either side were pitch black.

As she passed the hall door she heard light, sprinting feet spurning the gravel – something was coming towards her from the side of the house. She stopped, her heart fluttering. Was it some ruffian, through a careless word let fall, come to waylay her before her own front door? Something hard whipped her thigh. She bent quickly, panting, and a live wet thing was thrust energetically into her hand.

– Oh Mother of God! she cried, quailing, all her courage gone. Protect me.

Her fingers closed fiercely over the animal's wetted muzzle, and she held on until it whimpered.

– Be good, she whispered. Be a good dog now, she said, trying to calm herself. Now go down –

It was Lily's dog. The untrustworthy Alsatian Oscar. She let go her grip and a shadowy form fell back behind her, slunk away. She went on, her breathing disturbed. Now she was close to them: close to the lies she would have to tell them. The house was all about her; there the Warrens had lived, and before them the Goughs, and before them Timothy Daly at the beginning of the previous century, according to the Genealogical Office in Dublin Castle. And before Timothy Daly, others, no doubt, whom she had never heard of, for she had not been able to trace the house back to its foundations, searching in the Registry of Deeds Office in Dublin, in the Death Record Office in the Customs House, all to no purpose. There too her father and mother had lived, Bob and Lousa Langrishe, brought up a family, admired and respected by their Catholic tenantry. Her mother had turned Catholic towards the end of her life, and been buried as a Catholic in Donycomper graveyard. The bell of the Anglican church had rung for her as a last mark of respect. Two bells had sounded her passing. The heavy Roman Catholic bell in the churchyard midway up the main street of the village, and the high quick bell of Christ's Church within the gates of Castletown demesne.

As Helen passed the side of the house the cold wind struck at her face, blowing off the frozen fields, and there was their light shining behind the study blind. She went to the window and tapped on the glass and heard her sisters rising up in consternation. Then Imogen's voice asking *Who's there?*

Helen stood at the side door, exposed to the biting wind, thinking *They have become real old maids. Everything frightens them.* She heard whispering behind the door, the scuffle of their feet, then Imogen's voice called again:

– Who's there, please?

Silence.

– It's Helen (Lily's prompting voice). Let her in.

She heard the wooden bolt, heavy as a battering ram, being lifted bodily from its cradle and then the door was pulled open and she saw them huddled together, showing her their alarmed faces, and the lamplit hall stretching away behind to the foot of the stairs. She made an impatient motion with her gloved hand and went by them with her head averted.

In the airless study a coal fire was burning wastefully up the chimney. Ovaltine and a saucepan of milk covered with a plate, some unmatched cups and saucers, stood by the fender with her favourite cracknels. In this small library permeated with a dry heat they had spent most of the winter, hardly talking at all, the inner calves of their legs mottled brown, like burns on pancakes. They could not leave the fire on cold nights.

A book lay face down on Imogen's armchair; Lily was reading the *Evening Mail. Spanish ship 'Mar Canta Brisco' bombed and sunk in Bay of Biscay. Insanity plea in murder charge. Girl Killed at Dance.*

She watched herself in the mirror over the mantelpiece, framed in ornate mahogany, the bookshelves reaching to the ceiling behind her. She unloosened her bonnet and laid it aside, removed her gloves and capuchin. On her breast a cheap metal brooch held in place a sprig of wilted fern. She sat down, extending her frozen fingers to the blaze. She heard them struggling at the door, putting back the wooden bolt.

They came in together and began to hover around her, watching her, saying nothing. They wanted her to bring them a miracle and not the trouble she was bringing them. Staring at her pointed wellingtons, she said irritably:

– All right. Will one of you please close the door there, and come and sit down here? For God knows I'm cold enough already without having to stand more draughts. Will you listen to what I have to say? – because I'm only going to say it once.

When this was done, she said, staring at Lily's profile:

– Now, in the first place, that bloody savage brute Oscar who has already killed sheep, is out running wild over the countryside . . .

2

Helen awoke in sour white daylight. The day was already well advanced; she could tell by the direction from which the light came, weakly flooding the wrong corners of the room. The cold spell still persisted. Now she had to rise. She did not stir, but closed her eyes. Presently she felt something pressing on her feet. Looking down she saw two of the resident incubi and succubi crouching at her feet. The tabby and the grey stared at her with their afflicted eyes; their pupils, reduced to slits, bored into hers. They crouched side by side on the eiderdown in a design of outspread lotus flowers and ancient Egyptians, their bared claws digging into the worn material. They were old and far from healthy, one suffering from an abscess of the eye and the other from an ingrowing testicle. She tried to return their unwinking stare.

– Go away, she said at last. Get away. I don't want you.

They stopped what they were doing when they heard her voice; but in a little while began cautiously all over again.

– Go on, Helen said in a fretful voice, ruin the bed.

Why did they go on clawing it that way? They were feeling the fires. That was Imogen's expression. They were useless animals, always under her feet, crying to be let out, to be fed, to be pampered, to be let in, limping about. Once when he was young and frisky she had caught up the tomcat in her arms, pressing him to her breast. But his body, stiff as a board, had resisted all contact with her, and indeed she had some difficulty in recognizing him as the same tame domestic pet, who, though nameless, was through daily contact over the years known to her, more or less. He had strained away from her with a spiteful look on his face, covered in what seemed to be cat excrement which had come off on her hands and dress.

At times they brought in dismembered rats, thrushes and robins, disposing of them in a semi-masticated condition about the bed, where they remained until the smell gave them away. Then she would come with the fire tongs and the disinfectant and chase them away. Nothing was too disgusting for them.

She sat inert amid the down and feathers, resting on her back. Staring at different quarters of the ceiling and stucco mouldings as if at a spectacle worthy of contemplation. The night-light burned before the silver-plated crucifix. Above it the ceiling was pock-marked with a series of reddish-brown circles, where a tennis ball dipped in paint had been thrown again and again. Idly her abstracted gaze followed the circles outwards until they disappeared. The same old frieze ran round the room; in some moods of depression it became more real than life itself. It showed donkeys at the seaside, standing with heads bowed alongside their stout rubicund drivers, who wore pointed straw hats, standing barefooted in the surf, their trousers rolled up as if for wading. The donkeys' bridles trailed in the sea. About them on the narrow sandy shore children were running with vacant expressions of joy on their faces, by stranded starfish and sandcastles. She looked at it with distaste; nothing would ever change there. She lay still, attempting to purge her breast of all resentment, but her secret thoughts were bitter enough. The talk they had had on the night before had not been a success: they had slipped away from her arguments, pretending to understand, but she knew well enough that they had not understood, but had left the burden with her. They had stared at her before making inane suggestions. Hopeless, she thought, they know nothing. Not even Imogen, when it came to it. She would have to accept full responsibility herself, for them, for the disposal of the house, and for whatever would befall them after. In the middle of it all, to make things worse, Lily had jumped up crying There he is! and gone running out, hauling the big bolt out of its place with a great clattering and banging. Then her frantic cries outside: Oscar! *Os–car!* Come back here! And she, staring into the fire, had asked:

– And what's he doing out anyway, would you mind telling me? Who let him out?

Imogen shrugged her shoulders and said:

– He wasn't locked in. We forgot.

– Forgot? *Forgot?* That's good. Get her in here then before she's locked up herself. In God's name, who's worrying about a little thing like a dog licence at this stage in the proceedings?

At last Helen rose and began to dress herself, selecting for the day a fawn outfit. She pulled on her wellingtons and stowed away her town clothes in the wardrobe. Then she went to the window and drew up the Venetian blind. Looking out she saw clouds passing in a leisurely way over the hills. Cattle wandered across Mangan's long field, breathing out vapours into the freezing air. All was as it had always been, variations apart (the passing of her parents, the death of Emily), in the immutable order of events. She left the bedroom, stepping down onto the cold landing.

In the bathroom she ran some water into the washbasin, dabbing it over her cheeks and eyes, which refreshed her a little. Then she dried her face and hands, put the towel away, found a comb. With the greatest care she began combing. Long white strands came away in the teeth. The washbasin was covered with them, hers and other darker strands from Imogen's head. Lily was moulting too, but she combed her hair near the window, at Father's shaving mirror, and it came out there. Helen had held onto her teeth for as long as possible, until they too had to go; and now her hair, at one time so thick and lustrous, was coming out in fistfuls. Soon they would all be bald as old men, sitting around the fire at night, holy shows. From the window she could see the overgrown tennis-court and the high beech hedge along which Emily had trodden her path, and the dark knotty branches in the orchard beyond, so still. She left the bathroom, walking on linoleum, descended onto the main stairs. Where the banisters turned at right-angles, leading to the main bedrooms, she turned away, stopping outside a door. She rapped on the door of the small spare room into which Imogen had recently moved. Silence of the grave. Helen knocked again, louder.

– Come in, a muffled voice said at last.

She turned the handle and went in. The blind was drawn and the little room suffused with amethyst light, in which dust motes floated, sinking and rising. It was a narrow place with an alcove, shelves reaching from floor to ceiling on either side of the shallow fireplace; a table standing on one leg came out from the wall. One-third of the remaining floor space was occupied by a low bed over the end rail of which Imogen had thrown her clothes. Some empty stout bottles stood on the table and the room was permeated with the sickly sweetish smell of Guinness's porter. Helen stood on the faded mat, looking down on the dire confusion of the bed.

– Come up, Imogen, I must talk to you.

A disturbance of springs and squeaking castors began; then the bedclothes were pushed aside and Imogen's head appeared. Helen looked at her.

– What ails you? she said.

Imogen struggled up until her head and shoulders were free. She wore a loose shapeless brown cardigan with the stitching gone along one arm.

– Nothing *ails* me, she said in a peevish way. Why?

– You don't look so well.

Imogen drew the sheets that were none too clean up to her chin, staring down the bed.

– Do I ever look well? she said. I didn't sleep very well last night, that's all.

Helen seated herself on the edge of the bed. She wanted to say, You drink too much. Have you no dignity? She said:

– It makes all the difference to me (bowing her head), – a good night's rest.

Imogen closed her eyes and began passing her hand over her face, clearing away cobwebs.

– I was having a bad dream. I remember some of it.

Silence. She lay between the greyish sheets, eyes shut.

– Such a strange dream, Imogen said, passing her hand across her face several times. I dreamt that Christ's body was discovered in the Ural Mountains outside a town called Vlannick, which I don't suppose exists. But later on in the dream it was me they had unearthed. I mean I was Him, two thousand years buried under the earth. What could that mean, do you suppose? Are you any good at interpreting dreams?

– No, Helen said.

What sort of nonsense was that anyway? Christ; Russia; the Urals; bugbears and old maid's fancies.

At last Imogen heaved a heavy sigh and said:

– I think I'll just stay where I am for the time being. My stomach feels out of order today.

Well, God knows that was nothing new. All her life long she had been complaining about the state of her health in the same long-suffering voice, slurring her words, swallowing vowels, whole sentences trailing off into silence. She was beyond cure with her stomach cramps, her sick headaches, bodily fatigues, liver, kidneys, stones.

– Could I bring you anything? Helen said, avoiding her sister's eyes.

Imogen gave a wan smile, shaking her head. No thanks, really. She would try to sleep a little longer. She had no appetite, lived on very thin vegetarian omelettes sprinkled with parsley and apples with no pith which she cooked on a tin lid, the centres scooped out and filled with brown sugar.

And who feeds the unfortunate hens, pray? Helen thought. Or had they too grown accustomed to irregular hours of feeding?

After a further silence she said:

– I was thinking of visiting Donycomper today. It's after the anniversary. Someone should go.

Imogen stared at the ceiling over the door without saying anything. Breathing through her nose, adenoidal, she lowered her eyes until they were focussed on the clothes thrown over the bedrail.

– How would you go?

– On my bike, Helen said.

Silence.

– Why not? Imogen said at last.

Helen turned away. Her sister's battered shoes were arranged toe to toe by the bed. Her hazel stick was in the corner. She had her active and passive days. Yesterday she had been out marching. Winter was a hard time for her; then it took her ages to get up out of bed. She claimed that she was not such a morning bird, that she was brighter at night, which was debatable. It was painful to watch her getting out of bed. First one foot was slithered out to have its brown lisle stocking fixed to the arched toe, then rolled up to the calf, drawn smartly in and drawn up her thigh under the bedclothes. Half an hour might pass before the second leg emerged, just as white and corroded with goose-pimples as the first, to have its stocking fixed on the arched toes, and be drawn quickly in again. Then a long pause while she collected herself together, assembled her forces for the daily struggle, staring up at the ceiling with the light of human intelligence nowhere evident in the fixed stare of the eye.

At long last the bedclothes would be slipped aside and Imogen emerge, fully dressed save for her shoes, which she immediately put her feet into. She had a little touch of natural colour on her cheeks. An old love had put it there. The memory of past obscenities gave her that rose glow on sallow cheeks, when she was old.

– Excuse me, Imogen said, making as if to rise, I must pay a call.

Helen did not wait, but crossed to the door, letting herself out. Halfway down the stairs she remembered: hadn't she called on Imogen expressly to tell her something, ask her something? Yes, but what? For the life of her she could not remember. Her memory was playing her tricks. Was it something about the sale of the house, or something about the will, or what? She could not remember. No matter, it would come back to her. She went on down the main stairway into the hall.

It was three-twenty-five, and a dull cold day over the townland of Ballymakealy Upper, which is in the Parish of Killadoon, which is in the diocese of Celbridge, which is in the Barony of Salt, which is in the County Kildare, which is in the province of Leinster.

3

Taking her time, Helen cycled slowly by the wall of the Charter School. It ended; a hedge began; there was Muldowney's cottage sunken into the earth, then a banked ditch full of melancholy brown bogwater. Beyond, a ploughed field stretched away, with crows and plover dispersing over the black and stiffened furrows. A little way on and the road dipped downwards as the hill began. On the right was Killadoon front avenue, leading towards a remote white gate which she could not see. Down she went, her brakes half on, ringing her bell.

Raw air entered her lungs, struck against her face, gone rigid with the cold. Her eyes watered, so that it became difficult to see. Not that it mattered, she knew the way so well, letting the hill carry her down its gradual incline. The road swept by under her whispering tyres. The line of beech trees had long ago shed their leaves, now frozen hard against the foot of the wall. Over the docked hedges she saw a high stone house surmounted by a flagpost. Oakley Park. She rounded Paisley's corner.

The mark of his cottage showed in the wall. He had died or left and his home had been pulled down. The wall inclined inward to accommodate the shape of the cottage; now – tenant departed – the stones had been put back into the structure from which they had come. Mortar and cement, irregular white lines; in ten years of weathering all that would go unnoticed under the growth of fungus; in twenty years few would remember that Paisley's house had ever stood there.

She passed the Abbey and a moment later was entering the village. This was some time before five o'clock. The main street was almost deserted. This suited her, for she disliked being stared at. She cycled slowly up the main street, a fine rain falling in her head, past Brennan's the Saddlers at the foot of the humpback bridge. At the far end of the village, on the hill, the gates of Castletown stood open. Where the public way ended the long straight avenue of limes began.

Poor shops, sweet shops, the black convent gates on a grey colourless day towards the end of winter with the light gone out of everything. Helen dismounted and wheeled her bicycle into the church yard. She propped it against the flaking wall where the stone of an older church still showed. An elderly couple were standing gossiping on the path. As she approached she heard:

– It's only the poor who have to work hard for their money.

– Aye.

– That's generally the way.

They saw her and stood aside, bowing as she passed between them. She crossed herself at the holy water font and entered the porch. The door swung to behind her, she advanced into the quietness of the church. High white pillars went away towards the high altar and its two side altars. White flowers and unlit candles on the main altar made it cheerless and remote, flanked by crypto-Celtic mosaics. Smell of incense, church woods, varnish and floor polish; smell of holy oil, waxen candles, heady smell of the pews. A bit stifling. Like what? Angora wool?

Two statues of saints were posted further down the nave near the pulpit. Bridget, with flaming cheeks, the patroness of the County. St Patrick in bishop's mitre, heavy vestments of saffron and green extending his bishop's crozier, two fingers of one hand blessing a non-existent congregation. The church was empty. No ... Two parishioners in black, doing the stations, were whispering there, bringing their beads to their lips, genuflecting, their lips moving. They moved on slowly, one behind the other.

Helen advanced along the nave on the Epistle side, her rubber-soled boots making little sound on the tiles. The holy lamp suspended on elaborate chains from the vaulted roof hung before the Blessed Sacrament. Its diminutive ruby flame burning in oil behind protective glass glimmered and wavered, dimming out only to shine forth again. The priests' cards were turned face inward on the heavy purple velvet of the confessionals, Rev. Fr D. Binchley, PP, Fr P. Pierce.

Behind, trapped in their heavy frames, the figures of the Saviour and Simon of Cyrene reeled along under their cross in muddy coloured bas-relief. Votive candles were burning on a brass stand to one side of the curate's confessional. As she approached, a candle went out on the stand, sending up a blue spiral of smoke. Helen fumbled in her purse for a copper. She dropped it into the slot, found another candle, lit it, setting it up where the first had gone out. Walk whilst you have the light, that the darkness may not overtake you. Bridget's protuberant eyes watched from her post by the pulpit. Piously disposed in a nun's black habit, gilded at sleeve and hem; heavy rosary beads hung at her waist, set stiff against the drapery of her robes. Before the high altar the crimson light flickered, sank, and went out. Helen passed behind a pillar.

Above the cross narrow stained glass windows, representing the Holy Trinity, ascended towards the timbered roof. When she was halfway down the aisle the holy light shone forth again. She genuflected, entering one of the centre pews. Drawing off her gloves she knelt upright on the wooden boards. Closing her eyes she brought her cold hands together before her face, and prayed that she would see her way clear in the troubles that lay ahead. Before her closed eyes, minute, irradiant, the holy light moved, shifted its position; the altars drew closer.

She uncovered her face at last, opened her eyes. The blurred altars receded again. She sat back. On the plaque before her was inscribed, *Pray for the Donor*, and a name short and flat – *Dumphy*.

On the surface of the river running out rapidly below the bridge a grey cloud formation advanced against the current, making no headway. As Helen watched, the weak winter sun, piercing for a moment the overcast, shone down through a narrow break in the clouds. The light penetrated the water, shone down through the paler clay that was rising from the bed of the stream.

Partly submerged branches floated aimlessly by, going under only to rise again, covered in slime, twisting and turning in the pull of the current. The river was coming down in spate as the snow melted in the hills. The rising water had already gone over the sandbar – silt from one of the five arches – swamping the grove of willows. Subsiding into it, their glistening branches dipped and waved, coppery red.

The water was up to the coping stones on the outside arches. Filling and emptying as the flood went through, it created a prodigious watery commotion that shook the bridge to its foundations. Helen saw a sign whitewashed over on a riverside wall: Celbridge Engineering & Motor Works. The corrugated tin roof had rotted in places along its eaves.

In the distance, marking the end of the village, the mute brown bell tower of Christ's Church rose above the roofs. She saw the tops of the high limes on Castletown avenue. Behind her, the light fled across the bridge, over the wall, onto the river, and away.

She looked down on dull greenish waves, choppy water in a freshening breeze, and the occasional flotsam going out under her feet and on down past the lawns of Major Kirkpatrick's estate. She had the bridge to herself. A short while earlier an old ragged woman had come with a sack from the Temple Mills direction, bent double under the weight of firewood she bore, escorted by two small children and a dog. They had gone off on the Hazelhatch road; the dog followed them, running from one ditch to the other, until all vanished over the horizon.

Helen turned to face the opposite parapet and the empty mill beyond. A yellow cinema poster was flapping on the wall. She stared across at it, but could not make out the title. She stepped off the pavement with the intention of studying it at closer range, but had not taken two steps onto the road when she heard the blare of a motor horn and the drone of a machine approaching rapidly on the Lucan road. She hesitated in the middle of the narrow way, not knowing whether to go on or turn back. A single footpath served the bridge, and she had just left it. It was too late to turn now. The motor van, changing down to second gear, rounded the corner and was upon her. She stayed where she was, smiling at her ridiculous position, putting a bold face on it. It was Rourke's bread van. The driver stared at her through his flyblown windscreen. The van had stopped; he beckoned to her to cross. She did so. With a great noise and mangling of gears the van passed her, the driver, a small crabbed man in a brown cap with a cigarette butt behind one ear, saluting; turning right by Broe's shop the van went on up the village.

The ruined mill faced her over the parapet wall. The clock had stopped at seven minutes to eight. Celbridge flour and woollen mills. The windows of its four storeys had fallen in under the weather, and the crows and jackdaws had taken over. Across the river from it, at the end of an ivy-covered wall a squat stone building overhung the water – the old Abbey school, now a National school.

Helen bent to read the cinema poster. *Forbidden Heaven*, featuring Charles Farrell and Charlotte Henry, was showing at the Electric Picture House, Newbridge. Romance and pathos among four human derelicts. Prices of admission, 4d, 9d, 1/4d. Wednesday and Thursday, March 10 & 11. She bent lower, intent, read with difficulty the supporting programme. *Strike it Rich*, with George Gee and Gina Malo. She sighed, lifted her head, saw the schoolhouse with its leaded windows and mossy roof. She preferred it to all the other houses in the village, this little edifice of stone on the Liffey.

The wind coming off the water was perishing cold, blowing into her face. She turned away from it. Human derelicts, she thought grimly, it's about us. Her big green pushbike was propped up by one pedal against the far kerbside. She stepped into the roadway. It was time to go.

Arranging her bulky taffeta skirt about her, she mounted, pushed off downhill from the crest. Turning left by Sammon's Bar and Select Lounge, she turned onto the Lucan road, pedalling as hard as she could go, bound for Donycomper cemetery. Less than a quarter of an hour had passed since she had come cycling in. Already she could see its graveyard trees in turmoil. Her father and mother lay buried there; her sister too; all the Langrishe *moribundi*.

4

Helen stood in the nave of the old church at Donycomper, and for the first time that day felt at peace. It would all come out well in the end, no doubt. She moved from under the semi-circular arch. In the side chapel she came upon an open vault. The slab lay half off and a bleak and fugitive light, penetrating the hazel and ivy which grew in profusion there, fell on dust and stony ground below. The surface of the slab showed marks of osier wattles which had supported it when under construction. The partly obliterated inscription read:

epulchre is The
ial Place of The
mily of Alens of
ALENSCOURT

Helen peered down apprehensively into the open vault. It gave off a certain smell. Dusty roots, a piece of oxidized metal, brown bones of dead animals, the scant dropping of the living. Alenscourt: what did the name mean to her? It might have meant something once. She straightened up, listening, thinking, My poor memory's going. Sure enough, – a little way off behind the broken wall of the church, water was running over the bed of the stream.

Helen left the church and stood on the mound upon which it was built. She remained there for some time, her feet among nettles and coarse grass, staring about. Beside the broken door a holy water font had filled with discoloured water upon which floated a few wizened mulberries. The church was roofless. She had often speculated on its age, but without coming to any conclusion. One of the side walls had cracked from top to bottom in a wedge-shaped breach wide enough to allow the passage of a bullock. A rusty lawnmower, once perhaps used on graves, stood on its end against one wall in the company of a labourer's scythe with a thin brown blade.

The headstones were sinking into the grass. She began poking at one with a stick and the toe of her boot. In a little while the inscription stood out clearly enough. With the point of the stick she traced the words, *Lieth Body of KANE, who departed this Life 26th of April* 1738. As she straightened up she heard close by the sound of teeth chattering. Crossing to the window she looked in under the knags of ivy that pressed down with all their weight upon the broken walls. The teeth chattered again. She looked down. On the ledge within stood a wreath of fireclay flowers and a white dove, one knocking against the other. The glass dome had cracked and the flowers were shattered. Helen touched the trembling bird with her gloved hand and the sound stopped.

She went out by the side of the church where a hazel tree sprouted from the wall. A plaque below it said: Erected by Stephen Coyle to the memory of. Here lieth his father George who departed this life. May 18th 1790. Aged 76 years.

Helen made her way down through the nettles into the cemetery proper. Coming upon one of the lanes she progressed slowly along, her feet making no sound on the carpet of leaves. Her memory of place was poor: she found she could not recall where the family plot was situated. Poor names and places, they were too much for her, they would have to get on without her. She went down a lane of cypress and yew, reading names on headstones. Mahoney, Kevany, Kane, Russell, Rourke, Doyle, Dease, Darlington, Dempsey, Tyrrell, Mooney, Tisdell, Cotter, Ahern chiselled into marble, granite and limestone in a hand that no eye could evade, no heart go unmoved by; not elegant or grand, no, but this was her place nevertheless, and these were its people.

She continued on, reading where she would. In loving memory of my daughter. Maura Russell died 1st of December 1931, aged sixteen years. Interred in old cemetery. Christ have mercy. Helen turned into a path to the right and continued on at the same funereal pace.

The long-handled shovels of the roadmenders stuck out from a cypress tree. The inscriptions mutely spoke to her. In sad and loving memory. She halted before a headstone. Salus per Christum. Lloyd Christian died December 1935. Deemster 1579. Ronaldsway, Isle of Man. Son of Robert Calder Christian and General David Elliot. Thus without abuse he bore the grand old name of gentleman. In the raked ground at her feet a border of frozen Michaelmas daisies trembled along their double rank. From where she stood she recognized the next plot, for it was theirs. She took four more paces and came level with the grave-plot.

In Loving Memory

Louisa Kathleen Langrishe, died 9th May. Springfield, Celbridge. And Robert Langrishe, died 17th September. There they lay with Emily. Mother's grave had been opened to let her in. Mother, long dead now, dissolved into the first principle of earth. Emily. Emily stricken with phlebitis, with 'white leg', painted it with belladonna on a feather, like George VI. She looked a sight. That fellow she was attached to; an awful thick lug of a fellow all dressed up sitting at the fire with nothing to say for himself. Hold me in thrall.

Emily cutting rhubarb in the garden with a breadknife. Early Albert or nameless garden rhubarb, good for the blood and bowels. The salts by her bed. Cream crackers laden with butter. Her diffidence, refusal. A high chair. Her bewilderment when it was all over. The rumble of a solid heavy door. Lie heavy on her, earth, Helen prayed, for she laid many a heavy load on thee. They lay in each other's arms at last, under a plain monument with no Celtic cross, no flames perpetuated in stone, wrought about with shamrock, no images of the Bleeding Heart. Over them the wind blew.

And their beloved Daughter
Emily, died 3rd March.
R.I.P.

They were on the altar list of the dead and in November of every year prayers would be offered for the repose of their souls.

When my turn comes, Helen thought, another headstone will be needed, for there's no more space on theirs. Those who are dead now lie in earth, the living linger here; so much the worse for them. Earth voided by earth, gnawed by worms. The cypresses above her head stirred in the breeze. The beeches over the road groaned under their weight of timber. All swayed in the same wind, uttering the same cry: In loving memory, in sad and loving memory. Words could not express more.

Helen heard the sound of footsteps coming towards her over the gravel. She looked about but could see nobody. The breeze died down. An evening calm invaded the cemetery. The still trees had begun to lose their outline. The footsteps came on, dragging and heavy. She saw the stooped figure of an old man moving behind the trees. Helen shifted her ground somewhat from the Langrishe plot, not wishing to be associated with her own dead. She waited, her eyes fixed on the opening through which he would presently come. He came on slowly, turned into the lane, came on towards her at the same snail's pace, not lifting his head, carrying a gardening fork under one arm. Between them a miniature whirlwind danced on the path, spinning on its tail. Then, its energy spent, it collapsed at her feet, leaves, dust and straw.

He advanced towards her, head down. Was it the gravedigger come to prepare tomorrow's grave? He drew abreast of her, stopped, raised his eyes, then his hat. A bent old fellow in a ragged surtout was doffing his hat to her.

– Grand evening, Helen said.

– Tis indade, grand, thanks be to God.

He waited for her to speak again.

– Tell me, she said in a formal way, do I trespass here at this hour?

The old man grounded his fork.

– Not a-tall, M'am. Yarra, not a-tall. Sure you have it all to yourself. The gate's open for all them that want to.

Helen bowed. Well and good, she was not trespassing. He was not the sexton.

– Tis grand an quiet here, he said. All you do hear all the year round is the birds an the Shinkeen flowin by.

In the silence she could hear it rambling over the bed of the stream. She said nothing. The Shinkeen. After a short silence he spoke again; he was a gabby old man. Was she looking for any in *par*-ticlar?

Was she? Emily Norton Langrishe, dead, of whom hereafter; peace to her *manes*.

– No, Helen lied, no. I was just admiring the ruins. (The old church, its ruins submerged under the dark green vegetation that had overgrown all.)

She made a half-turn as though she would walk on, looking quickly at him.

– Them ould runes, he said, nodding towards them, sure they're countless years old. They do say that there's a priest's tunnel laden from there –

– Yes, Helen said politely.

– Into St Wolstan's beyant. Into the ould Barony of Salt itself. But sure arne't there priests' tunnels everywhere in Catholic Ireland? he said, staring about him with a slow wandering gaze, rubbing his chest with one hand.

– Don't let me interrupt you, Helen said after a silence, if you have work to do.

Oh faith he had. Wasn't he on his way to a grave that needed attention for an anniversary that fell on the following day? Hadn't he his fork with him?

– I see that, Helen said.

– Aye.

The old man thrust his fork under one arm.

– Then let us move on, Helen said with resolution.

– Aye.

Together they advanced slowly along the gravel path, Helen casting about in her mind for something to say. She could think of nothing bright. When they had gone about twenty yards she hazarded:

– If the Alens were buried there – as I see they were – how old would that make it? That old church?

He halted, resting the prongs of his fork on the ground. Leaning his weight on the handle and massaging an unshaven chin, his uncertain rheumy eyes sought hers. Helen avoided his stare and looked instead at his hands, knotted with swollen wormy veins, fidgeting on the handle of his implement.

– You have me puzzled there, he admitted at last.

She said nothing to that.

He added:

– I've heard said it goes back into the . . . middle sinturies.

He stared hopelessly at her with his colourless eyes, wringing his labourer's hands, making her feel uncomfortable.

– Oblige me and put on your hat, she said, and let us move on.

They went on.

The days, the wonderful summer days when she had gone unescorted into St Wolstan's grounds; and come upon a lofty garden wall with flues; and an urn on a granite pedestal inscribed with the legend, 'As dying, yet we live,' dated May 1st 1756. Down there a narrow stone bridge of picturesque Irish antiquity spanned the river, the old bridge erected by John Ledecer in the early fourteenth century. At one time she had had ambitions to write a history of the whole area, tracing back the names, the grand estates: Swift and later Grattan at the Abbey, Speaker Conolly at Castletown, Charles Napier at Oakley Park. But nothing had come of this. It all lay in bits and pieces in three big green notebooks. Her grasp of history was poor; she could not assemble the material she had collected, no, not in any coherent way. In the course of years the evidence itself was disappearing back into the ground, like the headstones in the graveyard. The landscape, so indifferent to its history, the bloody battles waged upon it and for it, still turned its back upon the living.

They had come to a halt before a grave. A family interment place surmounted by a seven foot high Celtic cross, the plot surrounded by a cement ridge raised a half foot above the rutted grass.

The old man unbuttoned his surtout and brought out from an interior pocket a loose brown paper parcel which he laid on the ground to one side of the grave. Then he produced a dibber and put it by the parcel. Throwing back the wings of his coat, he spat on his hands, grasped the fork with both hands, and had the prongs into the hard ground with a deft thrust of his boot. She watched him. The furrowed brows twitched under the brim of his battered rimless hat, and he grunted and mumbled to himself as he worked. Helen looked away. Among the dark and precisely spaced trees, calm in their massed outline, blackbirds flew hither and thither with restless cries. Beyond the ditch a heifer was butting its skull against the bars of a gate; she heard the impatient dragging of its chains.

– Aye, he said, bending and weeding, all you ever hear is the birds, or the bastes out in the field beyant.

She took a step closer to him.

The bastes out in the field.

– Donycomper, she said.

– Aye.

– It's an odd name. Is it from the Irish?

– Tis, he said indifferently, so I hear. I was never a great hand at the language meself, although the dear Lord knows we had it baiten into us often enough.

– And Celbridge. Is that from the Irish too?

That he didn't know; all he knew was that at one time the coach road had gone through Castletown grounds by the river bank. The present road had cut through the old graveyard.

– The ould graves are all lost beyant in the Major's place, he said, pointing. Mind you, I'm talking now of the times before the Daysus an the Goffs an all the grand nobility ever set foot there.

– Is that so? Helen said.

– Yis, said the old man. An that's takin you back a fair stretch.

She caught his wild eye and looked away. She had little contact with the common people and felt uneasy in their presence. Imogen could talk to them; she could not.

– I recall meself when the mill was workin, the old man said, an the lads of the village drawin good wages. Aye, an I recall when there were gintry living above in the Abbey – the Langdales. Bedad I do. Twas the Dutchman before them who built on them outhouses, stables an yards . . .

– Who? she said, beginning to lose track. Whom do you mean? Bartholomew Vanhomrigh?

– Yis, said the old man after a pause, that might be the name. A Dutchman it was. Vanessy's da.

The voice droned on without ceasing.

I am under the trees, she thought, under the old Donycomper trees. I hear water flowing. It's the Shinkeen flowing by. He called it the Shinkeen. This old man is speaking to me, telling me all over again the history of my home that I never bothered to know; or, if I did by chance know it once, did not bother to remember. He will never stop talking. I hear it all. No doubt irrefutable facts about dead people and places which still exist. I hear it. In my head I hear it. Do I? No, I hear nothing, remember nothing, am nothing.

– You have a great memory, certainly, Helen said, allowing a little feeling into her voice.

He was pleased with the compliment.

– I have bedad, he admitted, flattered. I'm over eighty, but me memory an me appetite are as good today as ever they were. I've always enjoyed good health, thank God.

He went on talking, his tongue wagging over the history of Ireland. He had lost a son in the Great War. Was it the presence of so many graves? . . . He could remember it to this day: his son and the groom from St Wolstan's had decided to join up together. One freezing morning they had arranged it on the Pond Walk. He would remember it to his dying day – the morning in 1917 when his son had walked into the house and told him that he had decided to go to war. They were in France for the last six months. His son had joined the Irish Guards. Brogan, the groom, had gone into a cavalry regiment, and had been killed almost at once; buried on foreign soil. His son had seen service in Flanders and after in the Dardanelles where he had met his death before the Turkish batteries.

– Oh dear God but it was a terrible waar, the old man said. Terrible murder. The mudde and the filt an the cowld. Me son Tom, God rest his sowl, seen grown min in the trinches cryin with the cowld.

A sudden breeze disturbed the tops of the trees. The old man, kneeling by a grave, lifted his face briefly towards hers, then went on clearing the weeds and dead flowers in a leisurely way. He also went on talking. Soon she had lost track of what he was saying.

– Pepperin the thransports! (they were back in the Dardanelles). Sure the Turks knew. Them bloodthirsty ruffians. Of course they did (holding up a fistful of weeds). They were waitin . . . (shaking earth from the weeds). They mowed us down with their macheen guns (throwing the weeds away) . . . Dear God.

He opened the paper parcel and took out some wall-flowers.

– Brogan is gone, he said, an me own son Tom, the Lord have mercy on their sowls. I was very great with him. An now he's gone. An me own son. Aye, the pair of them dead an rotten these twenty years. Dear God.

Catching up the wooden dibber in his free hand he poked out fiercely an uneven line of holes in the newly turned earth of the grave.

– And if I had another, he said, glaring up at her, would I send him off to waar?

Helen shook her head.

– I would not! he cried, flinging the dibber aside.

He himself had no desire to see the great world. Starting life as an under-gardener in Castletown, he had gone as a young man into Guinness's brewery. In 1902 he was earning good wages. £3.11.0 a week, considered good money in those days; seeing the 'Transport people were only drawing fifty-five bob.' In the brewery his health had broken down; he was accustomed to fresh air and city life had not agreed with him. Taken ill, he had gone to hospital in Dublin and undergone two operations for sciatica, the stitches bursting after the first. Surrounded by medical students Sir John Lumsden had walked through the wards addressing the patients whose names he had marked down on a list; asking the men how they were and assuring them that they would be up and about soon.

– Oh Guinnesses know how to look after their own, the old man said with pride. Of course they do – or they wouldn't be Guinnesses!

He asked her did she know how Sir Arthur Guinness had started. No, she did not.

– Here in Celbridge! the old man cried. Yis. A gardener an his son here, brewin for them above in Oakley Park. They say he got the knack . . . the formula you know, just be accident. They had guests and there was a big dinner prepared, but didn't he go an burn the brew. The two of them were in fear an tremblin when it was served up for fear they'd be dismissed. But bedad it was highly praised instead. That's how it started. They had the first mix there at the back of the church.

– I could never touch it, Helen said, meaning the porter.

– Ah but it's not a drink for a lady, the old man said. But it's a lovely soft drink all the same, for a labourin man. A rale male in itself. Sure with your soda bread an your spuds an your porter, you wouldn't lack for anything. No indade you wouldn't.

– No, I suppose not, Helen conceded.

– He was a Ranger in the Phoenix Park after, the old man said after a pause. An will you look at him now.

He went on clearing the grave, making a good job of it, talking the while. In St James's Gate brewery they had started a trade union movement at the turn of the century. The first in Ireland. And into this he had paid union dues until he had to go to hospital. In hospital he had fallen into arrears with his payments, but as soon as he came out he had started to catch up. But as soon as he had paid up all that he owed, the union itself was disbanded. The brewery heads had threatened to cut all wages, irrespective of whether the men concerned were union members or not, pointing out that their employees were already drawing wages substantially higher than any others in Dublin, or in Ireland for that matter. And this had quashed the union movement.

She listened with only half an ear, since labour disputes were of scant interest to her. Besides, he seemed to be talking to himself as much as to her, as the old tend to do. He began complaining about the condition of the cemetery. There were too many trees in it in his opinion, endangering the valuable headstones and crosses.

– Wan good wind, wan good storm, an some of them'll be down. You'll see. The storms come here in February an March, an throughout November.

And the land, he had strong feelings about the land, in itself so rich, yet so ill-portioned out, in his opinion, and the muddle of government at the root of it all. (The grave-plot was in order now, neat and tidy for the anniversary that fell on the following day. Three rows of russet-coloured flowers nodded to the inscription which she was too polite to read, for it would have meant going forward and staring at it.) The old man went on talking. If the young men were compelled to work the land, stay on the land, and work their farms and holdings, as God surely intended, wouldn't that halt emigration, the bane of Ireland? Wouldn't it go some way towards it? It had been a mistake to abandon the compulsory tillage scheme. And now there was De Valera's economic war. (Helen could no longer listen to him. The gist of it all was that the country was in a bad way, but this state of affairs could be remedied, if the right men were put in charge. In politics his heroes were John Redmond and Michael Collins.)

– They had to shoot Collins to get the present crowd in. Sure that's well known.

Was it well known? She had never heard of it. So many had been killed in one way or another. Sinn Fein buffs, Dada used to say.

All that bloodshed; and for what?

5

Imogen closed the door behind her and walked into the room. The place, unoccupied since his death, had a stale forgotten odour, the walls bare except for a calendar for September of 1928, and a paraffin lamp much corroded with rust, which hung on the wall at a level convenient to the eye. Wardrobe and bed stood where they had stood in his lifetime. The bed was stripped, the wardrobe empty save for a pair of old-fashioned shoe-trees, jointed to fit a pair of boots. When the door swung open she was confronted with the wan image of herself standing there, her eyes meeting those other eyes timidly and irresolutely; a faded woman, no more young, all dressed in grey.

She brought her hand to her breast, summoning a look into her eyes. Those other disgruntled eyes peered back at her, the expression in them secretive, the brows drawn down. Stealthily she pushed the door to until it clicked shut; then she turned the key in the lock and moved away.

His chair, upholstered in green leather, was drawn up to the writing-desk. She sat down at it. There were some pens and pencils in a trough of shallow glass, a black marble paperweight, a pair of nail scissors and a ball of string. The ink had turned to powder in the inkwell. She sat there, staring at a whitened mark on the wallpaper of maroon and purple where an article of furniture had been taken away and sold. Under her hand a thin layer of dust covered the worn leather of the writing surface. The drawers contained documents and papers relating to the estate, neatly collated and sealed with the tapes of Goodbody & Son, the Dublin solicitors, and a few packets of Players with a couple of cigarettes in each. For some reason or other he never finished a packet of cigarettes, but threw it away with a few left in it. Imogen swept the desk clear with the heel of her hand and pulled open a drawer at random. She took out a folio notebook bound in cloth with the title 'Rent Book' written on the cover in her father's precise sloping hand. She opened it without much interest. The entries related to rent payments for the three lodges. The June of the last year of his life. *Front lodge: T. Boyle.* Then a neat page of ticked off figures below, paid and receipted, two pounds five per month. *Back lodge: Herr Beck. As agreement.* Imogen turned a page rapidly and read: *Ballymakealy Uppr. Lodge. Collins.* March-April-May rent in arrears. And a figure after that. Do not look back, she counselled herself, her eyes on the entries. Sporadic ones for January and February. She recalled the ashen-faced one-armed lodger, ex-British army, who had later expired of cancer at Peamount Sanatorium. The cottage had been condemned by the Health Authorities for not having any sanitary arrangements. The roof thatched in parts where the slate had fallen in. It had stood near the ring pump, below the toss bank where the men played on Sundays after twelve o'clock Mass. The outline was stilll there, the kitchen flagstones and a few bricks of one side wall left standing, a charred stump of the chimney. As agreement. She closed her eyes, tore the rent book along the binding, dropping it in two halves into the waste-paper basket. When had the Keegans come? They who paid their rent, such as it was, on the nail, five shillings a week. The other lodge lay empty. After father died it had been Emily's responsibility to see that the tenants paid their rent as it fell due; but Emily was dead nine years.

Imogen pulled out another drawer. Odds and ends – cheque stubs made out to the Royal Bank of Ireland, old receipted bills from Ahern the butcher, a cutting from the *Leinster Leader* yellow with age, an Ordnance Survey map of Springfield lands folded and refolded so many times that it had torn along the folds, with other articles of no value. She took into her hands the folded page of yellowing newsprint, opened it out. Imogen read: *Mrs Louisa Langrishe was a native of Celbridge parish and associated herself with its social and cultural activities for a number of years. She was a survival of the dead-and-gone generation dating back to the mid-years of the last century and had borne to the end the imprint of her generation, the grand old simple faith, the abounding charity, the pure unsophistication, the gentle manners and the big, kind heart of the women of the olden days. Those who knew her when time was younger and fortune smiled upon her way will recall the benevolence and generosity with which the late Mrs Langrishe fulfilled her duty to the poor and stricken, and how joyfully she responded to every call upon her resources towards the alleviation of public and personal distress. Never was there a better or more thoughtful, considerate, and kindly neighbour than she, never was there a truer or more sincere friend. Passed from a world in which time, change and development have completely altered the ideals to which she clung, the late Mrs Louisa Langrishe entered into the Kingdom of Eternal Life, there to enjoy the reward of her faith and virtues. R.I.P.*

Imogen put it by. The sour smell of the old paper, the stale smell of the room, long unaired, closed around her. She sat there, empty of feeling. Kindly and considerate. No, a hard cold woman really, who kept her feelings to herself.

Mamma, her hair fluffed out, sat in a chair with wooden arm-rests, the grip of the knitting basket looped over one arm, listening to what the Major had to say for himself. He had come looking for impartial advice. How strictly or how leniently should he behave in a dispute he was having with some of his tenants – a family. By accident she overheard. Mamma was staring at him over her spectacles, the knitting needles keeping up a rapid tempo, rasping against the dress she wore, some heavy material like bombazine. As he stated his case she was yanking out more and more wool. You decide for me, Louisa, the Major said. You decide.

When she spoke it was in a thin, affronted voice, tradition speaking through her. You know your own business best, she said. But if you would take a fool's advice, I'd say not to hesitate. Put them out. They won't thank you for doing them a kindness.

Old Clooney had spoken rightly when he said that the gentry had the law at their own feet. Mamma, that upright, stern-principled, cold woman, never showed her feelings to her children. Had she any feelings to show?

Imogen opened another drawer, taking from it four or five pencils with blunt points or no points, and a pencil sharpener shaped like a small globe of the world. She found a clean sheet of paper, began to pare them into it, her thoughts elsewhere. Coloured whorls of wood parings and ground-up lead fell as the globe revolved in her hand. She spread the pencils fanwise with their sharp points out, took up the sheet of paper, folded it in two, tilted the contents into the wastepaper basket. Then she wiped her hands in the paper and let it go, took up the pencils and set them on the serrated glass together with the small blue globe of the world.

She bent forward and touched a hidden spring in the upper part of the desk above a row of cubbyholes and a concealed drawer slid out towards her. She took from it a legal document with its red seals broken, spread it open on the desk, and put on her reading glasses to read a paragraph that interested her. She read: 'and if my money cannot be had, which is due to me, then I leave to my daughter Imogen the two hundred pounds (£200) which is now in Mr Kennedy's safekeeping in Dublin, and until she be married the interest thereof shall be to pay the rent of the Capuchin Chapel in Dublin. And if Imogen die before she be married then she leaves the above amount for the Order of Capuchins, that they may pray for her soul.'

Signed Louisa Langrishe in her mother's business-like hand. Imogen replaced the paper in the drawer. Her father had shown her the secret drawer when she was young and innocent enough to sit on his knee without offence. None of the others knew about it; and there she kept her private effects. Her mother had explained that the inheritance had come originally from property in America. It was Langrishe money, she had none herself. But even so this inheritance would not last into the third generation. Neither Emily, the eldest, nor she, the youngest, would ever see a penny of it and to that they must be resigned. Imogen had smiled, listening to this, hearing it only as a precautionary tale, intended to teach them the value of money they themselves had not earned, or possibly intended to act as a curb on whatever rash spending they might be inclined to go in for once they got their hands on their inheritance. But Mother had been speaking no more than the truth. The inheritance had not come. Offers of marriage had not come. The money they had, it had dwindled away. Where had all the fine life gone to, and what would they do now? With fingers pressed to her cheek she stared at the rusted paraffin lamp, which told her nothing.

How many times had his hand extinguished that same lamp in her presence? Many and many's the time. Lowering the wick, his face tilted at a judicious remove from the hot funnel, the little flame sinking and his voice murmuring in the darkening room, bidding her good-night.

She passed silently out through the doorway. Looking back, her hand on the door-knob, she saw his strikingly lit up eyes watching her, his face like an actor's face on a darkened stage, his tall humpbacked shadow crowding over the ceiling as she closed the door quietly behind her, she heard the quick *huff* of his expelled breath as he blew out the light. Then a heavy sigh behind the door; then the creaking of bedsprings; then silence.

The tin reflector was corroded with reddish-brown rust, the glass funnel in an impaired state, also coated with dust it had hung there all those years. All the years of Father's death. He had a shy way of caressing her. Joining the first two fingers of his right hand, doubling up his thumb at the joint and bending the joints of his joined fingers, the action of a blessing, he held them to her face which she inclined to him. He pressed his cold fingers to her hot cheek. Otherwise he rarely touched her, never kissed her, although she was supposed to be his favourite. He affected some gallantry for the prettier young ladies. He ran alongside her on the main garden path, holding steady the handlebars of her new bicycle, his free hand flat on the small of her back. But whatever bond there was between them had not survived. As a growing girl, when she had sat on his knee, she had sensed his resentment at her putting her hot bottom there. She was the beauty of the family, Mother had said so, plaiting her long black hair. You are the beauty, she had said, brushing and combing, her mouth full of hairpins, but Helen has the brains.

He had surprised her naked in the bathroom admiring her figure in the long glass. She had not heard him approaching in tennis shoes on the landing, and he had caught her with her arms up in a pose – rounding the door to be confronted with her shame, eyes blazing. Crouching, her hand out for a towel that slid from the rail and fell, she had wailed, red as a beetroot, *Oh get away! Get off, Dada!* He was shocked; she could see that. This female flesh of his own blood and engendering, a living being with adult desires, with face distorted, was strange to him. He turned about without a word. His steps retreated back along the landing, down a short flight of steps, off linoleum onto carpet, descending silently into the hall. Her handsome father.

Was he? He had a sensible face, hardly to be called handsome, but almost so. Pale blue eyes that tended to water under the stress of emotion, on his thin-skinned temples two soft veins pulsing, and on either flank of a narrow forehead a neat row of sausage curls. He wore the choker collars that were the fashion then, well polished tan boots on his feet, the soles oiled to render them durable and supple.

In company he was always careful, if there was no ashtray to hand, to deposit cigarette ash in the turnups of his well-tailored sharply pressed trousers. He was very polite, liked to remain unobtrusive, and kept himself to himself as much as possible.

He wore a black hard hat with a curly brim, clapped onto place with studied precision, and had a wardrobe full of identical tweed suits – herringbone of autumnal beige. The suits had small neat collars and mothballs in all the pockets. For he had a great dread of mould and decay. His carefully pressed trousers hung on separate hangers. In chill weather the suit which he intended to wear that day was aired in the kitchen oven and brought over Biddy's arm to his room as he shaved himself. He used a cut-throat, getting up a great lather, thrusting out his chin at his own reflection in an oval shaving mirror that came out from the wall. He pomaded his hair. With the tweed suit would come a freshly ironed shirt, his collar-box and cufflinks.

In summer his dress tended to be more relaxed and casual. When the days were warm enough he wore a flannel suit, sear and yellow with age, a tennis shirt, bow tie, panama hat and a pair of tapering cricket boots very wrinkled about the insteps, shedding their pipe-clay like a snake shedding its skins. He pursued his studies in the summerhouse, remaining there all day, with the scent of honeysuckle and rambling roses coming in the windows.

The time came when he gave up all pretence of running a farm. The estate was managed by a land steward who had come from Longford with him, Tommy Flynn. He applied himself to meditation and study. That was the life he had elected to live; a mild, protected life out of the way of things. But while he was broadening his mind the estate went to rack and ruin. The wonder was that he didn't die intestate. He had advanced theories about farming which he attempted to put into operation before Tommy Flynn took over. It hadn't been a success. One morning she had seen him issuing orders to the field-hands gathered in the front yard. Grouped about him they were listening open-mouthed. He spoke rapidly in his thin voice, striking his thigh with a switch for emphasis, pulling the ends of his waistcoat down, shooting his cuffs, studying their inscrutable faces. Yis, sur. Yis, sur. When he became excited his voice grew reedier: a voice sharp and high-toned – disagreeable. The men did not believe in his new-fangled notions, not even they could follow them. He began waving his hands then, powerless to improve or change anything – loose at the wrists, the gesture that scatters fowl. *Well, to work men, to work! I think we understand each other now. We have wasted too much time talking.* Their inscrutable faces. Yis, sur. Yis, sur. They had not understood him and went out of the yard looking puzzled, as well they might. They came trailing back at odd hours, disappearing into the harness-room. Punctually at six o'clock they brought out a bucket, dipped it into the open tank, washed their hands and necks with axle grease, put on their coats, cycled off down the back avenue, leaving Tommy Flynn to close the heavy yard gate, take his concertina down off the nail and sit there in the cool of the evening, his back against the wall, playing traditional airs.

Then father died. It was in the autumn. He died when no one was expecting it. He had caught a chill out in the rain and thinking nothing of it, had neglected to change out of wet clothes, developed acute pneumonia and was dead within a month.

A fire was lit in the big bedroom facing the front drive which had formerly been his wife's room. He would not stay in bed, not at first; and then not in that room at all. At the beginning of his illness he had sat before the fire in his dressing-gown, coughing, saying he was feeling better, staring into the flames, the fire tongs in his hand. He had difficulty in breathing, a most terrible struggle for breath in the early stages. Every breath seemed like his last. His poor labouring chest could hardly bring it up, and always coughing with a strained look in his eye. Being osculated, looking up at Dr Broadbent. The sound of a spoon striking the rim of a glass. The nurse in starched uniform always in attendance. And then, apparently over the worst of it, his condition steadily improving. Improving, but still weak. Sitting up, sipping drinks. Eggflips. Poor Father.

Out of bed he ate oranges, holding them over the fireplace, biting into one without bothering to peel it, all the juice wasted, sucking at the pulpy centre and throwing it away. Evidence of a wasteful, erratic nature.

Then the relapse. In the cramped little room above the hall, once a changing-room, his final illness began. During the oppressively long days that went away towards a Christmas that he would not live to see, he had lain propped up on pillows, calling them one by one to his bed so that he could talk to them. But he found that he could not so easily put aside the habits of a lifetime, and there had been long embarrassed silences. Her heart had turned to stone in that small sickly-smelling chamber. She avoided his eyes, the appeal directed from the bed which she could not respond to, her hand in his hand and what remained of his life ebbing away. He no longer read, he who had been such a great reader all his life, but contented himself with staring out the window, for he had his bed moved so that he could watch what was going on outside. From where he lay he could see the beech tree in the front field and the pheasants rooting in the beech mast and part of Killadoon wood beyond. The sun, with no warmth in it, reached the balcony at a certain point each day, never penetrating into the room, and when it receded from that point, that much more life had left with it. He watched the starlings flying over the field as the light went. They landed in a cluster all together, feeding with restless chattering; then one or two would rise, then all would rise and fly on again, changing their feeding ground.

Two labourers crossed the sodden field with a horse and cart. One walked at the horse's head holding the bridle, the other sat on the tailboard, a pitchfork between his knees. Creegan came to the door, cap in hand, asking:

– An how is the maaster?

– Ah Creegan, he's not well at all. It's just as well to be prepared.

He would not allow the curtains to be drawn day or night in the little room with the oppressive maroon wallpaper. Faded dimity curtains that had originally belonged to the Warrens. His window grew darker. His condition grew worse. A day was passing. He watched the light go with no expression on his face, staring at the curtains, the wallpaper, gazing out towards the hills, the sky's grey reaches. What occupied his thoughts then? How he had first come to Springfield House with a young bride from the Battery Road of Longford; what he had said then, how she had replied? They had come down from Longford; had trouble finding a suitable place; but the moment he saw Springfield he wanted it. He had two trees cut down, two elms standing in the plantation before the house, obstructing the view. When they were down the view opened out up to the hills. They could watch the smoke of the Blessington steam-driven tram ascending the hill on a calm summer's day, climbing all the way toward Blessington, sending up puffs of white smoke from its long funnel. All that was finished now; over and done with.

Now his life had become burdensome to him; he lost all interest in activities that had formerly engrossed him, no longer read, wrote or despatched letters, he who had been such a keen correspondent all his life, but sank back into a lethargy that persisted to the end. His presence paralysed her; she could not open her mouth to say a word. He wanted her to speak, open up a little, break the spell. She couldn't do it.

The radiator in the sick-room rattled and groaned. Another day ended. The dairymen in dinted slouch hats went past below the window at four o'clock in the morning banging their buckets, climbing the paling and shouting to the cows to rise. Half the circumference of the paling had been sold and replaced with wooden stakes and barbed wire. Father had got into the habit of selling trees. The walnut tree at the end of the garden was sold to a buyer for a timberman, sold by the foot and paid for by girth, in a package deal with two ash trees. A single man came with an axe and felled it into the back field. The buyer only wanted the walnut, for the two ash trees lay on the ground for over a year. They were sold eventually to Behan, a handyman from Clane. The other had wanted the walnut for veneering. A lone blackthorn in the front field came down. It was unlucky to fell blackthorn, but it came down. Also a tall ash with two forked arms in the front field by the back lodge, sold and felled. They worked until after dark cutting it up, lighting a fire at night, the sound of the crosscut carried across the field, figures about the fire and someone playing a harmonica.

The front field had been set for a month at £2 an acre for the aftergrass. Twenty acres. The dairymen slept in the front lodge. The cowmen. They were brothers. They slept in a stall in the back yard on hay, and got up at outlandish hours, smelling of milk. They themselves had the complexions of cows, russet pelts, very red hands and a white scum on their underlips; they wore sweat-soaked hats back to front, with the brims up. They were rough peculiar men who slept most of the day and had no life at all. Three tall urns were set up in the centre of the field. The delivery had to be in Dublin before seven o'clock in the morning, so they were up betimes.

Father's face turned towards her. She stared out at the shadowed hills. Baldonnel airport was there somewhere. At a loss for a word he turned his face away. The radiator rattled and groaned. The dairymen went past again banging their buckets. He asked for apple jelly. Thanks to the economically-minded Lily there was some on the shelves – six or more two pound jars made from windfalls. He had his apple jelly – a splash of red among the medicine bottles. He had flushed cheeks. The days must have been long for him, long days spent lying there with nothing to do but stare at the folds of the dimity curtains with the curtain rods askew, hearing the bells ringing from every quarter. That which has not been altered for a long time seems unalterable. The bell in Killadoon wood was thin-toned and rapid, ringing at one o'clock and again at six. The sound of Straffan Catholic church bell came with the west wind five days a week. The big heavy bell of St Patrick's Catholic church pounded out in the village. The thin Church of Ireland bell occasionally, further away, lost in its belfry. The sound of the bells from Maynooth College coming on a calm day. That was what occupied his time.

One evening he called her to him. He began to speak directly to her in a way he had not done for many years.

– Come here, Shell . . .

Going down by the bedside she laid her hand on the sheet and he took it in both his. In a weak voice he continued:

– Now you listen here. You be patient when I'm gone, Shell. Because in this world you will suffer more than the others . . .

The voice came from a long way off and what it was saying did not seem to bear much relation to her. The nurse brought him beef tea and stayed up with him all night.

One morning when no one was attending he drew his last breath. The nurse came in and found him dead. He died in a morning of such stillness. In the afternoon the motorcars were coming slowly up the drive. She had helped in the kitchen which was filled with the scent of jasmine from the shrub outside, after the rain. They went in to see him – a low murmur of condolences behind the door. Then the clink of cups and saucers when Biddy served tea and scones in the drawing-room. She had stayed a long time at the window staring out at the dreary aspect of dripping leaves and weeping branches. Rain fell with a drumming sound on the roofs of the cars with their Dublin and Longford number plates. She turned back into the room.

Life had gone out of him without a struggle. The nurse, no longer in uniform, was there. Her suitcase was packed and ready in the hall. She said that he had gone peacefully. She repeated this. It was well received. The Catholic ones said, Thank God for the grace of a peaceful death. The Protestant ones shook their heads. The rain stopped. The cars departed, sounding their muted horns at the gate.

She took his intolerably cold hands and parted the clasped fingers. They were flaccid, wrinkled. She bent, holding her breath, to kiss his forehead. It was chill and moist. His eyelids had blue veins. The aquiline nose and jutting Adam's apple belonged to a face that she had not seen before. Old Mrs Henry had laid him out. Extending from his chin to where the coffin intervened he was dressed in stiff white biscuit-paper. Every individual hair of his head was standing on end. About him there was a total rigidity, a pulling inward. You be patient now. She bent again, took his hands, gave him lily of the valley, kissed him. The dead man considered his indifferent length and upturned toes; the *vis mortua* of his departed spirit blew coldly on her. Nothing now. Helen, with her queer notions, had stayed out all day, cycling. She came back late when the coffin was already on trestles at the rear of Celbridge church. There was only the impression his head had made on the pillows there for her to see.

Imogen put the documents together again, replacing them in the back of the drawer, her secret place, pushing it to until the mechanism clicked shut. Then she heard car tyres turning on the gravel before the house. A motorcar had come up the front drive and was pulling up before the hall-door. In the air the murmur of subdued voices.

Lady Brooke of Pickering Forest calling on Lily to take her on a country drive. Presently car-doors were slammed, the engine started up, and they rolled away down the front drive.

She sighed, rose from the chair, crossed to the full-length window. Letting down the catch she pulled the frame towards her. It came creaking in, shedding pieces of plaster and white-paint; she went out into the murmurous evening air.

Evening falling; a ruddy opulence of sky. The Overland was disappearing among the trees. It went on out of sight, leaving behind a lone cyclist pedalling towards the gate. A tall stiff woman on a high roadster. Imogen thought, *Who . . . ?* The double blare of the horn sounded imperiously at the gate. Then she recognized Helen, en route for Donycomper. The sound of the engine faded towards the village; the cyclist followed the motorcar out of sight.

Imogen stood on the balcony under a ruddy opulence of sky. A great field spread itself out before her, bounded on three sides by limestone walls. In a couple of hours the light would go. In the distance a mist from the river was slowly crossing it. The front field intervened, then the unclipped hedge before the road, then the wall; then Mangan's field. Soon the light would be gone. She rose so late – that was all that remained to her of the day. In the summer it would be different: she would rise with the lark. The sycamore would be out, its white flowers full of bees, the cock pheasants coming in over the wall from Killadoon. Then she remembered: the house would be up for sale. Potential buyers would be tramping through the rooms. Helen had said so. Seventy-two acres in good heart. Co. Kildare. Extensive stabling. Good shooting. Old-world orchard. Of particular interest to bloodstock breeders and followers of the hunt. Jackson Stops & McCabe. She was looking at this peaceful March landscape for the last time. These things she would not see again, no, not in her lifetime. She rested her hand on the balustrade and looked about.

Soon the evening flock of crows would come flying over the house, to go down in uproar into the wood. In the twilight the Angelus bell would ring a mile away in the village, *Angelus domini* coming on the wind. But not yet. In the declining light the trees of Killadoon were dark and leafless. A late spring. In the lee of the wall cattle moved among nettles and twigs, some straying across the field, others in more deliberate assembly close to the wall. She could distinguish the ruins of the Hell Fire Club on the hill where Speaker Conolly and gambler Buck Whaley had caroused of old. The days had begun to draw out. Brief and cold for her who rose so late they were soon over. Twilight would begin in the late afternoon. She heard the cries of blackbirds going in a flurry through the side plantation and the whole countryside blurred and trembled before her eyes. It had not always been so. Far from it. At one time she had seen the hill and sky with quite different eyes. In those auspicious days her blood had been on fire. On fire, then left to go out slowly, loath to go of its own accord.

She thought: the trees fall, the palings are sold, nothing changes, the house stands; we depart. Tendrils of Virginia creeper. A pile of russet leaves in the corner of the balcony rigid in decay. Light goes. We depart. Of that time, what do I remember now? What can I recall if I try? Was he good to me? Yes. He was good to me; good for me; kind and considerate. I was living in a daze before I met him. He brought me to life.

6

The Angelus bell began ringing from the village. It was six o'clock. Time to go. In the darkening graveyard now they drew apart. The old man pulled off his hat and turning away from her addressed himself to his evening prayers, blessing himself in a slow purposeful manner. All was over. Calm in their massed outline the cypresses stood. The strokes of the bell hung in the air. Soon it would cease ringing.

She saw a patient bald pate of a dead glossy white and a few scarce hairs about the ears. She thought, He thinks I am a Protestant. Let him. His ostensibly pious attitude irritated her. He stared ahead into the gloom, moving his lips, in a rapt pose that spoke for the properness of his faith, the rightness of the scene, the edification of his example. She saw that he was indeed old; old and tired out after a lifetime of service and labour to masters who had not always been easy; he would not mind setting his burden down in consecrated ground, and be buried among his people; buried with Tisdell and Darlington and Dempsey and the rest. Helen looked away.

Everything was losing its outline now, ruins and trees. She heard a pheasant's choked-off cry, abruptly terminated; then silence. The thick smell of the weedy grass came up to her. Out of the corner of her eye she saw him bending his knee in an arthritic genuflection, then he went on praying with downcast eyes. She felt herself growing resentful of him. She began to move off, finding again the main path that led towards the gate. Imogen might be worried and would set out after her.

The old man stood by the tree. He finished his prayers, blessed himself, put on his hat again; looking about he caught sight of her some way off, heading for the gate. Knocking off the earth from his fork against the butt of the tree, he crammed paper and dibber into his pocket, shouldered the fork, set out after her at his best pace.

She passed out through the cemetery gate. Her bicycle was there, leaning against the wall. She wheeled it to the side of the road. Her foot was already searching for the offside pedal, when he banged the gate. Few visitors come through this gate.

– Ave-nin, Miss Hillin!

She stopped and turned about. He came limping towards her. Three paces off he stopped, staring at her.

– Ah you don't mane to say you've forgotten me?

Helen stared at him. Who was he? She didn't know him from Adam. He had pulled off his hat and was crushing it in his hands.

– I'm afraid I have. Who are you?

He made a wry mouth.

– Ah indade to goodness you oughtn't to, seein I worked for your daddy for well nigh-on ten year! Don't you remember Josey Feeney, your old gardener an boilerman?

No, she had not remembered. Names and faces, they were escaping her, they were too much for her.

– Are you Joseph? she said in a faint voice. Yes, I remember you.

But she had not remembered him. Resentful of any display of emotion, she was grateful for the twilight; but wished it would end. It was embarrassing.

– I well remimber her sittin out on the summer sate with a big bowl of atin apples. When I kem into the yard with a fine jack rabbit for her dinner she didn't say a word but took a howlt of him be the hind legs an handed me a napple. A napple! the old man said with grudging admiration for such parsimony. Oh I'm telling you she was the right haro!

– Who? Helen asked, at a loss.

– Miss Emily.

She wished it would end. It was embarrassing.

– Springfield! Feeney said in a loud voice. Them were the days, Miss Hillin! God be with the old days!

– Yes, Helen said.

– Sure everything is changed nowadays, Feeney declared. Aye, an not altered for the better.

She said nothing, standing there with bowed head, twisting the loose vulcanite handgrip and wishing it would end.

– Many's the time I heard your poor daddy, God rest his sowl, singin and laughin to himself above in the fields, Feeney said. Oh a grand smart hardy little man.

Will you let me go? Will you let me be? We are paupers like the rest of you, except we live in a big house and enjoy credit. But we can't pay our bills any more. There's nothing to eat in the place except a few maggoty snipe hanging up in the larder. For all the eating we do, we might just as well not eat at all. Porridge and tea, tea and porridge. Heavy old stirabout that lies heavy on the stomach all day. Will you let me go? Bog-shares, bog-shares. The smell of manure in straw. Pale and faint, weary and watchful. I have no life in me.

– Colonel Clements had them riz.

The which? ... the one-storey houses of stone among the Council cottages. The herd's house in the demesne. No life left in me. No life at all.

– An yourself? (Nothing would silence him.) Do you sing a-tall yourself now, Miss Hillin?

– Sing? Helen said. I don't sing. What gave you that notion?

He came forward a pace, peering up into her face.

– Well indade to goodness you used to. Sing! Aye, like a bird.

A foggy morning; a miry plain; cold mists from the river traverse the field; Papa lies in bed dying. Springfield in the old days.

– It was a gramophone. Only records.

O Moon of my Delight. I Hear You Calling Me. Lo Hear the Gentle Lark. Oldtime waltzes and slow foxtrots.

– A grand high voice you had, Feeney persisted. Ah yis.

Galli-Curci. John McCormack. What does it matter now? Let him think what he pleases.

– An Miss Imagine? he said, putting a heavy stress on the middle syllable.

She could see the pale blur of his face watching her, vaguely outlined against the cemetery wall.

– She's well.

– Ah. An Miss Lily?

– Well too, Helen said.

– Ah, now isn't that grand for you!

They're there, that's all I can say. I try to keep out of their way, as they do out of mine. They have their own worries. We never had much contact at the best of times, nor anything much to say to each other. I can't stand the sight of Lily any more.

In the gloom two birds were wheeling and crying over the road. Then a single blurred pale shape, moving fast, a plump pale projectile, flew past low over her head. She felt the rush of air on her face. It went floundering off into the cemetery, and by the wall a single white feather came floating slowly down. An owl perhaps. But were there owls in winter? All her life she had lived in the country and yet knew so little about it.

Darkness had fallen. The workmen were cycling home. A group of them passed, coming from the Lucan direction. Their heavy boots, pale where the caked mud had dried, showed up in the weak beams of the carbide lamps as they went trudging round in the thrust and turn of the wheels. Since eight o'clock that morning they had been labouring in the fields, in cattle byres afloat with cattle dung, in the bottoms of ditches (the wheels were turning slowly), and now they were bound for the pubs. Feeney saluted them gravely:

– Night, men.

But they did not return his salute. They had not heard him. With hardly a sound they passed, the beams of their lights trained on the road, leaving behind them a faint sulphurous smell of wetted ashes.

– I must be going too, Helen said.

She set her bicycle lamp, adjusted her skirt, bade him goodnight, mounted, prepared to go.

He watched her cycling down towards the mill; then going down the dip; then gone out of sight. He stood there, confronted with the shell of a riverside mill on the river silent half a century and more, the roof fallen in in places, stood there as if mesmerized.

– Ah, tis a pile, he said aloud.

Shouldering his fork once more he set off towards the village, the lights of which were already beginning to shine through the bare scattered branches of the trees.

7

In Helen's room the Venetian blinds were half-drawn, the bed unmade, and two mangy dispirited-looking cats stared at her from the bed, while a third was licking something from a plate balanced precariously on some books on the desk. When this animal saw Imogen coming it jumped down and glided away.

She crossed to the window and drew up the blind a foot or more, admitting more light on the writing-desk, then seated herself at it. Sheets of paper heavily scored and corrected in her sister's slipshod hand lay there and a book which Helen had lately been reading, open with a marker between the leaves. Bending, Imogen read: 'then our long drive through Drumlanrig woods, with much talk from her (careless of the shower that fell, battering on our hood and apron); in spite of my habitual dispiritment, and helpless gloom all that summer, I too was cheered for the time. And then the dinner itself, and the bustling rustic company, all this, too, was saved by her, who turned it into something . . .'

Imogen stopped, pushed the book away. She tried to memorize the position of the objects on the desk, one in relation to another, before she began her inspection; then abruptly pulled open a drawer by her right hand.

Photographs, brown with age, face up. She took them out; four. The first showed a mine shaft rising above a hill upon which grew sparse scrub. There was a hut in the foreground, and before it a young man with a boater hat under his arm stared from the picture. Above him there was an inked cross on the print. The second showed a very plain housemaid clasping her hands to her abdomen on a flat rooftop. Her hair, parted in the middle, was frizzed up; she affected a white flower at the crown; her ears protruded, she had heavy eyebrows, her face excessively powdered, and she had the heavy slumberous loose Langrishe jaw. Her eyes, perhaps out of diffidence, were half closed. She looked like a man dressed up. The third photograph showed a boxer in a gymnasium, stripped for action, presenting his admirable profile to the photographer and his long reach to an unseen opponent. His dark hair was sleeked down, he wore a pair of shorts, tennis shoes, dark socks – an object of admiration to a number of heavily bustled ladies standing in edifying poses along the wall of the gym, below the Stars and Stripes, the Yale pennant and other unidentified insignia. On this print, on either side of the boxer's legs, was written in ink: *Jimmy Britt?* The last picture showed the rail tracks of the mine, the same precisely as in the first photograph, but now leading towards a narrow tunnel in the centre of the scrub-covered hill. The boater-hatted young man was posed before the tunnel, resting one foot on an item of rolling stock, leaning forward, chin in hand, pensively regarding the camera. He had the soft, well-bred appearance of a young gentleman of leisure.

Imogen put her hand back into the drawer and drew out a document which when unrolled revealed itself as a shares certificate impressed in gold leaf, with a dark green torch shooting forth static green flames, over which was printed in black lettering the legend

LANGRISHE CONSOLIDATED
MINING COMPANY

Issued to Robert Langrishe, dated September 24th a good few years past. She spread it out. The centre sheet was watermarked in gold, stamped with a beaten gold seal upon which was embossed the title, *Langrishe Consolidated Mining Company, Arizona*, and in the middle of the seal, *Incorporated* 1915. It was a certificate for 3,720 shares of capital stock, fully paid and non-assessable, transferable only on the books of the Corporation by the holder in person or by Attorney upon surrender of the certificate, properly endorsed. A fanciful illustration showed the mine workings, the narrow gauge railway, the shaft and sundry cooling towers belching smoke, the whole set among mountainous scenery. Par value ten cents. Incorporated under the laws of the State of Arizona. Serial number 93. Imogen put it away.

She thrust in her hand again; and this time brought out to her surprise something she had not seen before. A single carbon copy of a sheet of typescript, torn down the centre in an irregular line, the left half of which was missing. She put on her spectacles to read.

non
moment ago was; if you were aware
present or other examinations
or made you waver in your opinion,
e? No, you wouldn't.
ay, you can exaggerate sweating
s a far more important factor
sweating at one examination
erent things, – what the frame of th
t, whether she was nervous at that
mean the woman was full up after

e state of her nerves? It might.
ve a neurotic case without any of
s? Yes, it could.
it may be held to you, when these
you know the woman's full history
before? I don't know what you
tory because she gave me details
d past history since childhood.
patient for numerous years would it
be a help?
Delaney who knew her for close

ient. His evidence was that he met
accident but never beforehand
ing her as a patient, I suggest to you
her as a woman for twenty years and
ion to judge her genuineness than you
e.
examination of her? I had two
to to my satisfaction.
think I could decide in that time.

Imogen read this through twice; but it yielded up nothing. She could make nothing of it. She replaced it in the drawer which she then closed. With a steady hand she pulled out another drawer, the contents of which were already familiar to her, and took from the back a bundle of letters tied together, addressed to a Herr Otto Beck at a Munich address. They were in her own handwriting. She untied the bundle. A folded sheet of lined notepaper lay on top, and this she opened out. On it was written: 'This parcel of letters relates to the two happiest years of my long and insignificant existence, although those years were accompanied by uncertainty, and by the absence of anything that could constitute present happiness.' The tone was pure Mary Berry, although the handwriting was her own, when she was thirty-nine. She put it aside. The only letter he had ever written to her was there, addressed to Springfield with a Dublin postmark. He had been engaged in tutoring, earning a little money, staying with some people in Pembroke Road, Dublin. She opened the letter. The hand was unforgettable: angular, bold, the n's and w's were gates being trampled down, each imperious line dashed down almost on top of the previous one. She read: 'Today I amused myself watching the kangaroos at the Zoo. They are such strange creatures. The mother had her young with her, which kept coming in and out of the pouch. They have an awkward fashion of courtship. The buck hobbles along next to the chosen female in such a manner that the head and upper body seem insignificant, they look like big grey wagon wheels rolling slowly and deliberately over bumpy ground, next to the rabbit-shape of the female, who appears to be indifferent to them. But alert all the same, ears cocked. A truly prehistoric scene of fornication in its slowness and cumbersomeness. I have often considered . . .'

She stopped reading, laid the letter open on the desk, smoothing out its creases with the palm of her hand, and stared at the wall before her. Today I amused myself.

After a while she folded the letter neatly again, replaced it in its envelope, thrust it back with the others. Scheming, schemer . . . the letters in a certain way arranged, as if casually . . . Traps, all traps. She's sly. She took out some of her own letters. They never reached the Munich address, at least Helen had saved her that. One day she had put them away in a certain place, in a curtain, where Helen had come upon them, read and appropriated them without saying a word. Imogen took one out and read: 'What's travelling like? Are you tired of it, or is the capacity for novelty worn out before the things are?' Had she written that? How many years ago? Had she been happy then? The hot days of the long dry spell; the so-called dog days. Otto seated on a kitchen chair inside the cottage door in the evening sun, smoking his pipe, in shirt-sleeves, collarless, dreaming of something. Otto on his knees sowing seeds in the wet beds behind the cottage. There was a man of double deed, sowed his garden full of seed. She had brought cuttings from Springfield gardens. Lupins, bellflowers, balm of Gilead, blue spiraea, Cupid's dart, snow-in-summer. He had touched her behind that first night on the avenue; had drawn close to her affections by stealth. She read: 'I am no good without you. I have been so terribly lonely. It is my dearest wish ... My own dearest, I feel how uncertain I am without you. Tonight I sit here and can do nothing except mope and drink gin. There is so little now-a-days. Not that there is so little really, but so much of one closes up – I mean me. I listen to Helen and her world is so small and narrow, the world that she calls art. Of course she doesn't talk an awful lot to me, as I am one of the sub-intelligents. I've been reading, would you believe it, *The Wings of a Dove*. I find much of it badly written, or rather not written well enough; a man trying to describe shades of feeling beyond his range of expression. If only he had Proust at his elbow. Would that be right?'

She read to the end of the letter and put it back in its envelope; drew out another one, opened it:

'... I've not been too well ... but no further sign of trouble from that quarter, or any other part of me ... I wondered if my little indisposition had been a bit of ...' She read on a little further. And then:

'I still think the only cure for living is drinking. No, I am quite serious. Why else is it that ideas become so very much clearer when you've had a drink? Is it because the shambles of life falls into the background or what? It must be very simple. After all the animal traits become clearer, why not the mind also?'

The animal traits become clearer. Imogen read on through the four-page letter, depressed by its assumptions. She had been parading herself a little, trying to impress him. It wouldn't have worked. Not with him. She read: 'What do you think, is the world big or is the world small? I myself have become very small; tight and dull and even immune to my own meaner moods. It's the old oppression I knew would creep up on me. And then to have the energy to throw it off – well, I just haven't got it.'

She read to the end; selected another; read:

'Just to be on my bicycle again on a long clear evening. It's years since I've made use of an early summer evening. But now I find it impossible to fully enjoy anything. I say "now" and that's a laugh, – as if at any other time it had been otherwise. For even before there was always something to upset the happiness we had. Some foolishness or some quarrel; only this time I was in the future. The roads were the same, the hills the same but my eyes and my heart are two different things and between them they give me no peace, all the misery of the world staring out of my eyes, something that is an essential part of me, I cannot escape it. What can I do? "Come to terms" – that doesn't mean anything. It sounds as bad as "Know thyself" and all that rubbish. The only things that help are thunderstorms or very strong winds that blow on one. The sun is no good, for it opens everything out. I want to remain closed.'

She went on reading. The memory of things – are they better than the things themselves? It had grown dark outside, and the light coming through the window hardly sufficed for her to see by. After a while she got up, adjusted the blind to its former level, moved her chair in close by the wall, took from the mantelpiece Helen's spare bicycle lamp, reseated herself, turned it on. It cast a feeble enough light, but sufficient. Helen returning would not notice it from below. Imogen selected another letter.

'I have gained a stone in weight. It is very obvious, as I bulge all over the place, but feel very comfortable . . .

'Days are passing and I am getting more and more anxious. Weeks, months, years could go by. My dearest sweetheart, my life, do not think of me, if you think . . . think unkindly or say that ever on this earth . . . and then I would gladly . . . but feeling so guilty that I don't know. I might convince myself that it was too late, better to turn back forget that it had ever . . . so that I am sending you . . . I who am in no position, to say the least of it . . . well, is that asking too much? (She read rapidly, skipping words, phrases, her elbows on the table, hands at her temples, her head close to the indiscreet scrawl.) . . . I sometimes wonder . . . try to be frank, trying to be honest, but whether there could be meaning in it, that's another matter . . . There is a river near Parthenay called the Thouet . . . so how is one . . . or did you perhaps mean something else? Oh my dearest love bring me to Chapelizod again and we will . . . destroy the happiness we had . . .'

She read down to *and if you are free*.

She felt something painful stirring in her, behind her ribs for an instant knew its timid pressure. A younger Imogen, not heart-whole, dressed in organdie and with bare arms, beckoned. She did not offer to read on, but remained sitting in the darkened room, her eyes closed. Destroy the happiness we had. She had tried to keep it, sustain it at maximum force; but it had left her. Below a bicycle passed slowly on the gravel. Helen was back.

She folded the four pages, thrust them in their envelope, took the bundle of letters securing them with two rubber bands and pushed them back into the drawer, closed it, got to her feet, turned over the cushion, re-arranged the objects on the desk so that it looked now just as she had found it, more or less the same disorder prevailing. The sound of a drawer clicking shut in a darkened room. A woman rising hastily, thrusting away documents. Imogen hurried, lamp in hand, to the door, opened it, extinguishing the light.

Through the low window on the landing another faint light was advancing towards the side door. It shone over the covered tank. Helen was already in the yard. She would have to move quickly. Moving back into the room, where a faint light came through the window, she went forward until her outstretched hand encountered the mantelpiece. No time now for finesse, no putting it back exactly where she had found it. Helen could think what she liked, think that it was the cats. She thrust the lamp in among other unidentified objects and moved back towards the door, advancing crablike, her right hand outstretched before her, leading with her right foot – one step forward, then bringing up the left foot, heel to heel with the right foot, then the right foot forward again, the left foot brought up, heel to heel, and so on until her hand met the cold surface of the wall. The open door was to the left. She found it when her hand went through the opening. She stood on the step in total darkness. There was no light in the yard. Helen was putting her bicycle away.

She could see nothing in front of her, only pitch darkness. The landing, the lavatory door opposite, the near window overlooking the yard, which could have guided her steps, had a little light come through, all lay in utter darkness. She might fall and break her neck on the stairs. She must go back and take Helen's lamp again in order to get down.

She turned, groping her way back, three, four slow blind steps. Until there it was again, the hard edge of projecting cast-iron. She introduced her hand with some guile, ultra-careful, among miscellaneous objects, jars, toiletries, useless things, fumbled for it; anticipating it before she found it, a certain shape, shallow black tin cold to the touch, minor protuberances of flanged cup and milled edge; in a word, the precise shape she could recognize, by touching.

Close to, close enough for her to fancy the still air disturbed by the softly shuttling motion of its pendulum, a measured, resonant, liquid-sounding stroke announced the presence, close to her face, of a good-sized clock. In the dark it sounded loud. You'll never find it. Breathing hard, she thrust her hand here and there among the vanities on the mantelpiece. An unidentified object, evading her nervous grasp, fell, and was shattered to bits in the grate.

She listened, straining her ears. Silence. Nothing. With a shaky hand she tried again. This time she found something likely. It was it. Her fingers quickly imprisoned it as the door below opened with a familiar dragging of its hinge.

She lost her head completely then. The object she had in her hand was not a lamp, no such thing, only a hairbrush. She had forgotten on which side of the clock she had left the accursed thing, and in any case would never find it in the dark. She thrust her hands here and there, breathing fast. Additional objects rained down. She was beginning to doubt seriously whether she had left it there at all, when she found it. Snatching it up she made for the door, had the lamp working, and was through. Helen bolted the door below leading into the yard, and advanced along the flagged passageway. Imogen advanced on tip-toe on squeaking linoleum above her. At the end of the landing, on the wall, light flooded from the lamplit hall below. She went down four steps, crossed to the carpeted main stairway, and fled up towards her room, just as Helen, tired out from her expedition, set foot on the lower stairs.

8

I hear the wind in the high beech tree and the wearisome grinding together of its great boughs. Night comes. The darkened house is breathing . . . windy, bronchial.

Soon we will be old. Old, ill and poor; and when we die no one will mourn for us, or afterwards remember us.

I am cold. So cold. Here I languish under blankets and eiderdown. Nothing stirs. Sounds die out. I have grown accustomed to the cistern. It's in my head. I am freezing. I am dead with cold.

I fold my arms across my breast, crossing them, the right hand over the left, the wrists touching, fingers resting in the hollows above the collar bones, my mind at rest. I am resigned. Gradually my respiration comes slower and slower. Disturbed by the air coming in at the top of the window, the Venetian blind blows in, then collapses against the frame. Silence. Then blows in without a sound. Again collapsing with a slurred sound, regular as breathing. The whole house creaks and groans. The mice escaping the cold have invaded it, for I can hear them. Time passes. I smell a bad smell. The Venetian blind makes its sound again. I hear a hoarse barking not far away. For a little longer he keeps it up. Where? Lives on what he can kill. What can he find in the ditches when times are bad? Nits, field mice, frogs, cress. Silent now. Travelling. Night-prowling fox after our hens. Far away in the Council houses a dog answers. Now he can go in. Nothing disturbs me. Nothing has been forgotten. I go over in my mind the trivial events of the day. Nothing has been forgotten. Good.

Heedless of so much, ignorant of so much. So much. So much. All my efforts to be one thing, be other than I am, of no avail. I know, I know. And there are things which one wouldn't say to a person's face which one could say behind that person's back. The broken objects in the grate. The letters all mixed. I knew right well that she had been, poking about as usual.

The stench, it's from the candlestick by my head. A smell of hot iron and tallow. The candle must have burned down to nothing and gone out. So I must have dozed. I like to read last thing in bed. It sends me to sleep.

The noise of the cistern fills the landing. Its rusty dinted ballcocks are half out of the water and the lid that might have silenced it is off. Running away, it fills my head. Water leaking continuously away, gallons of it, sufficient to fill a tank, two goodsized tanks. More, more. A small lake. A reservoir. There's a reservoir in my head.

Isn't she the incompetent article all the same? I at least carry the responsibility for all on my shoulders, and for myself too, but she couldn't crack an egg without spilling it on the floor. She has been poking about again. One of the cats is gone.

Could I even be sure if I leave him alone again that he wouldn't be torn to bits in the door, lacking the sight of his one poor eye? No I couldn't. She's a nosey-parker. What kind of fool does she take me to be? I'll stay here and never go down again. I'll stay where I am; because I can't stand the sound of people walking about above my head; because everything in the world has begun to irritate me. I'll do that. I'll arrange the chairs here so that I can move from one to the other, from bed to door. I'll stay where I am, for sooner or later the step down will kill me.

What kind of abject fool does she take me to be? I have eyes in my head to see. I am up to all her tricks. Those letters of hers. Never posted nor delivered nor ever intended to be, some of them left much to be desired from the point of view of grammar and spelling, others from the point of view of common decency and restraint, any kind of restraint, syntax, grammar and punctuation apart, our name apart, making a spectacle of herself like that. With her lardy suety face, I don't know what he saw in her.

And then, and then, far away out of reach of memory, I have a dream that something in me responds to – well, regret for what cannot be changed, grief for what will not come back – all that, nonsense perhaps . . . but I too in my way . . . I too . . .

There now, what's the use of poking about in the muck, raking up all the old resentments? Leave well alone. That's poor advice no one would thank you for. I've done it throughout my miserable existence and look where it's got me. But wouldn't you think she'd have got tired of it? If God himself called down to her to come to her senses. That fellow. He never loved her. Never. She must have known. Well, she had her lesson. A hard enough lesson. *Are you tired of it?* ... Or is the capacity for *novelty?* All that tone of camouflaged entreaty. You'd imagine she'd get tired of it. My own dearest I am no good without you. Your lovely body. If I were close enough. Love of all my life and all my senses. Induce where. And all my senses. What kind of talk was that?

No, I'll speak up against the German if it's the last thing I do, and in a court of law too. Because if she was a real fool about him, as the dear God knows she certainly was, he was a downright ruffian to go and leave her. She might have died. She was never strong. It broke her heart. It might have killed her. She hadn't a care in the world before. Look at what he did to her. In the time she was with him, all the waste and expense. The waste and expense will not come back. What does it matter now?

... Your body, if it were close enough ... oh my dearest, my love, love of all my life ... and all my senses ...

The shadows move away. It's late. The cold penetrates my knees. It's from the earth freezing as the temperature drops. The Venetian blind makes its sound against the window frame. I lie in bed on my left side, my frozen feet pointing to the river, flooding down through the village, by Straffan, Stacumney, Leixlip, and all the grand estates. In the dark a church bell is ringing, the rope pulled by someone half asleep.

There's the wind in the high beech tree again, followed by the wearisome grinding together of its boughs.

On the night of the storm, how the wind roared through it. If it were to fall? It would hit the house, slicing through the walls. I'd be cut in two in bed, driven down through the floor into the kitchen. Lath, plaster, brick and stone would go down like tissue paper before such force. All night long it sways and groans.

The cry of curlew or plover comes down to me. Passing over the house at a great height, making for the hills, the gorse. *Pluvia.* Rain sign. *Pluvia.* Faint; once more. Passing; faintly heard. Gone.

I hear it, my face stiff with cold. All is dark. All life's extinct. My feet have gone dead on me. With rheumatic fingers I chafe the soles of my feet, solicitous of my corns. Nothing helps. The blood refuses to be coaxed down into my extremities. I give off little heat. The earthenware jar has slipped down out of reach. It had gone tepid. No matter. Outside the land is stiffening in the cold. The ditches are frozen up. Out of the atmosphere the cold descends. I can feel it approaching, tightening, colder than Yeniseisk in the black frost of 1736 when the temperature dropped 126° below zero and the birds fell down dead out of the air.

In the silence the room turns on its axis and all the sounds rush back to me. I feel lonely. I have coaxed a little heat back into my limbs. So my thin Langrishe blood still warms me a little. Now that some heat has come back, I feel less forgotten to myself. I am sinking. Good. Tonight I can hope for some sleep. I begin to prepare my mind for it by going over the trivial events of the day. I live here. The greasy road leads into the village. My village. My Kildrought. I cycled there for groceries 'to be charged for'. What more is there to say. It seems I have lived here all my life and will very likely die here. History begins and ends in me. In me, now, today.

On the banks of the ditches bluebells grow in spring. On stark cold days I cycled there, my shadow following me along the wall by the Charter School and the Gaelic football field, past the point where old Tommy Morrissy who carried the post for Colonel Clements was run over by the Edenderry bus, coming out of the long blind approach onto the road, killed him outright on the hill.

The days draw in. They are soon over. Soon over. The sun rises at eight-thirty; goes up over the trees. Low all day, it sinks out of sight before five. Dusk begins at four in the afternoon. Brief days, brief days. The mornings are dim and overcast, with no sun. Not mornings at all. It might be any hour of the day were it not for the sharpness, the coldness. Through these windows these eyes have watched, have seen. What I see oppresses me. I have looked at it long enough. All old disputed land. My home today. Written of in Exchequer Inquisitions and chronicles, in the time of Henry VIII and Elizabeth before him. She who, in right of her crown, seized of the Manor of Kildrought, alias Castleton-Kildrought, and one water-mill, all in the County Kildare. Mentioned in Parliamentary Statutes. In the Courts of Exchequer lists dating back six and more centuries. In rolls of forfeited estates. In deeds offices. Ordnance Survey records. Statistical surveys, Land Commission files. In private documents. In dead men's wills. Forfeited over and over again since the Anglo-Normans. And 74 acres of it mine today – a forgotten battlefield that means nothing to me. Nothing. The grand names and the grand estates. Castletown. Alenscourt. Donycomper where Madame Popoff lives, married to the White Russian. Killadoon where Miss Kitty Clements lives with her mother. The empty Abbey. Oakley Park. Windgates. Rose Lawn. Pickering Forest. Nothing. Napier. Allen. Kane. Conolly. Dease. The Honourable George Cavendish. John Graham Hope de la Poer, the 5th Baron Decies (who was it died in the flood?). As it was in the beginning, is now, ever shall be, world without end. Nothing. Invasion after invasion; occupation after occupation. Silent mills, bear testimony. Overgrown ruins, bear silent testimony. Round towers beloved of King John, bear testimony. Disused graveyards, bear testimony. Broken monuments of the Geraldines, bear testimony. Joe Feeney, bear testimony. History ends in me. Now. Today.

I am prey to strange fancies. Sometimes in the night I hear the central heating rattling, which is what it cannot do, with no steam going through it. Can it be that I imagine Feeney is stoking in the furnace room? No, I know that's impossible.

I wanted to scream with irritation when she began poking the fire. Couldn't she leave it alone? . . . leave it, leave it. (bending hand outstretched . . .) The noise of the fire tongs irritates me. Poking at the logs and coal irritates me. Just getting accustomed to . . . one thing . . . say a certain arrangement of fuel and glare . . . then the picture to be upset . . . different noises come from it . . . the fire burns briskly in a quite different way. Most exasperating sound of all is the clatter of fire-irons in the fender. Her idiotic attempts at order.

The ballcock is exposed and the lid is off. Stale brownish water, rusted metal, the smell of Scrubb's ammonia, that awful smell. Water running all night. It leaks away in my head. No wonder I'm short-tempered.

Side by side with the real world there is another. I believe that. The old man who carried the post for Colonel Clements was knocked down by the Edenderry bus and killed outright. An old man with whiskers, heavy topboots and a blue uniform. The front wheels went over him as he came cycling out of the blind approach to Killadoon. The long front avenue. Such a little old man to lose such a lot of blood. Old Tommy Morrissy.

I hear a disturbance in the radiator. The central heating is working again, fired by loyal Feeney in the furnace-room below. I hear the noise distinctly, the rattling in the pipes that informs me that hot steam is once again coming through.

The Venetian blind makes its noise again. Then all I hear is the ceaseless creaking and groaning of the old house, which goes on all night, from the foundations to the attic, and the scurry of mice. They have the run of the whole house. Much good may it do them.

Although the noise in the radiator has persisted for some time, the room is no warmer on that account. Presently the noise too dies away. The room is freezing again. I think I can control ... control – No ... no ... and gradually out of my mind everything goes. Everything. Except the belief that in order to be at peace with my Creator, the maker of me. Increasing loathing of all living things. The rottenness. Is it because I am ill? The rottenness. It's dreadful to think about. To think of them there is dreadful, sunken down. What can they resemble? Putrid by now; leaking; something one mustn't dwell on. The acrid stench of the potatoes in the earthen bank. Dusty tubers sprouting ears. This execrable life that yields not an inch.

I have never known the love of the body or of the heart. People think that I am bored with them but that in fact is not so. I come empty-handed to them and go empty-handed away. Senseless to lament what cannot be changed; but there you are – one does.

Something black, dreadful. Puddles of it leaking out of the coffin. Rottenness seeped up by the coffinboards and the earth. Ligament from ligament. Diminishing, disappearing, dried out by summer, become dry as dust. Death-moths. No longer in existence. Old Mr Johnston of Rose Lawn that died of typhus when sewage got into his well-water. A leakage. No longer in existence. Emily no longer in existence.

Waxen pallor of their faces. Befuddled heads. I do not like their voices, particularly Imogen's. Lily rarely opens her mouth. A rank sisterhood. Insipid. Yes, yes.

What portion of happiness may one expect, forgetting what it is like to have one's health, ill and only being able to think about that, the form one's illness takes, there's nothing else. When I look into the mirror now I see an old, old woman.

Today's trip exhausted me. Never again. I'm not able for it any more. A few turns in the garden. Like childhood again. The gruel. The taste's in my mouth of my childish days. Buddleia in a May garden. A blameless life. How perfectly useless everything seems towards the end of a blameless life . . .

The starlings come each summer to hatch out their eggs in the broken wall there in the corner of the rockery. A few turns there, that's enough. The line of silver birches behind the summerhouse. Long crimson flowers in spring, seen against the papery white texture of the bark which is in turn mottled with a brownish black discoloration. Fertilized by the wind. Breezes in summer. Calm day at sea. Silence. Then the surge again. That word. Surge. Summer sounds on a strand. Push of the tired tide, followed by the drag and recession of innumerable pebbles and stones. Grain going through a riddle. The breeze. Gentle sigh.

Small oblong cones. In the autumn the winged seeds flutter in countless numbers to the ground. In countless numbers. Line of beautiful silver birches. Silent now. Only the beech tree groans. All night long from its roots up it groans its deep persistent groan. I lie awake and listen to it. And it is with that sound in my ears that I am carried away.

9

The rockery and main garden grow wild; shrubs and grass hide the pathways; weeds proliferate everywhere. The rustic bowers fall in under the weight of rambling roses, and edging beds of rock roses advance across the unscuffled paths. Rain falls continually, pattering down on the beech hedge and on the orchard where the overladen branches of the apple trees have sunk to the ground. When the fruit rots off the branches meander at will across the overgrown paths. The entrances through the hedge become narrower, the place sealing itself off, closing on its rank grass, rotten fruit and swarming wasps. In the autumn Lily enters with a basket to collect cookers for apple jam, and loses it in the long scutch grass. A year goes by and she finds it by accident, useless now, rotted away by damp and partly devoured by slugs and ants. As if the place was now deserted, hedgehogs come out of the hedge in unheard of numbers and go about, an inch at a time, on the neglected lawns. (Imogen came upon one of them rolled up into a ball and mistook it at first for a mound of cowdung.) The tennis net, never taken in and now weighed down by the rain, trails its sad fringe. It sags across the court, discoloured by the birds, subsiding at last into the thick close grass that has already swallowed up a garden roller. Weeds grow on the sundial, the palm trees lose their fronds.

December snow breaks the windows of the greenhouse. Rot undermines the exposed roof supports and half of it falls in upon what has already perished there – tomatoes that nobody wants, a lone tea-rose, Belgium vine. The leaves of the chestnut tree dry up and fall in groups and singly. All that seasonal decay and dying fall to the ground, deprived of summer's light and heat. The leaves cover the wrinkled conkers, soon to be obliterated. And so all goes away. The field-hands share the gaberdine suits between them. Lily is cheated in a scheme for marketing Bramley Seedlings. Winter invades the garden and the orchard, coming down from the freezing sky and up from the ground, to lay all in waste before it.

Gaunt and famished like a wolf the neglected Alsation Oscar starves in the backyard ash-pit.

Indoors too there is neglect and decay. Worn thin and threadbare the carpets are cut up into oddments. Draped over the front paling and left there for a day and then dragged back into the wrong rooms. Helen puts her false teeth in a glass of water diluted with Milton. Grown very particular she thinks of all the things she cannot stand. In Lily's bedroom where a window stands half-open, rainwater has collected, leaving a stain on the perished carpet.

There, each in her own room, each with her own troubles, they lie sleeping in big brass beds headed into the corners and looking as if designed for suffering – dreaming of better times, of worse times. And so all goes away.

II
1932

'As it falles out, where sodayne flightes & frightes overcomes as
many as doth the armes of the adversaries.'

Sir James Perrott
The Chronicle of Ireland
1584–1608

10

'... she is pretty, truth to tell, wildwood's eyes and primarose hair, quietly, all the woods so wild, in mauves of moss and daphnedews, how all so still she lay, neath of the whitehorn, child of tree, like some losthappy leaf, like blowing flower stilled, as fain would she anon, for soon again 'twill be, win me, woo me, wed me, ah weary me! deeply, now evencalm lay sleeping.'

Finnegans Wake.

Otto Beck lay in the meadow, his back against the paling, enjoying his pipe, the last of the day, letting his thoughts wander. The sun had begun to sink behind the trees. It was going down at last, ending yet another day of hot and prolonged sunshine. His cherry-wood was drawing well. The mixture which he had blended himself, while not exactly another Cope's Escudo, was nevertheless a good strong smoking mixture, and one that gave him pleasure. He smoked his pipes in strict rotation. He had fourteen. The cherry-wood was his favourite. He had been up and about since six o'clock that morning and now felt tired and at peace. Country life suited him well. The tobacco smoke helped to keep away the midges, but an uneasy army of insects moving through the dry powdery earth at the base of the grass, the woodlice and ants in great numbers – these travelled over his person and were endured with stoical indifference; he was Lemuel Gulliver.

The light drained out of the evening sky, reluctant to go, mauve and violet over Killadoon. As the sun sank the trees along the back avenue rose up to meet it. It rested on timber, then went gliding downwards out of sight towards the hill of Ardrass. Beside him in its sack the white ferret stirred. Time passed. Twilight came down. He did not move.

Along the plantation the white scuts of rabbits jumped, vanishing into the shadowy hedge. The air was full of the noises that summer releases after dark. In hot clinging waves the sickly yellow smell of some flowering shrub came to him; – not magnolia, not rhododendron, but another, oversweet and overpowering. Above the meadow flew the bats. He had not shifted for the best part of one and three-quarter hours.

Then in the stillness he heard footsteps coming on the dusty avenue; a woman's light step was approaching from the house. He got to his feet and leant his back against the paling. He had met the Langrishe sisters and wondered which one it might be: Helen, Lily, or the youngest – Imogen. He decided to turn at the last moment and salute her, whoever she was. But she had seen him already. The feet slowed down, halted some distance from him, and a woman's voice called out in a high cultivated accent:

– Excuse me, but what star is that?

He turned and saw it was the youngest, Miss Imogen; she was pointing over the back lodge. He removed his pipe from his mouth, turned with deliberation, looked up. Clear sky, a single early star, *Abendstern*; through this the world goes.

– The evening star, he said. Venus. Always low and always the same – the first in the dark.

– Oh, she said, is that so? taken aback a little by the irony in his voice.

– I thought it was Hesper, she added after a pause.

– Hesper? he said. No. Unmistakably Venus, the brightest of the four planets . . . visible, that is, to the naked eye. A planet in fact, not a star.

– How can you tell whether it's Venus or not? she said. Aren't they all the same?

– The same? he said. The same as what?

– Why, the same as each other, she said, planets and stars.

– Decidedly not, he said. Planets are closer than stars, for one thing. And nine of them revolve around the sun, against a background of constant stars which do not move. How does one know it's Venus, you ask. Well, because it's brighter than all the other stars and planets, as you will see, and because it's in the position where it should be, if it is Venus, moving in the direction

Venus ought to move in. How, then, can it be anything else but Venus?

– I see, she said, absent-minded. I see.

Otto Beck looked towards Killadoon wood, whose timber showed above the front plantation, over the road.

– We could see Mercury tonight, he said, if Killadoon didn't interfere with the view. It's visible for an hour and a half after the sun sets in this hemisphere around this time of year.

She thought about it for a while with one finger to her cheek. Then, looking to one side of him, she said:

– I'm obliged to you for this information, I suppose. Who are you?

– I'm from the back lodge, Miss Imogen, he said. Beck is my name. Otto Beck, student. At your service, he added, bowing.

She came to the paling between him and the house and leant her forearms on it, staring into the meadow, not deigning to look at him directly.

– Can you inform me please, he tried at last, turning and waving his hand, – what's that shrub I smell with the nauseating scent?

He watched her go through the pantomime of drawing in a nauseating smell through her nose.

– Syringa, she declared at last, nodding. Yes . . . mock-orange.

He said he had never heard of that – syringa.

– Jasmine, she said.

– Ah, jasmine, he said. I see. Is that what you call it here?

She made no reply. They stared out over the meadow. The bats were scattering widely, dipping, dodging, apparently without purpose, uttering weak cries. All over the whitening grass the puff-balls went sailing. A bluish mist, bringing more heat, glided along by the dark plantation. Not once had she looked at him. She was dressed in a light belted raincoat, her black hair cut in a fringe low over her heavily made-up eyes. He saw a pale face in profile, dark lipstick on her rosebud lips, the features vague and shadowed, and he was conscious of her perfume. Her expression was wry, petulant; she was continually fidgeting and moving her body this way and that, her hands restless, touching herself with covetous gestures here and there, on hips, throat, cheeks, tendentious, patting her hair.

– And what brings you here? she said at last.

– Exercise, he said. I walk the avenues in the evening. It's so peaceful. Is that not permitted?

He hoped she had not noticed the sack; he had hoped for a little quiet ferreting in the cool of the evening, but had done nothing about it.

– That's no concern of mine, she said. I meant what brings you here to Celbridge. You are not local-born, are you?

– Far from it, he said. I come from Bavaria.

– Is that so? You speak English very well.

– Thank you. I learnt to speak it as a child. My mother was a great Anglophile.

He climbed the paling. Resting his forearms on the black iron rail he stared with her into the meadow. She made no further comment, and did not look at him either. He struck a match, relit his cherry-wood, which had gone out. He began smoking again, staring every now and again at her; but she ignored him. She was not interested. A breeze blew over the meadow. They might have been leaning over a ship's rail at night, strange to each other, uncomfortable passengers thrown together at the beginning of a voyage. Looking down he studied his right tennis shoe, none too clean, resting on the lower rung. She said nothing.

She was thinking: Not jasmine, not syringa, no. Philadelphus. A smell like decay. He doesn't know me, but I know him. He's a friend of Major Barton's son from Trinity College, Dublin. Dada allowed him the back lodge rent-free because he is poor and said to be gifted, and because he spoke German to Dada, quoted Schiller. He didn't attend the funeral because he left just before Dada died. He was supposed to be travelling on a scholarship grant, that was the story we heard. The lodge lay empty all that time. Now he's back again, in residence again. He never asked our permission, or, if he did, Emily never spoke of it. I knew his name was Beck. Beck of Bavaria. He has no visible means of support. He was arrested by the Guards of Enniskerry and Dada got him out on bail. He is writing a thesis, supposed to be. He doesn't know me or remember me, he has forgotten Dada's famous tennis-parties. We sat on the terrace watching the mixed doubles tournament. He doesn't remember that.

He looked at her. Vacuous stare; her thoughts elsewhere. In the silence an ass and cart went grinding by on the road.

What did Anglophile mean? It was difficult to follow him.

– I have never travelled very much, she said, to my great regret. I don't even know my own country very well, I am ashamed to admit.

– Ah yes, he said, only too pleased to have an opportunity of going on talking, I too would like to see more of Ireland. It is a beautiful country. To see Tara where your kings and queens are buried. How many dynasties lie buried there I wonder?

– Only here, she said, with a tutor, and then at a boarding-school, then at Parthenay, *Deux-Sèvres*, near Poitiers. And then back in this house. That's all.

He wondered, was she a little *hard of hearing*, but cleared his throat and managed to say politely:

– Yes? You have been abroad then. Do you speak any French, Miss Langrishe?

– I was beginning to think in French, but now I'm losing it again. One gets little opportunity for practising French here.

He began to knock his cold pipe out into the palm of his hand.

– Let me hear your pronunciation, he said, master to pupil.

– *Je sens toujours les houblons mouillés des pluies*, she said, nasal, in a strange woman's liberated voice.

– First class, said Otto Beck.

She heard the noise of a cart going by so slow it was like a noise in her head; the grating of the ungreased axles against the side of the cart, its laboriously turning wheels which hardly seemed to move, both wheels turning so slowly, these were sounds from a dream. It carried her back.

The grass of the meadow had grown high, and him there with his shirt off, scything thistles, the bones of his white back moving to and fro, pistons in their proper sockets, the strength of him, and the sun on his red hair shining like fire. His arms moved methodically from side to side, his ribs contracted, bulging through the skin, and the thistles and grass tumbled down.

She had come out of the shrubbery with a bowl of blackberries but was too shy to approach him. He stood sharpening the curved blade with professional sweeps of the whetstone, the hair over his eyes, his scythe at rest, its point in the ground. She noticed that his pale skin could not take the sun, which was quite fierce, for an Irish summer.

Or again, in cool air, imagining himself alone, Otto walked through the mist of spray by the weir, his hands in his trouser pockets, whistling, imagining himself unobserved. Unseen herself, she had watched him cutting his initials in a tree with his pocket knife, which hung from a little chain, with a dark wood handle and a bright well-sharpened blade. The pink skin of the yew tree exuded a little moisture after his attentions. And it was still damp when she came to it and saw his mark.

Dada surprised him sunbathing stark naked in a wheatfield with a book covering his face, and gave him a good talking to. Dada sat under the old yew tree in the garden reading Petronius Arbiter and the *Elegies* of Propertius. He wore a pointed sunhat of yellow straw, and had a notebook and pencil by his side. Dada had sunbathed too, in the orchard. The conical point of yellow above the low grass near the hedge was all that showed. He sat on a rug there. She had heard the drone of Latin. His *concise* hat. She had blushed when told about shameless Otto in the wheatfield, remembering another occasion, a small guilty mirror on a chair; the humiliating exposure of her first shame. She thought: Nevertheless I would neither be here nor elsewhere. His restless eyes devour me. Mine meet them, and I flinch away. He has a small flat head and a fox's face. One thinks of sharp teeth and a lolling red tongue; his expression never changes. He runs his tongue over his dry lips like a fox cleaning its chops. His small-boned body and animal nature suit that first image of him I carried away as a silly girl; a still face staring from among the leaves. Not stepping on a twig, alert, ready to pounce; the fire of life is burning in him, – lust and cruelty too. He seemed an outlandish, a legendary figure, that face among the leaves, the skin stretched tight, in a word, holding onto or separating branches: the hunger of life. Does he cut his own hair? It looks like it. His shirt is open three buttons down and I can see curly man's hair. It's a faded blue shirt, I saw it in the daylight hanging on the line. The buckle of his belt shines with fire when he moves in the sun. He wears dirty tennis shoes without socks, this Naturalist in corduroy with bottle-green eyes and red hair. Who ever heard of a German with carroty hair? His melancholy fixed expression; he stands so still, always in awful clothes, this time trousers with faded tide marks about the fly. The baggy corduroys fold at the knees and at the glossy seat, the tongue of the buckle bites into the leather about his narrow waist and stretches the eye-hole. His shirt is open. Vengeful manner, cruel lover; he stands a long way off, his eyes blazing, stretching out both hands for me. I wouldn't mind being his trollop. Him to be cruel to me, as such men are reputed; he could do anything he likes with me. What else is my soft white useless woman's flesh good for? What else? I hear the leaves shake; the branches part and he's upon me. I am coming, my dearest . . . I am coming!

Over the meadow the white night moths were scattering at random, this way and that, flying and falling thick as feathers. The ass and cart had gone slowly out of earshot.

Do you want to get me down here, have your way? Who knows? From his manner it seems a possibility. Dare I? Dare I? A shot in the dark. I am not frigid, far from it, let him try. Take me by the shoulders, pull me down, here on the grass verge. The other two are like corpses already. Nobody passes, nobody sees or cares. Pray, Sir, did you ever meet a lady who is now a sort of specimen of a bygone world?

She turned then and they stood face to face. He saw a little ravenous pointed face under the fringe staring at him, and saw her breasts rising and falling beneath the tightly-belted coat.

– Yes, she said, almost inaudible, the filaments firing in her eyes.

– I am not very well equipped . . . he stopped and began again. I am not very *elegant*, but could a poor needy tenant offer you refreshment . . . tea, or perhaps a drink?

– H'm, she said, looking quickly away, softly striking the paling with the flat of her hand. Do you want to compromise me, making such an offer? You, a bachelor, alone at night.

– Oh I am harmless enough, he said in a mild way. I respect a woman.

You have your cheek, Mr Evening Star.

She stood away from the paling, staring down at her feet, thinking about it.

She thought: No, not now. We played until the evening then. A wonderful summer's day just as hot and long as today. The endless evening and the thrushes singing at the end of the garden in the walnut tree. I sat next to him in my new Switzer's dress of candystripe silk. He couldn't get enough to eat and was too polite to stretch. He seemed to be starving. His hand touched mine when I offered him, and he accepted, lemon angel pie. He touched me once; he has forgotten it. Yes, now.

He had noticed a rabbit track in the grass leading directly to where he stood. Where the track left the meadow and crossed the dust of the avenue, a wire snare was set on a forked twig, the stiff noose about the opening. He was wondering how he had not noticed it before.

– Look here, she said in a decisive way, the house is nearer. Do you mind if we go there instead? I could perhaps offer you something. That's closer, and less compromising. What do you say?

He said he didn't mind.

– Good, that's settled then. I'm sure Biddy won't mind. You may take my arm if you wish.

– I am thirsty, he said.

She made a gesture of offering him her arm. He looked at her without moving, suddenly hang-dog.

– I won't eat you.

He took her arm – that is to say, put his right wrist into the crook of her left elbow; and together, in step they moved towards the house. She moved in a rhythmic way on high heels. He felt, through the conducting agent of his arm, the shudder of her spine and ardent hips in motion. As they came onto the gravel before the house, he saw the high rooms lit up already, and heard the sad sound of a gramophone playing in an upstairs room.

– That's my sister Helen, she said.

The music stopped, as if Helen Langrishe were listening. Miss Imogen detached her arm from his with diffidence, climbed four steps and passed into the hall of Springfield House. He followed her, conscious of certain allurements offered to his eye: the narrowness of her waist, her movements on white high-heel court shoes, the proud swell of her calf.

The hall smelt of furniture polish. He walked across a tiled floor of pink and blue squares. Going before him, indicating the open door on the right, she said:

– Please go in. I won't be long.

She stopped and turned. He inclined his head. It was not exactly a bow. Behind her the stairway led up towards the bedrooms. She turned on her heel, beginning to loosen her belt. Facing the open door was another closed door across the hall; beyond it a flight of steps led away to the kitchen quarters. She went down a step calling back:

– Sir, would you drink tea?

– Yes, he called, I would, thank you.

– Biddy! *Biddy!*

Her high voice below. He walked forward, his image advancing to meet him in the long mirror over which hung the crossed swords of dead British officers, with faded tassels looped about the hilts. Hair on end and eyes blazing, an apparition in a loose open shirt and sagging green trousers went to meet him. Nature's lay idiot and no error.

He halted before the glass and attempted to put himself to rights. He, a poacher admitted on terms of equal footing into the house of Irish Ascendancy, admitted under false pretences, must try and comport himself with the best dignity he could. The music started again upstairs, louder, nearer. Otto Beck began to examine his surroundings, to see what he might expect in the way of hospitality.

A dark print the size of a barn door was suspended by its heavy gilt frame from the picture rail. In it, minute human figures were swarming towards a walled city on fire in the middle foreground. Groups of soldiery fought on the walls of the town, and others in outlying parts of the countryside, while here and there isolated individuals were engaged in bloody hand-to-hand combat in waste places before the walls. The fires that raged in the city were reflected in sulphurous storm-clouds which came down low over-head. It was night; a city besieged by night. In the near foreground a semi-naked man with a toga concealing very little of his person was in the act of climbing from a weed choked morass. An assemblage of urns and heavy burnished platters of gold were scattered about on the grass. Was this a looter dumping his spoils, or an honest citizen hiding his own property until the coming of more settled times? It was not possible to say with any certainty. On his flexed male leg, white and stringy, the muscles bulged in desperation; and on the dark surface of the stagnant pool a green scum lay thick. The Sacking of Rome, Otto thought. He looked away from the carnage. Facing the war print was another of a later day, in monochrome. A line of cavalry galloped at full tilt out of the picture. The Scots' Greys? The Charge of the Light Brigade at Balaclava? Otto bent closer and read: 'Scotland for Ever', after the original by Lady Elizabeth Butler. The music upstairs stopped in mid-career. Had she lifted up the needle?

Four small pictures hung below the cavalry charge. They were set in narrow black frames, human figures worked on fine silk. Beneath the glass that faced the open hall door stood a black lead sarcophagus studded with bolts and bars, with handgrips at the side, supporting a vase of white geraniums. Below the charging bugle-blowing sabre-waving Greys was a hall table of mahogany, and on it stood a blackamoor in wood with a high gloss, three handspans high and black as night, lightly clad in slashed trousers and outsize earrings, extending a lacquered tray for letters, invitations, bills. Against the wall by the door was a monk's chest for travelling rugs. He opened it. Empty. Where the short flight of steps led down a brass dinner gong was suspended on its cord above a gong stick. He opened the door facing the one she had indicated. This spacious room was empty and uncarpeted. He was to discover later that only one room in the whole house was furnished in any style: the one she had pointed to; the rest were sparsely furnished or not furnished at all. Some were closed up and in rival stages of dilapidation and decay. Then he heard the sound of her footsteps coming back. He closed the door and padded back across the hall.

His feet sank into a thick green carpet in a high chamber which in the daytime would be flooded with light, but now was hung about with drapes and closed Venetian blinds. Two paraffin lamps cast a subdued light in primrose and green from under their swelling globes. A small marble-top coffee table stood by the sofa, and against one wall an open piano, with some sheets of music on the stand. He heard her delay before the hall mirror. And as she entered the room he was rising to his feet from the sofa. The music started again upstairs. She had removed her coat and brushed her hair for him. She wore a pretty dress, walking there before him where the air was so still, in the dim light and shade of a past which he had no part in. Now that he could see her more clearly he saw that she had a pale powdered face, the skin stretched tight across the bones. Her dress made a caressing sound, *riss-riss*, as she passed, and her scent, her displacement, followed; so many cubic feet of scented Miss Imogen Langrishe going *riss-riss*.

She came and sat beside him on the sofa. But not too close and so as to face him. She crossed her bare legs, her hip thrust out. Sideways on she faced him, one elbow resting on the arm of the sofa, the fingers of the same hand spread fanwise on her temple beneath the black hair, her eyes fixed on him. Her back was to the light. She was narrow in the waist, heavily made up, particularly about the eyes, remarkable eyes – depthless and glittering, full of expression.

Now, she said, You're the fellow who's been staring at me through the back lodge window, and I just want to know what you mean by it. That was what she wanted to say to him, but in fact said nothing; not a word.

93

11

One sunny, cloudless day unlike any other, Imogen walked the front avenue where the air was so full of the smell of turned hay, sweetish and dry. Stripped to their waistcoats the men were tossing it in the side paddock. Some children were playing there with dogs and there was a continuous movement in the field, the men in line abreast throwing the hay with easy, practised gestures. A field of stubble swaths, poppies and clover, with insects continuously rising. And in Imogen's body too there was unrest.

A week passed, then another, after that first encounter on the avenue. A month went by. Several times she had passed the lodge on her bicycle and seen smoke issuing from his chimney pot, but of Otto Beck himself there was no visible sign. She thought she had seen him once in the distance in the harvest field with the men saving the hay, but she wasn't sure.

Shortly after that they met by accident in the village. He was buying groceries in Broe's shop near the bridge and other customers were present. Otto, standing very upright by the wooden counter, gave his order in a brusque fashion to a stout red-faced woman. There was a heavy weighing scales on the counter and leaning against the side of it was an open flour sack with a big ladle stuck in it.

She was put out of countenance by the too familiar manner he adopted towards her, as though there was some sort of understanding between them, which was in the highest degree embarrassing before the local gossips. He was dressed as usual in corduroy, a brown suit with a belted jacket, very foreign-looking, the trousers sagging at knees and seat. And she noticed that the stitching of one of his shoes had burst along the lining so that the sole was almost parting company with the upper. The young serving woman did not address him as Sir or Mister. He addressed his insufferable remarks to *her* over his shoulder, putting her out of countenance. Unshaven and carrying a bicycle pump in one hand, the snake-like flex screwed into place, he rapped the various tins he required with the vulcanite pumping end of it in a peremptory manner. Give me this, give me that, he said, but never once said please or thank you. He addressed his insufferable remarks to her over his shoulder.

She endured this for a while, searching about in her mind for an excuse to leave. Then she said:

– I must go to the Post Office. Excuse me.

Outside his battered bicycle was propped against the barred window. Inside the shop some of them had turned and were gaping at her. She took her bicycle to the kerbside, spun the near pedal until it was in position, and mounted. She cycled a little way up the village, turned and went out as fast as she could. She did not look towards Broe's, for he was capable of rushing out and shouting at her. She got away safely however.

Instead of going straight on out of the village past the Abbey, she turned right into Tee Lane, passing the open rectory gate, the yard gates of Oakley Park and, at the end of the lane, the iron gate of the Protestant cemetery. A bearded puck goat was trapped against the wall by the dismantled parts of an iron bed; a makeshift pen. Its colourless eyes watched her go. The route took her out of her way – three or more miles. She felt irritated with herself and with him, but was at least spared the embarrassment of his company home. He was an upstart and that was the end of it. She resolved to cut him dead in the future.

One night Otto Beck left the back cottage door open and made his way to the plantation. He walked along the narrow path until he came to the foot of a high pine tree. It rose to more than a hundred feet, the first fifteen feet bare of any foothold or branch whatsoever. Alongside it grew a laurel, its upper branches caught about the big tree. Otto stuffed the ends of his trousers into his socks as though for cycling and swung himself into the laurel; from there he gained access to the pine tree. Above him now its branches sprouted out with the regularity of rungs on a telegraph pole. He climbed upwards hand over fist, a mariner ascending into the main royal.

As he went higher the branches grew thinner, set closer together. He had to climb round the circumference of the narrowing trunk looking for supports for his hands and feet. When at last he could climb no higher, looking down he saw the meadow set out innocently below him, the beech and the sycamore throwing their heavy shadows before the house. It was a clear night towards the end of July. The house stood in its own dark shadows. The two main bedrooms were on either side of the balcony, divided by the main hall, above drawing-room and dining-room.

A Georgian house covered in Virginia creeper, bay-fronted on its sweep of gravel; buttressed by side shrubberies and tall trees, beech and elm, with front and back avenue leading away to the lodges hidden among the plantation. The white cords on the half-drawn blinds hung down in the dead centre of the glass, as if set with a plumbline; and this precision of detail, to Otto's way of thinking, bestowed a placid air to the whole edifice, as though it were well satisfied with itself, its position and its times. He could not see the white cords now, moonlight shone on the glass, and the Venetian blinds were drawn. But he had seen the cords in the daytime bisecting the dark panes, and thought that they somehow indicated the true character of Springfield House – as of something well pleased with itself, set apart.

He saw the feeble light of a candle moving in one of the bedrooms, and guessed that it was Biddy Langan mounting to her night's rest. It was she who had served Miss Imogen Langrishe and himself in the drawing-room with all the suffocating screens and cushions. The main bedroom on the centre block of the house never showed a light, and that was the dead sister's room. The companion bedroom across the intervening balcony generally had its windows half-open, and within the room the paraffin lamp burned late, and he imagined that to be *her* room (now as he watched the light went out). In the bedroom of the wing beyond the windows were always closed and the Venetian blinds drawn, and there the light burned later still, for he had seen it at three and four o'clock in the morning when returning from a night's poaching in the upper fields. It was the room where the gramophone had played; there the recluse lived undisturbed. Aloft in his eyrie Otto Beck felt the wind changing, setting in to blow from a different quarter. Dying gracefully; getting up again; always shifting about. The fine spell was due to break, rain was on the way. He felt the coolness on his skin, playing about with his hair and chest through the thin shirt, as the tree, trembling down all its length, began to sway gently back and forth. He was swaying with it, back and forth in a good land breeze, lulled by a kind of topgallant's trance. He was up at a dangerous height, for he had climbed another rung of the tree and the top was bending.

When his work became arduous beyond reason; when he felt troubled, or despaired of his own company, which he did occasionally, when he longed to be free of Ireland, it was then that he liked to ascend into the high rigging and begin to rotate with the action of the earth, so that life, which had gone, could come back into the world again, and hope into his breast again, looking down at all the leaves straining in one direction in Killadoon, and the meadow running away below him.

In his crow's nest, safe from intrusion, Otto Beck observed the lie of the land. The grass was turning pale in the meadow and the lights going out one by one at long intervals in the house, until all lay in profoundest darkness. Beyond the house the sky was full of summer stars, through which he was sailing. Close to his face he saw a cluster of pine cones. He brought them down, pulling one away. The whole bunch came away with it. Falling from his hand they rained down on the laurel shrub below. He had one safe in his hand, examined it, then flung it out towards the house. It went away from him, spinning like a rugby ball, and went rapidly out of sight. At the same moment his eye half-caught something running in the meadow a few hundred yards off. A white flickering shape had come out of the shadow of the front plantation, ran with a jinking almost human action along the shadowed border by the paling; uncertainly perceived in dense shadows, progressing away from him, until it vanished into the haze. He stared after it, his heart pounding; missed it again, looking for it in the wrong places. He saw it then, further away now beyond the sycamore, a blur of white, just for a split second and then gone. It went in the winking of an eye, just as it had first appeared, back into the haze. His eyes watered as he stared after it, both arms about the swaying mast of the tree.

It did not offer to come back. The tree to which he clung, so precariously high up, stood becalmed and nothing stirred; not a branch, not a leaf; all the waving grass lay dead below; in Springfield House the lights were everywhere extinguished.

Then a breeze began to stir, he felt it first on his face, and presently the mist which had obscured the borders of the meadow, creeping about the branches of the sycamore tree where they touched the grass, rolled away to its furthest end; and in all that area nothing moved. Otto stared about him, then commenced his slow descent from the tree.

12

Late one night Imogen awoke to the sound of a restless stirring and a shuffling on the gravel, a loose slovenly tread of many hooves. The soft senseless plodding went through her. She lay still, listening, thinking, *In a little while I will* . . . Below something was shaking and buffeting the iron paling. Whoever it was, man or beast, possessed no ordinary strength, for at each onslaught the horizontal rails rattled to the foundations down the line of stiff-set uprights. Possessed of no ordinary brain either, to judge from the sounds that came up from below – now wild and vigorous, now exhausted and slow, now quick and eager – hopeful – now wild and vigorous again, now in slow motion, now irregular and indifferent, now wild and vigorous as before, working up to a positive fury of thrusting and pulling, without rhyme or reason, and very unsettling to listen to.

It was like that for a while, then not so any longer. No. Now an unwieldy object was being forced through the bars of the paling, which shook and trembled at its violent passage. She listened, straining her ears. Was it that, or was it something live itself that was attempting to force its way through the narrow opening, and either get off the gravel into the front field, or get out of the front field onto the gravel? She listened until she could endure it no longer, then drew back the bed coverings, put her bare feet to the carpet and went to the window. She gave the cord of the Venetian blinds a quick pull; the slats opened outwards, she peered out.

All along the hill bonfires were burning. The night was well advanced, indeed was nearly over. An orange-coloured harvest moon in its last quarter was setting in an unfamiliar place in a clear sky somewhere to the right of Killadoon wood. In its meagre light a brown landscape revealed itself, a dim umber print in old gravure.

The boughs of bush and shrub and inaccessible tree swam in a haze; haycocks drifted above the field, extending to left and right in parallel rows. The rabbits were out of their warrens, feeding on the wet grass. Out of the down-thrown shadows of the house that stretched across the gravel, slowly roving shapes emerged, advancing from darkness into light. She saw broad moving backs and pale horns; their hooves stumbled over the gravel.

A herd of cattle had come up the back avenue, off the road, through the open gate on their way to the North Wall and the slaughterhouses across the Channel. Some were frisky enough, butting into each other with their dusty skulls. One was pushing and pulling its neck over the lower rail of the paling (this was the noise she had heard); and others were making their way noisily through the side shrubbery in search of fodder. As she watched, one, taking fright, bolted back onto the avenue.

All were restlessly moving about and dunging up the place, as if some instinct had warned them that their hours were numbered. Imogen counted eighteen head even in her restricted range of vision, before she moved to the centre window; looking through the slats of the blind she counted upwards of twenty head. Some were standing on the grass margin with their heads through the railings, cropping the grass which grew there, out of reach of the mowing machine. Going to the window that overlooked the front drive, she parted the slats with her fingers and looked out. What she saw there greatly astonished her.

On the paling some way down the drive a man was sitting, with his back to the house, wrapped in thought, gazing into the field, ignoring the cattle and the damage they were doing. Was it because this was perhaps their last opportunity for fattening up that he was offering it to them without stint or fear for the consequences? Perhaps he was even considering ways and means of getting them into the field and at the hay? The cool cheek of him was beyond belief. *If only we had a man here*, she thought, *he'd send you packing in double quick time, Mister.*

He knew there were three unprotected females in the house whom he could safely take advantage of; yes, he must have known that. Would it be rash of her to call out, challenge him? What would he do? Curse her, round up his herd and depart? Refuse to stir, pretend he had not heard her, let them graze on? No. More likely he would come below the window, make a nuisance of himself. She could pretend to have a shotgun and menace him with it through the window. If she drew up the blind as loudly as possible and called out in her most commanding voice for him to quit the premises at once, taking his cattle with him, what then? It might not frighten him (seeing he was capable of grazing a herd of cattle in other people's land at night right under their noses) but it would certainly frighten the life out of the other two. A hullabaloo at night. If she had the courage to do it, and about this she was uncertain.

Flicking their tails, white-faced bullocks waded through the dust below. The herd sat on, staring into the moonlit field. He was hatless, wore no jacket; had no dog with him, no stick either, – which made him a queer kind of herd. Staring at his purposeful back, she could not decide what to do.

Once before cattle had strayed in off the road at night and perpetrated great damage in the gardens, dropping their dung everywhere and tearing up flowers with their hooves, leaving their trade mark even on the hall steps. They had forced their way through the side shrubbery into the big garden, crossed the tennis court, penetrating into the orchard on one side and into the rock garden on the other, where they did most damage of all. Tommy Flynn and Creegan routed them next morning. Much damage was done by the way they were driven out, – blundering over the flowerbeds and bellowing in their haste to be away from the persecution of Creegan and Flynn. Jammed in the gateway, they began climbing up over each other's hindquarters, breaking down the rustic arbour and bawling as the men laid into them with their ash-plants. Bursting free they had gone careering over the tennis court, leaving behind a new trail of wreckage. Father had been furious and no wonder. Creegan was blameless, he said, since he lived out, but Flynn was partly to blame because he lived over the harness-room and should have heard them. The real culprits were the gate-lodge tenants, neither of whom would admit their guilt. But the fact of the matter was, both had left their gates open all night, or (since they swore otherwise) had *allowed* them to be opened surreptitiously and a herd of thirty or forty head of cattle, en route to the shambles, had been redirected in – which was unheard of – and they must stand the cost of the damage. He had tried to say all this in a forceful way, even stamping his foot, but could only bring it out in a weak and ineffectual way which had embarrassed them and more than doubly embarrassed her. In the end, he footed the bill himself.

Imogen stood in her nightdress at the window. How queerly objects stood forth in the brown light. Stumbling and kicking up dust with their hooves, the bullocks moved restlessly below. She stood there for a long time, watching him. He did not move. His head was bowed, his face in shadow.

At long last he began to climb down. She watched him put his foot to one of the lower rails and bend, tying his lace. He wore tennis shoes. There was something about his posture that reminded her of someone she knew. She closed the slats of the blind and moved to the centre window, opening the blind there an inch. No matter which avenue he chose to drive the cattle down, still he must pass the house, and she might have a chance of getting a better look at him. At the other window overlooking the front drive he would perhaps notice the dark slit in the blinds, and possibly guess that he was under observation.

She stood on the bare boards close to the window, her breath coming fast, hearing the restless fidgeting and stirring on the gravel below, waiting for him to put in an appearance, her eyes never leaving the narrow judas. She could hear no sound other than the cattle lowing occasionally and stumbling about, and was beginning to think he had driven the stragglers out first, and would be coming back for the others, and so she could perhaps have a quick look at him going. Reaching out she took the cord in her free hand and pulled it sharply down; the blinds rattled up. Some of the cattle below took fright, although she did not take any notice of them, for all her attention was on the figure of the man who stood before her, by no means anticipated, down below, standing directly opposite the window, staring up, as large as life, at the abruptly opened blind. He seemed to be staring straight at her. (But could he see her from where he stood? – Surely only as someone in white, uncertainly perceived, standing back?) Her heart went pounding in her chest. She did not move or attempt to cover herself. He kept on staring straight at her. It was Otto Beck. Released from his student labours, his *lucubration*, he was enjoying a late stroll or more accurately an early stroll, for soon the moon would set. She felt herself begin to tremble, confronted with the fixity of his stare. He was looking straight at her, his face uplifted, caught in the surprised attitude in which the suddenly raised blind had found him.

Finally he shrugged his shoulders, made a gesture of resignation with his hands and moved on. He wore tennis shoes, a white shirt open at the neck, *lederhosen* shining with each stretch of his moving thighs. He passed silently before the house, advancing along the grass margin where it followed the outward curve of the paling, without looking at her again. He went on out of sight, forcing one of the heifers to give way, heading towards the back lodge. Imogen, dumbfounded, watched him go out of sight. What sort of behaviour was that? What could she think about him, except he was a scoundrel? He had, after all, certain obligations. The cottage had been let to him rent-free in good faith. He had never been asked to pay a day's rent in all his time there, Father had showed him every mark of kindness, making no demands on him either in kind or time, none whatsoever, his responsibilities were few, but he was after all the gate-keeper, or had been, and efficient enough in Father's time; and now he was just letting everything go hang. For all the great kindness done to him, this was how he repaid them. No, there was no gainsaying it, he was an out-an-out scoundrel, the same Otto Beck.

13

Why did I? . . .
Because I liked his manner; because I desired him to be happy; because I
wanted to give him something; because he had Father's eyes . . .

Rim-ram . . .

The lame pumping stroke. This was embarrassing. It had begun.
The limping stroke was caused by the iron side of the wheel jolting
against its loosened bed, seeking for a firmer purchase.

RAM, rim . . .

It took a little while for the water to rise. Then each labouring
stroke brought up a little more, up from the deep well in the yard.
The man from the back road who came three times a week to fill
the tank was standing in shirtsleeves and waistcoat on the rickety
wood stand just below her, turning the pump wheel, as per
agreement, so many revolutions per minute, labouring at it.

Rim-ram . . . rimmerrammer . . . rimmerrammer.

Grim-gram . . . grimmer-grammer.

Rim-ram.

Imogen heard water sloshing into the tank on the roof immediately above her head and was afraid to move or do anything,
because he would hear her; so she stayed where she was, at seat.
The evening sun had crept into a corner of the pebble-dashed wall
facing her, all the rest lay in shadow. The man laboured on. It was
tiring work. She heard evening swallows on the roof. Benediction
time. In the field beyond the bleach green someone with a high
voice called to a dog.

He had asked her, invited her, to go to the theatre with him in
Dublin. There was something on at the Gate. He had two free
tickets.

Jam, jim . . .
Jimmer-jammer, jim, jam.

Time passed. The ill-tempered labouring stroke went on. Grease oozed out from the wheel socket at the whim of the rising and falling plunger. So many revolutions per minute. The stroke of the wheel jolted hard against its shaking bed, stiffened as the tank filled. The revolutions were coming faster as he felt himself coming to the end of his chore, piling into it now with heavy blows. She could feel it going through her, the shock and repeated thud of the sullen plunger.

Rim-ram, rimmerrammer, ram, rim . . .

Time, time. She had joyfully agreed to go. Had with misgiving agreed to go. Because she liked his manner, because she wanted to know him better, wanted to be happy, because, in fine, he had Father's eyes.

RAM!

One last revolution of the handle and it was done. A fine spray of water fell past the window, and he was climbing stiffly down, walking away across the yard, pulling on his coat. She waited until she was sure he was out of earshot and rose up sighing, re-arranging her clothes.

14

As the lights were out in Agnew's and the doors chained, the pubs must have closed for the night. Through an ill-drawn blind behind a net curtain with a wheatstalk design, Imogen saw an old woman seated at a table, staring at her hands.

Otto was pressing her arm to his side in an intimate way, muttering to himself. They had little to say. The street numbers meant nothing to him; he was looking for a particular door. A cyclist passed them, going incautiously without a light. They walked under bay windows, by the offices of stockbrokers, notaries, a firm of whisky importers, until they came to another lane leading off at right-angles. This was a cul de sac. He stopped, at a loss, staring up at the street sign. Cope Street.

– Cope Street? Otto said. No. I'm afraid we have come too far. It's certainly not here.

They turned back again towards the river. Presently Otto was taking a key from his pocket and climbing a doorstep, vanishing into the blackness between the pillars; hidden there he attempted to fit a Yale into an unseen lock. She heard the furtive scraping as the key sought for entrance but the door would not yield. He had to admit defeat at last.

– It's the wrong door.

– The *wrong* door?

– Yes, or the wrong key . . . or both.

The next was wrong again. Three doors further down, more by chance than design, he hit upon the right one.

The heavy door gave silently inward and he disappeared into the darkness of the hall. Then the light came on and he was standing in the bright opening beckoning her in. She passed him thinking: Am I in my right senses, walking into this? Then the ascent. On each successive landing a warren of dusty offices led away. She saw doors with stippled glass panels and a board with a name and a time set aside for lunch. *Fogra. Sean Brett, Collector of Taxes.* A faint light came down, from the stars, the night sky, through the skylight. Then he switched on another light and she could go on up. He took her elbow and guided her in. Speaking close to her face, he said:

– Watch your step now.

A bit late for that, she thought, avoiding his eyes, trying to assume a calmness of demeanour which she did not feel.

They were in a low-ceilinged studio white as a bone, with two window recesses, potted plants, a trestle bed.

– Make yourself at home, Otto said.

Trying to compose herself she inspected the plants, bending over them, drawing off her gloves. They had a certain weak perfume. What were they? she asked, her back to him. They were not *endemic* were they? He stood in the middle of the room, smiling, watching her. No, they were not endemic, but tropical blooms pilfered from the Botanic Gardens in Glasnevin and not expected to last. The absent tenant had used them as details in a painting.

She looked at the four walls bare of all decorations. There were no paintings. Otto pointed towards one of the corners. In the shadows a massive easel stood on its iron castors, holding out in its wooden arms an iron jaw liberally besplattered with oil paint. Its upper cross-pieces cleared the ceiling with only inches to spare. Concealed behind this guillotine a collection of unmounted cavases were stacked face-in against the skirting-boards.

Imogen sat on the sofa. He struggled out with an armful of paintings, dragged a cane chair under the light, propping one of them against its backrest. She looked at it without comment. He set up another, glancing from the canvas to her, then back at the painting – a nude. After exhibiting six paintings, all nudes featuring the same dark gypsy-like brunette exposing surprising areas of her person in voluptuous attitudes of abandon and repose, he asked her did she like them.

– *Well* . . .

The dark model's hands were behind her head, fingers inter-locked, lifting her heavy bust, cleft in twain by a ravine, bringing out the shadowy tufts of her armpits and her more darkly shadowed escutcheon of shame.

– . . . she's bursting out of her skin.

Otto smiled a private smile, but made no comment. He gathered up the paintings again and put them back. From behind the easel he asked her would she like a drink.

– Yes thank you. That would be nice.

He came out dusting his hands. Excusing himself he left the room. When he had gone she stood up, re-arranging her clothes. She laid her handbag on the sofa beside her; he would have to remove it if he intended to sit there. Staring about, she lit a cigarette. The whole place gave off a curious indefinable odour. The light was shining discreetly through a cylindrical canvas shade that was painted red and hung awry.

She heard him prowling about in the kitchen. Presently he came in carrying a tray. He put in on the floor and began to prepare drinks. She inquired whether the artist was a *professional* or not?

– Oh yes, Otto said. Yes, you could call him that.

His parents, millers from somewhere down the country, had allowed him two years to make his way. If he succeeded in that time, well and good, he could go on supporting himself. If he failed, he would have to go back into the family business. At present he was travelling in Italy on a scholarship grant; the place was theirs until he returned. How long would that be, she wanted to know.

– There you are, he said, handing her a stiff gin-and-tonic with a slice of lemon floating in it. – Oh, all summer, off-hand.

You have a neck, Otto Beck, she thought, if you expect me to stay cooped up here with you all summer.

She sat sideways on to him, her knees pressed together, staring at him over her drink, wondering was her skirt at a decent length, trying to appear calm. Otto looked masterfully into her eyes and raised his glass to hers.

– *Prosit!* Your health!

– Yours, she said faintly, avoiding his eyes, and took a sip of gin. She sat balancing the glass on her lap, smoking, trying to decide what sort of threat glittered in his cold blue eye. He began talking of astronomy. Only the night before he had been observing the planet Mars through binoculars from the front field. Towards the end of the month it would be lost in the evening twilight. Venus was now rising as a morning star in the north-east. It was a fascinating science, he said, holding her with his lizard's eye, astronomy. He had an almanac and Gall & Inglis star atlas at home in the lodge which he would be only too happy to lend her at any time.

He went on, no stopping him. Jupiter and Europa. The white girdle of cloud about Venus, the ways of the circumpolar stars that can never set, the absence of twilight on the moon, the presence of Variable Stars in the sky, so unpredictable in their comings and goings, fit subjects for beginners with inexpensive equipment, the bright star Betelgeuse, the Great Galaxy or star system of which even the sun was a member, eclipses and equinoxes, the Solar System with its thirty-one known satellites, the methane and ammoniac (marsh gas) vapours that obscure Jupiter from our eyes. Jupiter, in opposition to the sun on such-and-such a date, rising at sunset and setting at sunrise, hanging low on the horizon. She stared at him with a frozen face as he leant forward to dollop out more gin with a liberal hand, getting rid of the rinds and peels.

So it went on. Star time and clock time, stellar degrees of magnitude. Fraunhofer lines. Thermonuclear reactions. Kepler's law of planetary motions. *Pickering*'s New Selenography. For her benefit alone, she who could make so little of it.

By the time he had said it all the night was well down, the bottle of gin three-quarters empty. He might have gone on talking all night, but just then by a merciful stroke of providence, the doorbell rang.

– To go no further than that, said Otto, draining his drink to the last drop.

They waited for it to ring again. And sure enough after a short delay it rang again, more insistent this time. In the silence that followed Otto heaved a heavy sigh and rose up, drawing the Yale key from his pocket. He went out wrapping it in his handkerchief. Crossing over to one of the bedrooms overlooking the street he pushed open a window and she could hear him calling down:

– Have you no scruples, waking people up at one o'clock in the morning?

Then he must have thrown the key down into the street, for presently the window was banged down and Otto returned, closing both doors behind him.

– Who is it?

– Only Shannon and his trollop.

He did not offer to sit down, but stood as if in deep thought. Then he said:

– And now if you will excuse me . . .

Imogen bowed.

– I must attend to nature, Otto said.

He turned on his heel and went out again. Now I am lost, she thought. A door slammed. Brief silence.

She heard them coming up, making a great disturbance on the stairs. Raised voices, and bursts of laughter, a man and a woman ascending in high spirits, getting louder as they drew nearer. The cistern started flushing as the lower door opened and Otto was calling out. She heard their voices answering below. They were coming up together. A woman's high voice, laughing at something Otto had said. Imogen waited for the door to open and the introductions to begin but instead they trooped past into the kitchen.

The studio door opened and in came Otto, not saying a word. He crossed the room with a firm step and disappeared behind the easel once again. She could hear him rummaging there. What was he after this time? He brought out a reading-lamp and set it on the floor to one side of the sofa, plugged it in at the wall socket and switched it on beside her. Then he went to the door and turned off the main light. A lair for love and no mistake.

– More intimate, he said, coming towards her. (The next moment his arm had encircled her waist.)

She had to unloosen her long hair for him and take out hairpins and let herself be kissed. She kept her eyes open and did not respond too ardently. Otto's face, seen at close quarters, repelled her a little. Too long. In the darkness. Give in.

– What is it? he said, low and heartfelt. Do you not trust your Otto?

His quiet manner had deceived her all along. He was persevering and sly. I'm frightened now, she thought, that's the trouble. She had a feeling that her breath was bad. Certainly she was no licentious courtesan swooning on silk and velours. No Europa. She felt him hot against her. Better to be sure than sorry. Unprepared for his. Where the needle goes the thread follows.

– I long, Otto said. I have longed for you.

She held onto his hand, all in disarray, hair about her face, her breathing disturbed. He kissed her on the throat as she stretched away from him and, hotly, on cheeks and eyelids.

– Permit me.

– You mustn't, she said. Don't.

Then he made a serious onslaught upon her person. It was too much. Pulling back violently, her head struck hard wood. He immediately let go, giving her an opportunity to free herself. She held him at arm's length with her hand on his chest, feeling his pounding heart. She said:

– Now listen. Please. We've gone far enough.

– No, he said.

He wanted too much; he wanted to take off all her clothes.

– *Ich möchte losgehen, wie aus der Pistole geschossen.*

– No, she said, without understanding. Oh no, pushing his hand away.

He said bitterly:

– Will you give me nothing but your mouth?

– Wait, she said . . . don't *harass* me.

Sitting with bowed head, moving her finger in the palm of his open hand, she began to plead her condition, inventing it on the spur of the moment – a woman's ailment. Otto, impervious to innuendo, closed his hand on hers, insistent, not taking the hint at all.

– Is that *all?* I don't mind.

– What do you mean, is that *all?* she said, dumbfounded (she knew nothing). Isn't it enough? I can't oblige, and that's all there's to it. It's my condition, my time. The last flowers of the year.

– Permit me, Otto said, insatiable, stretching out his hand.

She struck it down.

– No. You're a naughty man. I'm finished with you.

Behind the wall the loving couple were banging pans and raising a shout. A cork was drawn smartly and they cheered.

– Well, you're full of surprises, he said, I must say. Full of them. I don't understand you. But I see you mean it.

– I mean it all right.

Holding her hand in a brotherly way, altering his approach, deceitful to the last, Otto told her that she could at least get a good night's rest on the bed, while he, much as he regretted it, would doss down on the sofa. How would that suit? She kept her head bowed, considering the catch in this proposal.

– But you wouldn't, she said. Now would you?

In the darkness he would beg for her hand, would hold it with his lecherous grip, would insinuate himself into her favours, would glide into her bed.

– On the floor then, Otto said, baring his bad teeth.

– No.

– Oh my God! Otto said.

– At the same time, she said, taking his hand, you can't very well sleep out in the open, now can you?

She watched him pour another drink. Ah you're wicked, you'd get round me if I gave you half a chance. I know nothing.

– But you must have friends here in town, she persisted, pleading now.

Otto gulped down his drink.

– Be reasonable, she said. You can't sleep here any more than I can throw you out – not unless you have somewhere to go, that is.

Looking morose, he said that he knew an intern in one of the hospitals who would likely be on night duty, and he could have the other's room.

– Forget it, he said, staring at his empty glass.

Could he make her coffee?

– Now that's a good idea, she said.

She could help him make it. Otto stood up, hauling her to her feet. She said, looking at the cramped bed:

– Still, I don't see how we could have managed, all the same.

– We would have managed, Otto said with conviction.

Yes, she thought, at the price of my maidenhead we would have managed. She followed him across the passage. The kitchen door stood ajar. Inside, the woman's high voice, consciously seductive, full of *appoggiatura*, was saying:

– And then the nurse said try that. And it was green blancmange. God I couldn't *touch* that.

Otto hesitated a moment, then pushed open the door.

15

Oh but it's true, Barry, the woman said, leaning glutinously on the last word.

She had an emotional throb to her voice, bringing the words up from her stomach. The speaker was seated with her back to them at a table littered with the remnants of a late meal. They were drinking stout and whisky. The other – the man, in his early forties, corpulent and with a sly look about him, his eyes set close together – was supporting himself against the table, picking at discoloured teeth with the aid of a match. He opened his eyes wide when he saw them coming in, indicating to the woman that they had visitors. She turned to face them. Medium in size, not young nor exactly pretty, but very animated – a hot-faced sprite with a wet avaricious little mouth. She wore a leather eye-patch.

– And who have we here? she asked, pouting her lips, staring with her one good eye at Imogen.

Otto introduced them: Barry Shannon and Maureen Layde.

– This (inclining his head in her direction) is Imogen Langrishe, a friend of mine.

Mr Shannon brought out a chair for her and she thanked him and sat down opposite Miss Layde. Mr Shannon addressed himself to Otto, showing his teeth in a series of meaningless smiles. Maureen Layde interrupted them. She had an excitable manner, very vivacious in her gestures, using her hands a lot, squealing with highpitched laughter at the feeblest jokes. She had a skin like porcelain, auburn hair cut short and one brown eye with a great dark pupil that stared at Imogen as though she were not there. She had just come out of Clonskeagh fever hospital. A bout of scarlet fever had laid her low. She addressed her remarks mainly to Otto and Mr Shannon, performing for the men. Otto rested his back against the dresser and drank for the most part in silence.

With a temperature of 102° Maureen Layde had heard in an adjoining ward a frail female voice say, 'Martha, Martha, I'm not well a-tall.' And after a silence another female voice, frailer still, had asked, 'What's the matter, Dolly dree-am?' And Dolly Dream, lower still, as if she were dying (mimicked to the life by the narrator), had answered in an expiring voice, 'I can't feel in me toes an' feet.' The story was told well and they all laughed, all except Imogen, who smiled a polite smile.

– We have just come from *The Father*, Otto said.

– Oh, Maureen Layde said, where? At the Gate?

– Yes, Otto said, the Gate.

Maureen Layde began to speak disparagingly of one of the cast of the play.

– I met her just before I went into hospital. I believe while they were rehearsing this play you saw. She spoke of the *sole meunière* she had the night before at the Red Bank. The day after she was down with stomach cramps and Christ knows what else – all told in great detail. Well, those are not matters of much interest, fish and flatulence, what?

Imogen stared at the cracks and grains of the deal table, shifting about her glass. They were malicious, both of them. So it went on. Otto said nothing, making steady inroads into their supply of drink. Imogen sipped her gin and felt ill at ease. The names meant nothing to her. Maureen Layde sat presenting her good profile to Otto. She had a shiny black reticule on her lap into which she was continually dipping for cigarettes, chain-smoking, offering none around. She was doing most of the talking.

– Oh him, she said, tart enough – he's Byron. That sour distinguished face of his tells you he's different. He pays a woman twenty-two compliments and then expects her to go to bed with him.

She lit another cigarette, letting the smoke trickle out of her nose onto the table. They all laughed. She put up her chin and smiled at the ceiling. They watched her. Then, from Otto:

– The man who consummated his marriage on the sofa before dinner.

She said:

– Oh but he's not married, is he?

– I mean Byron, Otto said.

The voices droned on.

Otto was criticizing the makeshift decorations. An arrangement of cords coming down from hooks on the ceiling was fixed to a wooden floor base like the strings of a harp; behind it a very dirty gas stove, the overflow trough thick with hardened grease; some cluttered shelves, a stone sink full of unwashed plates. The walls were dusty and discoloured, broken by a single cramped window overlooking Dublin roofs.

– Oh Otto, Maureen Layde said, if you don't like my kitchen, would you like my bedroom any better?

Shannon asked Imogen whether she knew Lord Longford, a direct question followed by a direct silence.

– No, I don't, actually, Imogen said then.

It was the first word she had spoken.

– Why not? Maureen Layde asked.

Imogen said that she had never actually met him. Mr Beck had pointed him out to her, standing in one of the side aisles of the Gate, very stout, with cigarette ash on his waistcoat, and she had been surprised by his appearance, mistaking him for one of the programme-sellers, and slovenly dressed at that.

– You noticed that? Maureen Layde said.

Addressing no one in particular she said:

– I was beginning to think she couldn't talk.

They had finished off a crate of a dozen Guinness and now were starting on a second. The end of the gin was in sight.

Maureen Layde said that she had been to one of Lord Longford's theatrical garden parties where he had distributed cream buns and sherry and sung the Polish National Anthem at four in the afternoon. She would hear nothing against him.

– Isn't it curious, Otto said, how much your national theatre owes to the landed gentry? First Lady Gregory and Edward Martyn, and now Lord Longford.

Shannon nodded into his drink with a sage air, pursing his lips, the corners of his mouth drawn down, as though he had tasted something bitter. Blue cigarette smoke hung in the air. Maureen

Layde's carmine mouth never stopped opening and shutting. Imogen averted her eyes. *What can he think of me, becoming more and more torpid as the night wears on?* . . . Imogen with her copper rust blouse and her prim faded ways, a colourless cloak of unobtrusive mildness. She hadn't a single thing to say to them.

Then she found herself smiling with her head down, smiling because the alcohol had gone to her head, as she knew it would, and because Otto was so serious and sober-minded and well-informed. Shannon was picking his nails. Maureen Layde shook her curls from side to side, turning upon Imogen her singular stare.

– When they are swarming, Otto said, they go straight up from the hive, climbing anything before them, and then they'll sting all that gets in their way.

He, Otto Beck, naturalist, had once read a very interesting work entitled *Bybel der Natuure,* by the Flemish authority on apiculture, Clutius, remarkable for the distinction of its woodcuts and its many graces of style. He had read also Ludwig Buchner's essay *Mind in Animals*; and did they know, for instance, that it was a German who had discovered parthenogenesis in bees? Dzierzon, a clergyman. Shannon repeated the name *Dzierzon* as if it might have meant something to him. Otto's father Reinhardt Beck had kept an apiary in Bavaria when Otto was a boy, giving him an opportunity to study bees at first hand in the family home at Starnberg.

– Starnberg? Shannon said. Is that Starnbergersee?

– Yes, Otto said, the lake.

– That's in *The Waste Land*, Shannon said, you know. T. S. Eliot.

– So it is, Otto agreed.

– In the mountains, there you feel free, Shannon quoted.

Maureen Layde gave him a sharp look. He turned away from her and it was Imogen's turn again to encounter his vacant smile.

The voices droned on.

Otto was talking about hereditary traits, natural selection and the like; he invited them to consider the futility of making amatory conquests – the sheer amount of hypocrisy and lies that went into it, when the man 'in the right season and unbeknown to himself'

117

(the right season for the woman, that is) is always and ever
'negotiable' as Otto put it, 'to a woman's needs.' So that all the
fumblings to get there, to get what they both wanted, that was all
so much humbug.

– Dear Otto, but you're awful! Maureen Layde cried, delighted.
You're a terrible man, making us all sound like bitches on heat.

As she said it, she turned upon Imogen the full malice of her
stopped-up eye.

– Husbands with horns sprouting out of their ears, Otto said.

A big vein stood out on Shannon's forehead and his eyes were
starting from their sockets. Gripping a bottle of Guinness between
his knees, he was straining manfully to pull a difficult cork.

– Take the case of Mahomed the Second, Otto said.

Shannon wrenched the cork out, and thrust the neck of the
bottle into Imogen's glass before she could say nay.

– Gold for the body, Otto said. Dandelion soup.

– German idealism . . .

– *Comédie de mœurs* . . .

– I look very nice in the morning, Maureen Layde said, syrupy,
you should see.

– Oh I could well imagine, Otto said, closing one eye.

The blurred voices reaching her ears from afar. The room
would not stand still. None of it made sense any longer. Her face
felt stiff, from alcohol, from smiling. Her movements had become
slow and ponderous as though she were supporting heavy weights.
Their faces too had become blurred, acquired hazy secondary
outlines; she closed her eyes.

– I think the only reason they talk about the Sacré Cœur,
Shannon's voice said, slurring his words, is because it's situated up
there at the top of Montmartre, tha's all.

– Need you always talk such shit? Maureen Layde said.

– Now if only we had a bottle of Kummel . . . Otto's voice said
out of the fog now swirling, we would be happy.

The mere mention of more alcohol made her gorge rise.
Sometime later she caught the word *Simla*. They were discussing
the Spice Islands now and how the thieving monkeys came down
in the cool of the evening and stole the fruit from the market stalls.
At *Simla*. In a pained voice Maureen Layde asked:

– Why doesn't *she* say something?

– Ssshh now, Shannon's voice said, leave her alone. Azy does it.

Maureen Layde said belligerently:

– She hasn't opened her mouth yet, except to inform us that she is not acquainted with Lord Longford. I don't give a fuck whether she is or not. Sitting there sulking.

– Nobody's sulking, Shannon said, trying to pacify her.

– This one's sulking.

Imogen opened her eyes. They were all staring at her. Shannon, embarrassed, coughed.

Somebody's chair-leg scraped on the floor. Imogen, feeling faint, closed her eyes. A threatening voice spoke close to her ear:

– It's you I'm talking about. Wake up. Say something. Condescend to that much, will you?

She said more, much more. It was most humiliating. Then it all stopped, went far away, even the voice that was baiting her. The room swung round. Something was approaching, a kind of milky translucence. It came closer and closer. Her eyes filled with unshed tears. To her lasting shame they brimmed up in her. She tried to rise, deliver some crushing retort, but could think of nothing, her head full of cotton wool. Instead, she laid her forehead down on the table between her hands, not hearing the crash of glass on the floor. And, deaf to all entreaty, wept copiously – spectacularly drunk.

16

When Imogen opened her eyes she found herself lying fully dressed on the studio bed. Both windows were open, the red canvas shade stirring in the breeze.

Presently she heard footsteps approaching the door. It opened to admit Otto, carrying a tray. He approached her, full of solicitude, across the worn carpet.

– Here's your coffee. A bit late in the day. How do you feel?

He set the tray down on the cane chair.

– If I stay still . . .

– Yes, that would be best. Drink some of this stuff.

It was scalding. A feeble bell began to ring, far away, in her head. Such humiliation she thought, her face frozen stiff, such humiliation, that one berating me, her contempt for me, drunk and aggressive, really horrible.

– Have they gone?

– Yes, a while back. Gone to bed.

I have feelings like the rest of them, she thought. Who had the right to speak like that? Hateful, hateful, and such damned cheek.

– I didn't take to that one, she said, meaning Maureen Layde.

– No, I suppose not, Otto said.

From his right-hand jacket pocket he brought out a box of matches and a pipe, stared at them as though they did not belong to him, replacing them without a word in his left-hand trouser pocket. He sat on the edge of the bed.

– She didn't take to you, either, as you may have perceived. Still . . . she's not such a bad sort.

– Oh, Imogen said in a thin pointed voice, is that so? Glad to hear you say so.

– She's had a hard time, living on the breadline. A little above it one week, a little below it the next. And in between times Shannon gives her a dog's life, making up to all the young ones. What they see in him I wouldn't know.

– I would have thought it was the other way round, Imogen, thinking of the dog's life, said, – judging by what I saw tonight.

– Well, no. She gives him some backhanders when she's drunk, which is often enough. Besides, he would be on his best behaviour in front of you. She toured Ireland with a repertory company, a very mean affair by all accounts. *The Lily of Killarney, Jane Eyre, Peg o' my Heart* and stuff like that, for which she was paid perhaps two quid a week. She worked as a kennel-maid for less. She says she likes dogs, that she understands them. I can't abide the brutes myself.

– And now?

– Now she goes about with Shannon, and is unhappy, I would say.

Imogen said nothing.

– I wouldn't take that outburst of hers too much to heart. She didn't mean all she said. It was only that she wanted you to talk. Saying nothing sounds – (he stared at her, at a loss for a word) critical. She thinks you are – upper-class, in tendency at least, anyway a bit high hat. But she doesn't know you, and she was drunk, so forget it.

– Easier said than done.

– All right, Otto said, rising. She hasn't it in for you. I spoke to her. And doesn't remember much of it, and won't remember any of it in the morning . . . nor should you. Now I think it's time I left.

Bending over her he kissed her in a perfunctory manner on the forehead. She kept her eyes open, saying:

– My breath's awful . . .

He left then. She listened to the sound of his descending footsteps. Then the hall door slammed far below. Now she was quite alone. All was quiet. She finished the coffee and got up, undressed to her shift and fled into the bathroom. She undressed completely, laid her handbag on the edge of the bathtub which was none too clean, someone had thrown coffee grounds into it.

She washed, took from the rail a towel that might have seen

service as a dish-rag. A man's tattered bathrobe hung behind the door. She wrapped herself in it. It had a pervasive smell of sour maleness. She searched for toothpaste, fearful of coming upon the shameful things used to protect illicit intercourse from the consequences, but finding nothing, not even toothpaste (none of them washed their teeth, or took precautions), she applied Pond's cream to her face, neck and hands.

When she had completed her toilet she left the bathroom. Crossing to the studio she dropped her underclothes inside the door, then re-entered the kitchen. The place stank of staleness – perfume, cigarette smoke and drink. There was a broken glass under the table. She pulled down the window as far as it would go – perhaps a foot, washed her hands in the overcrowded sink, switched off the light and left the room, taking with her the cheap Timecal clock. She laid this on the pile of underclothes and made her way to the convenience on the lower landing.

When she returned she was walking in a daze of fatigue. She re-entered the studio, collecting all her clothes she draped them over the bamboo screen at the head of the bed, and wound up the clock. Four after four A.M. The alarm handle had gone, no matter, she would wake early enough.

She drew in the catch of the near window and switched off the light. In the darkened sky the stars shone out. She put the clock under the bed. With a rush of water the cistern began its frantic flushing below on the lower landing. Removing the dressing-gown she got into bed, pulling the blanket about her shoulders. There were no sheets. Turning on her right side, facing the window, she prepared for sleep. She heard, last thing, somewhere a door closing quietly. All over her she ached. The floorboards creaked. Were there fleas? Stirrings began behind the partition wall: murmurings, the jangle of bedsprings. That one, she thought, already drifting away far from herself, far from Anglesea Street, that one insulting me like that, unforgivable. Had she been jealous because Otto was a better-looking man than her ferrety-eyed Shannon? Was it that? Was Otto a better lover? *Stuck up* – she had said that, among other things. I am *not* stuck up, she told herself.

The shadows of the leaves stood motionless on the ceiling. Soon it would all be over. Soon she could sleep. *If you were here, you would have to teach me everything. Maybe I'd be good at it. Good for you, too.*

Good for him, who did not care for platonic attachments. What must he see in me? she asked herself, behind the lies I told him about my condition. What am I for him? A woman with a high waist, a skirt with too many pleats, an awkward manner with men. Is that me? It isn't me. Very well then, if I want to keep him I must change my ways. I'm weak, silly, don't know my own feelings.

She heard sounds behind the wall – the swish of a woman's undergarment being hastily removed, the creaking of bedsprings. A moment later the bed creaked heavily again – that was the man getting in.

The shadows of the leaves began to wave against the ceiling; they moved stealthily across the grey plain to which she had set her face; more and more were pushing onto the ceiling, stretching their thin branches. Behind the partition wall the woman groaned. Then the man's deeper voice murmuring; then all falling away into silence. In a sudden crowding and whispering more and more leaves were there, massed on the ceiling, jostling together; their subdued whispering filled the room. Then all parted, fled away. She could feel herself drifting; soon she was sleeping. In the early hours of the morning she thought she heard footsteps. The steps went off towards the river. A heavy person – a woman. But it was only the alarm clock under the bed, and in the grey sky already the cold morning stars were out.

When she opened her eyes again, the sun was shining on the wall. At first she had only a confused recollection of what had happened; but gradually it all came back to her. She had been insulted, had not stood up for herself: losing all dignity, she had been drunk, and ignominiously so – that was enough to be going on with. Otto, apparently, had not seen fit to interfere. Very gentlemanly behaviour indeed. He had introduced her to those people, saw that they did not hit it off, and then abandoned her. So much for him.

She felt hot and clammy. Stretching out her arm she found the clock. The tired old heartbeat of the kitchen time-piece still clouted out the hours. It was time to go; she must dress immediately and get away before he came. She stood up, wrapping herself in the blanket. The floor fell away from her. With heavy head and uncertain feet she moved across it, the floorboards moving under her. Her eyes ached; she felt wretched.

In the mild morning outside hooves stumbled on a cobbled way. The jingle of harness, men's voices. Going to the near window she pushed it open. Looking down, holding the blanket about her. She saw a small cobbled yard at the rear of warehouse premises, and a groom in hobnail boots leading out a docile roan mare through an open double doorway. The sun shone on the top of the wall where valerian and ash saplings sprouted amid the grass and weeds. He led the mare into the sun and turned her about. A pale clerk in brown denim overalls emerged from the shadows of the stable door. Leaning on the door jamb he brought out a packet of cigarettes, studying alternately the sky and the groom, now working with a currycomb on the mare's thick mane. Imogen stared down at the three figures. The groom was collarless, his neck muscles bulged as he worked. The idle clerk spoke:

– Good morning, he said, going to be a grand day, if it holds up.

– Aye, the groom agreed, aye. Grand day indeed (a male alto) ... Whoa there, me beauty! he cried, bringing a meaty hand down smartly on a generous roan flank ... Grand day for a big blonde.

Imogen drew in her head. A church bell began striking the hour. Nine o'clock over Dublin's hazy city; rare air, the beginning of a soft summery day, with a blue haze over the roofs.

She had the feeling, standing there by the open window, the heat of the coming day warming her face and bare arms, a premonition that henceforth her life would be entirely different. She dressed in a hurry, not bothering to wash, tidied the bed, then took her handbag to the mantelpiece. Propping her hand-mirror against the books she studied her face. She looked a fright. Attempting to freshen up with rouge and powder, she painted her lips and combed her hair, which still smelt of stale cigarette smoke. She put away her compact case, looking around to see whether she had forgotten anything, then left the room, descended the stairs. She did not encounter him coming up. Behind the doors they were already at work: she heard the heavy pounding of an office typewriter. She went on down, expecting every minute to run into him. But she did not meet him. Passing the board which informed her what she already knew, namely, that Sean Brett, Collector of Taxes, had an office on the second floor, she stepped down two steps, into the street.

17

Tollis peccata . . .

Bowing to the altar and striking his breast thrice with slow, ample gestures the priest prayed, *Agnus Dei, qui tollis peccata* . . . He bent forward to kiss again and turning blessed the congregation. Loosely girdled, he wore a chasuble of rose on velvet, the embroidered cloth-of-gold on the cross caught the light as he turned back to the altar where a couple of wax candles on either side of the tabernacle burned with a steady flame.

The priest replaced the ciborium in the back of the tabernacle and turned the key in the lock. Under the hem of the long linen vestment which he wore, the last six inches of a pair of black trousers were exposed, ending in a pair of well-polished black boots. He paced back and forth on the altar, praying *in secreto*, dashing aside a page of the Missal, murmuring Latin, blessing the congregation, turning back to the Missal, going to the book to turn another richly ornamented page, laying aside the silken bookmarks.

Kneeling on the top step, two altar-boys were holding up the priest's vestments from behind. He prayed *in secreto*, then genuflected and held the Blessed Host aloft for all to see, and the little bell was rung sharply by one of the altar-boys. Then the priest was raising the chalice and genuflecting and the congregation with all their heads bowed were praying. And then the priest genuflected again and the bell rang again, a single tinkle, and it was over.

One said 'the Canon of the Mass': strange canon. The priest murmured the Latin, *Per omnia saecula saeculorum* . . . and that too was strange. A strange phrase, a trickling of slurred consonants and vowel-sounds in his mouth. *Saecula saeculorum* . . . did it mean world without end?

He had a short while before distributed Holy Communion at the altar rails. Imogen knelt at the back of the church among poor-class women in shawls and labouring men who made no attempt to follow the Mass but were engrossed in their own devotions, their lips moving, telling their beads.

Agnus Dei, qui tollis peccata mundi, miserere nobis. Agnus Dei, qui tollis peccata mundi, dona nobis pacem. Thou who takest away the sins of the world, grant us peace. The priest kissed the altar and raising his eyes, he extended, raised, and joined his consecrated hands, bowing profoundly to the crucifix.

Resting on the lower altar steps and briefly consulted when the need arose were two printed Mass cards. The Missal rested on a stand covered in silk corresponding in colour to the vestments he wore.

– *Dominus vobiscum*.

– *Et cum spiritu tuo* (the altar-boy's obliging treble).

The priest closed the book and descended the altar steps. At the foot of the altar he began, *In principio erat Verbum*, the last Gospel, glancing at the altar-boy, putting his shoulders back, fingers hooked in the fall of the robe, his voice low and confidential as if for the acolyte's ears alone, then loud and strong so that all could hear.

At *Et Verbum caro factum est*, the congregation knelt noisily, with an outbreak of coughing from the men. And then it was all over and the priest was walking out adjusting his biretta, bearing under burse and veil the chalice and paten, the altar-boy going before, both passing out through a side door into the sacristy. Imogen stayed on as the church emptied.

It was quiet after the people had gone. A few devout old ones remained for the Stations. Presently a sacristan in a rumpled surplice came and extinguished both candles with a long-handled candle-snuffer. Bluish smoke curling upward, fading vanished. He took away the Missal, making a profound obeisance before the altar. A door was shut fast, with the minimum of noise, and unbroken silence closed around her. Now there was nothing for it, she would have to go; rising she genuflected and left the church. In the porch votive letters begged favours or returned thanks for favours received of St Anne, a pale saint whom girls in service could safely approach.

It had rained while she was at Mass, a passing summer shower.

Part of the sky was overcast, the rest serene. And the day began for her then, a day of wandering about in a daze without purpose.

By high inaccessible walls a gang of boys struggled for possession of a small rubber ball in a National School yard near the Church of Saints Michael and John. In the yard their cries and cheering echoed, from which higher and sweeter tones arose, one single high sustained bird-like cry of marvellous clarity, something not quite human, wild, free, burst forth like what? Curlew? Plover? They were struggling in a pack in the centre of the school yard as she went by.

She saw the motionless bluish green dome of the Four Courts reflected on the river and a blue sky overcast in part by cloud passing out towards Ringsend and the sea, a sombre court with recently mown green grass. On Inns Quay by the Courts of Justice she heard an itinerant trumpeter play 'Poor Little Angeline'. By Father Matthew Bridge on the again returning tide a sea-gull floated upstream. She watched until it disappeared under the side arch of the bridge. As she stepped onto the bridge an irrational feeling of hope took hold of her; all would turn out well in the end, no doubt of it.

An early morning mist was dispersing itself over the city. The pale greenish cupolas of the thirteen churches loomed above the mist.

A tall Civic Guard on point duty was directing the traffic from Winetavern and Fishamble Street onto Merchant's Quay. Wood Quay, Essex, Merchant's, then by Smithfield and Bolton Street into the narrow laneways abutting on Capel Street, the old wards. She went down the quays and into parts of the old Dublin where she had never been before. A flock of starlings crowded in the cornices of the City Hall on Cork Hill, hidden above the blackened columns, an unseen aviary of birds, heard above the noise of the traffic passing into Dame Street. She read on a plaque that Sean Connolly had died there in 1916. Mean dwelling-places under the shadows of the great churches. A fisherwoman with scorched face and brawny arms trundled a wicker-barrow up the hill beyond La Verna retreat house. Through an open door she saw a pile of coal reaching three-quarter way up a wall, a weighing-scales and an outsize steel cash register, an advertisement for Oxo cubes, a door at the back curtained off. She had entered the poverty-stricken area where clothiers conducted their business, their stalls open on the street. Cut-price articles of ladies' clothing were laid out on the shutters which did service as display counters, and a pile of well-thumbed fashion magazines. A drab line of muddy-coloured men's jackets and overcoats hung askew on a pole above the name James Liddle, stirring in the breeze that came up from the river past the Franciscan retreat house. She went past. She had no intention of returning to Anglesea Street; one humiliation was enough, more than enough. She did not wish to meet any of them again. He could think what he liked; his own behaviour had not been above reproach; she would not go back.

The Civic Guard stood there making a series of muscle-bound traffic signals as she approached slowly on the pavement away from the river. Turning his back on the vehicles converging from three directions, he signalled again, throwing up his forearm, his cape opening – a gesture quite imperial. Then he faced her directly and made a leisurely motion of the hand that she should cross. She could not move. He caught her eye, and gestured again that she should step across.

A thundering shook the ground as she passed before him; her head felt as if it was about to crack open; she saw a long pale face, his eyes were still fixed on her; greatly flustered, quickly averted her own. He opened his mouth to shout something at her, pointing before her. She refused to look in his direction but kept her head up, eyes averted. She heard a hollow pounding below the ground as she crossed the mouth of Fishamble Street and stepped onto the far pavement.

Do not look or he might think . . .

It reminded her of something; but what? In a moment it would come. The danger of falling, the sound of something struck, muffled subterranean noise, add to that certain irregularities under-foot (. . . probing, sounding, floundering, as if drawing a deeper breath); then it goes on, muffled, irregular – the sound of blows under the ground (here she was obliged to step off the pavement to avoid more debris). Her leading foot touched road. A sudden contraction of the heart for there it was; in a rush it all returned. Placing one foot before the other, avoiding the debris, with lowered eyes, she had suddenly been confronted with an open trench, a red ROAD UP sign, a glimpse of dismembered mains and the heads and shoulders of labourers below.

(*Water was pouring over the weir. It came on slowly, a leisurely current; gathering speed over the last fifteen yards it was sucked over the rim. A falling weight of many tons of water propelled violently down the sides of the weir. Its roar engulfed her. The muffled thudding of the ram came from the cement blockhouse, pumping water into the baths and toilets of the girls' Collegiate School half a mile off. Its pile-driven blows shook the earth. Qualms of one's being there, a dread of falling, drowning, going under with that sound in one's ears; it makes your spine tingle, the hair of the head stiffen, quickens something inside you, sweet and secret, internal.*)

So vividly by memory imparted; its roar engulfs me.

And then, safely past, she had left them behind her. The upturned perspiring faces, the sounds of the picks breaking up the road. Fearful of him setting out in hot pursuit now she kept off the main thoroughfares. He would hardly go so far, but on the other hand one never knew with him; he was determined enough to attempt anything, and she was taking no chances, not with Otto Beck.

Starlings fluttered above the louvres of the belfry on St Michan's Church. The din they made, an unseen choir louder than the traffic passing below into Dame Street, hidden among the cornices and mouldings in the High Court of Justice on Cork Hill. The scorbutic red face of the fisherwoman pushing a three-legged barrow up the hill beyond La Verna retreat house. Her hair was done in a bun, she wore white denim overalls soiled with blood-stains and fish scales, and hobnail boots. Fragments. *Disjecta membra.*

Graffiti on a wall in Bolton Street: 'P. Ray rode Kate Mulvey.'

All that she saw that day made a confused impression on her. An unshaven dwarf, ginger-haired, hump-backed, leant forward intently, his nose pressed against the window of a poor milliner's shop off Ryder's Row, staring at a display card of neat rows of small coloured buttons. As she passed, he watched her in the glass; when she had gone a little way past she heard him whistling between his teeth and fancied that he was staring after her with his hands in his pockets. In the shadowed yard of a foundry or vulcanizing works in Ryder's Row four giant tractor tyres, at least seven feet high, were propped against a wall.

Farinoco Pearls. The New Dessert. Dublin Copper & Brass Works. Pigeons now – not starlings – pushing each other along the ledges of the small barred windows in Chancery Street Civic Guard barracks. That Guard on point duty with his insolence. A grotto for the Madonna stood on a poor land island near Lamb Lane, no flowers before it, on a waste patch of ground, a padlocked shrine with a statue of the Virgin Mary in blue, safe behind bars. Outside drab establishments of the clothiers, the grey-faced consumptive-looking owners stood in the open doorways gazing hopelessly at all who passed by. She felt very tired. It was almost eleven o'clock and she had been on her feet since half past eight. She decided to take a bus out to Glasnevin and visit the Botanic Gardens. She could buy some food and have it on a seat there. Enjoy it alone. Pigeons crowding, all fluttering, murmurous presences among the mouldings and cornices of the Garda barracks in Chancery Lane, and fluttering about the slatted louvres of St Michan's Church.

Farinoco Pearls, the New Dessert, on the bridge a freshening river breeze, papers blowing in grimy dust, plane trees and Abbey Street, the hero of Trafalgar aloft on his smoke-grimed column, two Dalkey trams below starting level on slackened headrails, and the bells inside ringing, ringing for all they were worth, *tollis peccata, tollis peccata mundi.*

18

About the same time that Imogen was boarding a Glasnevin-bound bus, Otto, not far away, came out again into Anglesea Street in some confusion of mind, having found the nest empty and the bird flown, for not ten minutes before he had been confronted with her tidy bed, both windows adjusted half-open on the latch, a lost hairclip on the floor, a lingering scent of her perfume, her sad presence, and no information whatsoever from the two preparing breakfast, who said they had heard and seen nothing.

Nothing. He stood on the pavement before Agnew's public clock facing towards the quays, from which direction she would surely come, his eyes dazzled by the glare reflected from the roadway where four wet streets converged. It was impossible to see anyone approaching from any of those four points at twenty yards, due to the positively intractable force of whitish light that flooded the junction.

With an empty briefcase under his arm, he remained at his post until the hands of the clock stood at twelve-fifteen. But Imogen Langrishe did not come.

19

He asked me would I go to the theatre with him. He had two tickets. I said I would. We could have dinner somewhere. I thought in view of his pinched circumstances that he was considering something on the lines of a mixed grill at the Grand Central Cinema restaurant. But no. Would I *mind* going to a place called Under the Ocean. He knew the proprietor Gustave Warnets and his French wife Cleo. We could split a good bottle of German hock. How would that suit? I said of course that it would suit very well.

Dressing for the theatre in a high bedroom overlooking the hills, pondering on what lipstick to use, how to do my hair and what earrings to wear. The texture of my skin, so calm, beneath the powder and the creams. In profile in a wing of the mirror as I stare ahead. So still; a revelation: texture of forehead, cheeks, eyelids, mouth. Trying to calm myself. Why should I calm myself! Imposs- ible to wait. He is making a dead set at me. What shimmers on the ceiling? Sunlight in dancing waves on the white sand under the sea. Is that the spectrum? A drop of water magnified many times; now agitated, now still. Its rainbow-hued outer rings grow fainter, but condense in towards the centre, a block of white. The circles oscillate over the moulding; returning, they attempt to focus on the one central point that's never still. That was a funny name for a restaurant I said, Under the Ocean. (It begins to waver once more, to toggle, incandescent green and red of *Rosé* cannot lie still.) The Café Belge he said, under the Ocean & Accident Assurance Corporation.

The only time in my life when I am not ashamed to be one thing, proud to be that, his slave and doormat, in my chemise, massaging cream into my face and neck, deciding what to wear. I dress for you. White skin of my bare arms. Desired again. What about the grey moire dress cut tight about the bust and waist and then full? But, on consideration, he is poor, I think, and may well be embarrassed if I dress too well. My copper-rust blouse, then, with buttons down the front. (A bead of water glides slowly down the glass side of the jug of blue asters and ferns on the dressing-table. The wavering spectrum on the ceiling, in a sudden turmoil of reforming, breaks up, finally vanishes.)

The dressing and anticipation, the little deception we practised at the gate. He was waiting at the back gate when I was at the front. A long enough wait, hearing at long last the Edenderry bus coming and stopping at the back gate, and having to stand out then and signal. He was staring out the window at me. I sat a few seats in front of him.

Then having to endure the half-hour stop at Breen's Hotel while the long-distance passengers satisfied their thirst. He sat behind me. I could feel him there. The journey was endless. At last we came in sight of the city. At Conyngham Road terminus I alighted. A stop farther on he alighted, opposite Kingsbridge Station as though he intended to catch a train. To improve the lie he carried a briefcase under one arm. He wore a good suit. Walking to meet me. He bought two bottles of Dutch Lager at a bar and then we went together up the hill into the People's Gardens. The banks of flowers in full bloom there. Begonias, fuchsia, frangipani, polyanthus; red hosannas; and the stern stone bust of a national hero in a shady arbour.

All yesterday I was in a dream, with him walking me off my feet. We went into the Phoenix Park, following the path by the hedge that led past the Viceregal lodge, white-fronted, deserted, since Dev's appointed preferred to live in digs in Blackrock. Domnhail Ua Buachalla. The residence of the Governor-General of Ireland. Deer grazing near the Papal Nuncio's residence, indifferent to us picnicking under a tree. In the long grass bounding the polo grounds, gallantly laying down his coat for me, not offering to embrace me, although that was perhaps in his mind. In the distance the monkeys swinging in their cages in the Zoo. A magpie, out of the tree behind us, flew across the polo field, making for a copse of trees on the other side. He asked me had I ever visited the

National Gallery in Merrion Square. I never had. He promised to take me some time.

Figures in white moved behind the trees. We could hear the ball being struck, and the batsmen were taking a run, then a second. But the ball must have gone over the boundary, because they were walking slowly back to their creases. The umpire signalled a four and far away by the pavilion someone in white was changing a number on the black scoreboard. Fifty up. He said he had never heard of cricket being played in Ireland but supposed that it came from the British Army. The Gentlemen of Ireland XI, I said, did he never hear of Boucher or Ham Lambert? Otto said it looked a very futile kind of game to him, *in the long grass by the white palings that stream away*.

His aplomb at dinner, tasting the hock when the waiter poured a little into his glass. Quite brusque. Yes, that will do. He was entertaining. I could say nothing.

And then the play, about which I could feel nothing. The leather boots the actors wore and the queer smells floating over the footlights every time the curtain rose. And him peering into his programme, very critical of the acting.

And then it was over and we went out into O'Connell Street and all the theatre-going public going home and the Pillar Picture House emptying out. I knew we wouldn't catch the bus when we went for tea and delayed. He had no watch to consult. That feeling, of being with him at last and all left unsaid.

When we reached Aston Quay right enough the last Lucan bus had gone. We were to cycle home from Lucan. He had arranged everything. A lie probably, and too late anyway. It would have been a long walk from there, over the fields. The last bus from Maynooth had also gone.

Idling along Bachelor's Walk, telling me not to worry, that he knew a place in Anglesea Street where I could have a bed for the night. Then the metal footbridge under our feet and too late to go back. Here and now in Glasnevin, my decision to return home. It's no decision. Just to go home. Not even to see him.

Imogen left the Botanic Gardens at Glasnevin some time after five o'clock. Taking a bus back to the Pillar she crossed O'Connell Street and made her way past the Metropole Cinema.

On O'Connell Bridge, she saw the Edenderry bus already in alongside the quay, the roof stacked high with thick rolls of the evening editions. She took her seat midway down the saloon, half expecting to see him. But he wasn't there. It was still daylight when the bus moved off. The six o'clock bus to Edenderry was taking her home. She had a splitting headache, but it would pass off.

Lucan. Political slogans ('Up O'Duffy') chalked on the road near Lucan. At Celbridge. Papers and bicycles being unloaded at Breen's Hotel. It was happening. Delay again. Dan Breen's again. Her stomach quite empty. Then on again.

The Abbey; Charter School; Brady's corner, and all the time a great void in her stomach, since nothing was decided. In a way she could go home, let it begin again of its own accord, if it would. But she wanted that to end, the indecisiveness, the unreal part of her own life to end with it. At the front gate of Springfield she made no attempt to rise. The conductor ignored her, but some of the passengers at the back were whispering together. Coming up to the back gate, she thought this is quite ridiculous, but still could decide nothing. Better to stay where she was and willingly pay the additional fare to have the bus carry her away to Edenderry, right off into the County Offaly; with two pound notes in her purse that was enough. Turning, she caught the conductor's eye. He nodded, crouching, watching the road, and struck the bell with the flat of his palm. The bus began to slow down. When it stopped opposite Killadoon back lodge, there was nothing else she could do, she felt obliged to get off. Some of the others followed – she had not recognized them as locals. They saluted her. Bowing her head she began walking back towards Springfield back lodge, a matter of a hundred yards.

As she approached she saw smoke ascending from Otto's chimney. He was at home then. She came up to the gate, caught hold of it with both hands and laid her forehead against its hard metal bars. The dusty avenue led away towards the house, fifty yards on it turned at right angles and passed out of sight. Bluish turf smoke curled languidly from his chimney pot, going straight up. Evening sun on the walls, on the clematis. Otto did not appear.

Perhaps it was the woman who looked after him after all,

preparing his evening meal? Perhaps he had not come back but waited still in Anglesea Street. Or was phoning the hospitals, imagining her injured.

Imogen closed the gate behind her. She turned, thinking about it, and there he was, as large as life, watching her from the door, surprised in the act of shaving himself. She went towards him.

He was shaving just inside the door and held in one hand a shaving-stick, in the other an open cut-throat razor. He wore only *lederhosen*, his chest and arms naked, the former matted with ginger hair. A small mirror hung on a nail behind him. He laid aside the shaving-stick and picked up a towel, wiping his face, watching her. She stood before him neither brave nor abject, neither his slave nor his doormat, hardly herself at that moment. Dropping the towel onto a chair he swung around, moving the razor in an abrupt arc before his chest, the last of the sun dazzling bright on the steel. Never taking his eyes off hers, he snapped the cut-throat shut, palmed it, thrust it out of sight.

– Well, you're full of surprises, I must say . . . full of them.

The last favour. Ignorant of everything, every blessed thing. Larded with compliments. Pleading to be let in. The bed sagged in the centre, half a brick supporting one leg whose castor had gone. Here; now. Honeysuckle fragrance. Imogen, prone on the bed, in disarray, her hair touching the ground, was pushing a matchbox along the floor with one hand. She said, her voice muffled in the sheet:

– *Vous êtes un homme ou quoi?*

Otto went towards her. He would soon convince her on that point.

Mauvais quart d'heure. Received in ignorance and then downright pain. Will not move again. God Almighty. Will not move again.

She returned to the house as darkness was falling. Had he made love properly? She didn't know. It had afforded her no pleasure. Something had come out of her. She had entrusted to him her rigid virtue, given something which she was relieved to be rid of, with or without pleasure. It had become irksome to her. She was a fullblown woman now.

20

And you, he wanted to know, you are well off? Rich Irish heiresses?

She had to laugh. Irish heiresses.

– Indeed no . . . Do we look it?

– Oh now I don't know, Otto said, considering. Certainly your manner – the house . . . leads one . . .

– No, she said. No indeed. If it's my money you're after, you'll be wasting your time . . .

Silence.

– We had it once. At least Dada had it. Money and position and a name in this county. Look at us now. I'm afraid we have come down in the world considerably since those palmy days.

Down in the world. Palmy days.

– Please? said Otto, who at times liked to suggest that his grasp of the language, its idiomatic usages, was not as comprehensive as it might be.

– Oh you know, she said, when we were well-to-do.

– I see.

In the silence something stirs in the tree: a bird stirs: a leaf falls.

– Palmy days, Otto said, reflecting. Curious expression.

It was a clear night in the summertime in the first summer of their courtship, at a time when they were still a little strange to each other. They were sitting under a horse-chestnut tree near the front lodge, talking. Talking of what? Of themselves and of their lives before they had met.

Born in Bavaria of comfortably-off parents, Otto had lacked nothing as a child. His father Reinhardt Beck, a retired chemical manufacturer. His mother was Viennese and 'very interested in the arts'. She played the piano. *Etudes Symphoniques. Hungarian Dances.* Schubert, Mozart, Schumann. She and Otto played duets. They lived in a big house in Starnberg, near Munich on the lake, Otto and his younger brother and their parents. What was his father like?

– Astringent, Otto said. A well-set-up tall white-haired, stern, upstanding, firm-principled man, with a great chest on him, a commanding presence and a sunburnt face like a brazen image – I remember him as being over sixty and always frowning.

– You were brought up strictly?

– Strictly, yes.

When the time came for his formal education to begin he was packed off to boarding-school in England. The school was on the coast. – I remember lots of box-hedges and dogs, Otto said. He could have gone to nearby Schondorf, a better-class German boarding-school, but no, his mother had set her heart on him being educated in England, so England it had to be. He had not been too happy there.

– Clipped speech, Otto said. Clipped hedges. Trimmed sails. The cold touch that kills. *Morgue-anglaise.*

– Yes. Imogen smiled at his manner.

– All the fashionable Englishwomen on the beach at Southend getting set to read Vicki Baum.

He had returned to Germany. The war began. He was conscripted. He fought on the French front with the Bavarian units, attached to a machine-gun group. This was towards the end when all was already lost and in rout. Each of them had to carry parts of the gun. The supply of ammunition was erratic, the rations scarce and bad. He was eighteen years old.

He had suffered; been wounded. A hand-grenade thrown during an attack had come over the parapet and lodged between two sandbags; it exploded as he tried to get back. He sustained injuries on face and hands. The trench had been taken. Carried in great pain behind the Allied lines he had seen, or imagined it, grass growing on the deserted Belgian trenches.

Then the long months of hospital. Wheels of pain. In the long months of convalescence his parents sent him food parcels.

He had snapshots of the western front. One of himself laden down with field equipment, in regulation boots and Kaiser Wilhelm coalscuttle helmet in a redoubt floored with duckboards, protected by a high parapet of sandbags, leaning against the door of a dugout. The picture of him standing there alone, exposed to danger, touched her to the heart; an Otto she had never known stared at her from the yellowing print, lips compressed in a resolute line, prepared to shed his last drop of blood for the fatherland.

– Blood, Otto said, looking down at his clenched hands, *Blut* . . . I felt nothing, only weakness. It was pouring out of me. I thought I'd been blinded. I could feel it here (he closed his eyes) but, if you understand (opening his hands, spreading the fingers), couldn't see it soaking my uniform, going into my boots.

– Oh! she said, oh, alarmed by the violence of his face, and her heart turned over.

He had another snapshot of a section of No-Man's-Land after a bombardment. Muddy rainwater filled the shellholes. It might have been in spring or summer, for grass and weeds grew on the rims of the craters, and although the trees in the middle and foreground had their tops blown off, a misty clump of poplars in the remote distance were in full leaf. On the back of this photograph he had scrawled with a still uniformed hand, '*View of mudshow after a bombardment*', dating it the twentieth day of January, nineteen eighteen.

When the war ended he made his way home to Starnberg. He remained there a year, recuperating, reading. Reading writers she had never heard of with strange dissonant-sounding names. Boehme, Kierkegaard, Grillparzer, Fallada. Adalbert Stifter ('one of my spiritual ancestors'), Trakl, Baour-Lormian, Gilgamesch, Hiob, Hoelderlin, Kleist.

– Hyperion, Otto said. Bellarmin. Greece. One of the greatest of the German romantic poets, undoubtedly so. Diotima, his great love . . .

Entweder-Oder.

The Bavarian lakes had been the setting for his own early amours. Starnbergersee; Ammersee, Tegernsee.

Starnbergersee – a summer resort for swimming, boating and sailing, twenty-five miles or so from Munich, a half hour ride on the train – was on the north side of the lake. The lake itself was set in a landscape of rolling hills and alps, with the Zugspitze, Germany's highest peak, visible to the south.

From the railway station you go out through a subway onto the treelined lake promenade, with jetties going out into the lake and many brightly-painted boat-houses where rowing boats, sailing boats and motor boats can be hired by the hour.

A yacht pulling in towards the shore. Forceful gyrations. Slackened red sails. A memory of hot limbs. *Ungezügelt*. Ilse Grube-Deister. Helga Endruhn, Anneliese Ramin, Barbera Kraus (the girl with the mole on her thigh), Monika Planer.

On Ammersee, further west from Munich than Starnbergersee and slightly to the north of the latter, lay the village of Andechs, famous for its *Andechser Bier* and its monastery, 'a castle-like affair built above the village and owned by the Franciscan monks'. There in the vaulted beer hall he had drunk the good beer with *Andechser Kaese*, a type of Limburger. Otto sat carousing at a long rough table with his companions, discussing Grillparzer and Gerhardt Hauptmann.

– Not quite the place to take a girl of eighteen or twenty, though, he said on reflection.

Barbara Kraus, blondest of sirens, adopted coquettish poses for the camera. He had a snapshot of her taken from above, sunbathing on a lakeside jetty in Austria wearing a tight-fitting wet black bathing costume that displayed her charms. And another taken at some celebration in an Austrian hotel – a crowded table of entwined young couples waving beer mugs and wine glasses at the camera and Otto in the middle of them looking quite demented with his arm around the simpering Barbara Kraus.

At Ondosa Bad, part restaurant, part swimming place, the changing-rooms had wooden walls with knots in the planks, some of which had dropped out or been made to drop out, so that it was frequently possible to observe the girls changing next door.

– The place is essentially made out of a series of jetties going out into the lake, Otto said, covered with planks about an inch or two apart. It provides also a tower with diving boards. A restaurant is attached, with steel tables arranged under big umbrellas the bases of which pass through holes in the tables and are supported in that way. It's pleasant there.

Summer in Starnberg with Ilse Grube-Deister.

– Tegernsee is a lake about fifty or sixty miles to the south of

Munich where the atmosphere is quite different in character, because it's in the Alps. There is a village of the same name, a very famous resort advertising itself as *Luftkurort* because the air there is supposed to have a high ozone content. I was happy then, Otto said. I had few worries.

He had enrolled as a student in the university of Freiburg. His professors were Edmund Husserl, lecturing on philosophy, phenomenological investigations, and Martin Heidegger, lecturing on philosophy. (*Mr Husserl*, Otto said, mock-pompous. Mr Heidegger.)

In its theological faculty the university taught Roman Catholic theology. Heidegger had not yet published his '*Sein und Zeit*', which was to come out under Husserl's editorship after Otto had left Germany. Many of the students were members or sympathizers with the '*Stahlhelm*' Organization, which Otto said had vague meandering semi-political views in a way related to Nazism. He himself was indifferent to politics, absolutely indifferent. A lot of beer-thumping louts, the wild men from Bavaria, in his opinion.

– Papen is Chancellor now with his Cabinet of barons, and a gang of beer-hall agitators trying to get them out. Roehm, Edmund Heines, the Strasser brothers, Esser, Streicher, Heydrich . . . Jew baiters and murderers, being egged on by Mr Hitler and Mr Goering. Without education for the most part, with their Nazi strong-arm squads, Gymnastic and Sports Divisions, their *Freikorps*. Rosenberg is their philosopher and their policy is pumped out by *Völkischer Beobachter* editorials – some of the more inflammatory written by Mr Hitler himself. You would have to read *Mein Kampf* to appreciate what claptrap it all is.

He had been at university when the Bavarian State Police fired on the Nazi Stormtroopers, ending the putsch of November 1923. He knew the place, near the Feldherrnhalle, a public building with Grecian columns facing the Odeonsplatz, where statues of the Feldherrn stood.

– The *Hofgarten* is close by, as I'm sure our friend Shannon would be interested to hear.

Troubled times in Germany, troubled times at home, inflation and unemployment. By the end of 1923 the rate of exchange with the dollar had risen from seven thousand to a hundred and thirty thousand million. In the worst inflation years after the Great War one loaf of bread cost billions of marks. The prices changed from lunch to dinnertime.

He could not stand his father, who had re-married. He had one step-brother: Friedrich. The step-mother was at home. Elke. Otto had left not knowing what he would do, hoping he could continue his studies elsewhere. It had been a bad time for him – wandering about. There seemed no hope. Then he had found sanctuary in Spittal. An unpaid job looking after goats and sheep in the Dolomites. On a good day he could see clear to Venice. He had a hut, privacy, let his beard grow, was self-supporting, met no one, talked to no one, was content. It had been a good time for him.

– I ate hares, Otto said. Plenty of hares in Spittal. Prepared with parsley, you know . . .

The villagers respected him. He was a good shepherd. There he had begun his life's work. This period lasted two years. By the end of it he had scraped together a little money, not much but sufficient. They were sorry to see him go. If ever he wanted a job, they told him, he could come back to Spittal. He left Germany in 1928 for England. He spent two years in London, starving, working on his thesis. He spoke of his days of poverty in London. He had slaved at his studies in an attic in Swiss Cottage during one long wet winter and one long hot summer.

– Under the slates during a heat-wave, Otto said, believe me that was no joke. It was a furnace. One couldn't breathe. A cramped fetid place with a gas ring and just enough headroom in the centre for me to stand upright, shaped like a hencoop and not much bigger. In winter I had to keep the window closed. In cold weather I had to keep the gas ring on. It didn't do my health any good.

There he performed his chores, managed his cooking, such as it was; potatoes, sauerkraut, cheese, sometimes mincemeat. It had a disagreeable smell. His clothes stank. He walked up Haverstock Hill under the dripping trees to the pub on the corner and then back again.

– By the end of the winter, my face was bluish-grey, and even a kind of green in parts, like mould on the damp walls of a cellar. But the rent was only four shillings a week.

A single dormer window grey with dust and London grime served for light and ventilation. He would prop it open on its bar, drag the zinc-top table on which he ate his meals under it, set a chair on top of that, arrange his books on another chair alongside, and sit dressed only in underpants, with the upper part of his body out of the window, looking out on a scene which could offer few distractions for one who studied as hard as he.

– Dead end-walls and chimney stacks, Otto said, and the perspiration running down my sides onto the chair. I had a damp towel over the back. The place was only just endurable, with my head out of the skylight and my arse in the oven.

– Poor Otto, she said.

– The life of a scholar, he said, fatalistically, – it's lived within a narrow compass, in mute abstraction and solitary drudgery. I lived there, if you could call it living, in that accursed garret in Swiss Cottage for two mortal years. The wonder is, it didn't do me irreparable harm. But no, here I am, as you see, sound in mind and limb.

– I'm glad, she said.

Otto in Swiss Cottage (a name which he said brought to mind the white cake *Streuselkuchen*); she could have cooked for him, looked after him.

– The cities I've been hungry in! Otto said. I was hungry in Munich when I left university. I was starving in London. And after that I went to Dublin and did some starving there. In London I'd walk the streets until I was dizzy, my stomach groaning for food. One day in the middle of that foul winter, I found myself standing in front of the tourist office in Regent Street, before their big plate-glass window. On display there was a photograph enlarged to the size of a door. You could see the black grains. From where I stood in my wretched condition it jumped out at me with the utmost clarity. It was a blown-up photograph of an island, Inishere, on the Aran Isles, photographed on a hot summer day. I stood there confronting it, and the reality came floating out at me. I had never been to Aran, but I was in it that day, in a field of daisies in Inishere. It wasn't a dead and petrified agency still. No, it was the reality itself that came out at me, breathed on me. I could see the detail quite clearly, summer grass and stone walls, the small allotments, the fields of daisies surrounded by walls put up by hand, a whitewashed cottage with a thatched roof sweltering in the sun, and beyond it miles of sea, a breeze going over it and low on the horizon the Clare coast. It was taken from an aircraft. I was in it, yet above it; I possessed it. The baked earth, the coolness out at sea, the wind on the surface of the water, cliffs, marine fields, depthless deeps, – I owned it all. I was it all. I felt about it as God might feel about the earth, supposing He ever looks at it. Feeling myself drawn down into it. Such a strange feeling. I pressed my forehead against the glass, staring at it, its heat and waves, its freedom on a cold bleak day there in London. I smelt the grass and the briny Atlantic and watched the breeze passing over several square miles of sea, all in silence.

– Next to it . . . or perhaps some way down . . . there was a *Patisserie* with a display in the window. I came in front of it. All the juices in my stomach were up in my mouth when I saw the food arranged there . . . the appearance of it. I stood looking at a barmbrack covered with poppy-seeds . . . it was a confectionery shop in – I forget the name of the street . . . behind Liberty's. The brack was glazed, you know the appearance. A bread roll with poppy seeds, – an egg mixture, a beaten egg, brushed with beaten egg. It all came into my mouth when I looked. The appearance, the egg mixture of a glazed barmbrack on a stand in the window of a confectionery shop behind Liberty's of Regent Street. I longed for it – I can't tell you. My guts creaked for it. My salivary glands were discharging liquids into my mouth. I leaned towards it, yearning for it . . . for ten minutes or half an hour I stared at it. I couldn't tear myself away. I stood rooted to the spot. Tears came into my eyes and rolled down my cheeks into my mouth and I felt my heart would burst. When one is deprived of some absolutely fundamental thing – the daily bread we pray for – then everything becomes distorted. The ravenous beast that's in you will not let you be. I went away and sat down somewhere and tried to calm myself. A quarter of an hour later I was back at the window. I went on looking at the food until all desire for it left me. All my need for it vanished. Can you understand that?

– No, she said.

– I didn't expect you to, Otto said. But had it happened to you, I don't doubt that you would feel the same. There's an elevation to it, a giddiness, a lightness in the head. One is burning, as sores that go septic seem to burn. You begin to reason strangely, half-mad with hunger. You want to leave all normal life behind you. There were times when I could have wept for myself. One grows feeble, so thin a thread holds you to life. The days turn grey. In strong sunlight the air is full of little black grains that fall. What do the aged listen to? What do the hungry? They are harkening to themselves – systems that are going out.

Terena McSweeney, Imogen said.

21

He led her along a ferny bridle path into the plantation. They came presently to a clearing where a yew tree grew. He showed her the place on the tree where he had cut his initials some years before, when he had not known her to speak to, when her father was still alive. And right enough, there the letters were plain for all to see, O.B., his mark and seal cut into the deeply fluted trunk which was flaking away in places. The initials were cut at eye-level in Gothic capitals. She traced the fading O with her finger. The knife-marks had almost closed, scabby now like a wound that has healed, the resin set stiff and hard: Otto, his mark.

– Ot-to, she said, peeling away a piece of bark, – you're the same front and back.

She wanted to say, I spoke to you when Father was alive. I did. At least a few words. I was just back from Parthenay. Don't you remember the tennis-party? The fat man who fell. The scent of the hop-plant. We sat on the terrace of the summerhouse watching the mixed doubles.

– Am I?

On the previous evening he had spoken of his struggle to continue his studies, independent of university, how it had been an uphill struggle – and indeed still was. In London he had met Derek Barton, a man useful for getting him German 'grinds' when he moved to Dublin. He (Otto) was making investigations into seventeenth century Ireland and Irish customs of that time, and earlier; engaged on philological studies into the story of Ossian, with reference to Goethe's time, the brothers Grimm, Hebbel, Hamann. He would like to show it to her one day, his thesis. She said she would certainly like to see it, or parts of it anyway, if he would translate it for her. He said he would be only too pleased.

They sat with their backs against the trunk of the tree, their shoulders touching, his warmth going through her. It was an endless summer evening going on for ever and she wore a summer dress of white voile, white stockings and shoes that buttoned on the instep, her neck encircled by a locket on a filigree chain; her lips, which Otto said were the shape of the young and beautiful Clara Schumann's, were painted with a new lipstick.

They heard the front door of the lodge opening and old Boyle throwing out his dishwater. He cleared his windpipe, spat, muttered something aloud, retired again. They heard the latch fall; he was in for the night. Turning about, Otto buried his face in her lap and she thrust her fingers into his long hair. They remained in that position, he breathing on her thigh, she moving her fingers up and down his back.

– That's good, Otto said. Go on doing that.

She went on doing it. She loved to touch his skin. His head was buried in her lap. His smothered voice said:

– *Ich rieche Liebe*.

She said nothing, not understanding.

– All right, Otto said, that's enough.

She stopped doing it. He turned himself about so that the nape of his neck rested on her warm thigh and with lips compressed stared up into the spreading branches of the yew. After a while she ventured to say:

– Otto, listen. This is a little embarrassing for me. But – how shall I put it? – I want to tell you all the bad things about myself which I'm ashamed of, so that you won't be disappointed when you find them out for yourself.

– Very well, Otto said, staring up into the tree.

A cow began coughing in Brady's field; a sodden crunching sound followed by a long-drawn-out hollow-sounding cough. Hou ... huhh ... huo! Then silence, broken by the slop and fall of dung.

– So be it. I confess to you that I'm ashamed of my laugh. I have a terrible laugh. Aren't Germans supposed to have no sense of humour? So perhaps you haven't noticed I have none either.

– I hadn't noticed, Otto said.

She said nothing for a while. Then she asked:

– Do you like children, Otto?

– Why? he said at last.

– Because I don't, she said. I never have. I hope we never have any.

– H'm, Otto said.

She looked down at him, touching his forehead. He brushed her hand away, frowning.

– Listen, she said, – you mustn't laugh at this, if I tell you. Promise me you won't laugh, because I can't tell you if you laugh at me. (Otto made a sign that he would not laugh.) Well, I had a fad at one time. I suppose you could call it that. I was always washing myself. I had a hot bath every night and washed my hands I suppose thirty times a day. (Otto, himself not over-fastidious about bodily cleanliness, grunted at this.) Now, let's forget prudery. Sometimes I took air-baths in my skin.

Imogen paused as if inviting comment, looking down at his eyes. But his expression had not altered; he made no comment.

– Sometimes I got it so badly, she said, I couldn't sleep. Oh my dear you have no idea. I got so hot and bothered I didn't know what to do with myself, almost sick with sadness for something I could not name. I felt that I could shed my human skin and turn into a lump of something burning. My cheeks, my breasts, the tips of my fingers, all over me the same. I had to get up, take off my night things and put on that old red raincoat you like and get out of the house before I smothered. I went into the meadow and across to the plantation, stripped and ran round in the nude. Even in hot dry weather it was damp at night, from the dew. Best of all was when it rained – to feel it pouring down. I'd crawl into the grass and lie on my back with my arms out and my mouth open, and all my feelings welled up and I wept buckets. Can you conceive of such behaviour? I tell you, I never knew what I was weeping for; a silly woman prancing round in her birthday suit, *avant voulu*, being indecent, weeping her eyes out for nothing, isn't it too ridiculous for words?

Darkness had fallen while she was speaking. A car went by on the road, its headlights on, travelling fast in the direction of Barbarstown cross-roads. Light streamed through the plantation, passing over them and away. The sound of the engine died away.

After that the place seemed darker, more hidden, secret. Otto sighed. Imogen, not looking at him, massaged his forehead, thinking her own thoughts. *Water runs down leaves and eyes, dissolving the salt of sweat, drowning the eyes.* Otto, with a tactfulness not usual with him, had said nothing.

– I started the habit by taking air-baths on the back avenue at night, parading up and down in my red raincoat at first, opening and closing it like a striptease *artiste*. But then, because nothing ever happened, I took it off and carried it rolled up under my arm and continued up and down wearing nothing but high heels and make-up, gulping air and pretending that some dreadful men were leering at me from the bushes. Many a windy night I paraded up and down there, red hot, trying to cool off. Some nights, after it had rained, I'd go under the laurel bushes and shake rainwater over myself and have a good shower. I liked it when stray cyclists went by, I wanted to shout after them. You could imagine what. I could feel it coming up into my throat.

– Once a single drunk went by. I could hear him coming a long time, muttering to himself, cursing his life and his Maker. I listened from my hide, the wanton in her pelt, hair stuck to my face, trembling like the hare that hears the hunter's horn and hounds. As he came up to where I was hiding I found myself in the ditch intending I don't know what foolishness – maybe to climb out and dance a fandango stark naked before him on the public highway. I wonder what some poor scandalized yokel would have made of that, falling off his pushbike with fright and shame? But as I was going through the cutting in the side of the ditch, two sober men overtook him, the nearest one close enough for me to reach out and touch his arm. I pressed myself into the grass and prayed to God that I couldn't be seen, for I knew then that I was becoming mad and reckless, and that no sane man in his right senses would have looked at me.

She stopped, looking down at him. He said nothing. She said:

– I'm tired of all this – drool and rubbish. I'm sure it sounds dreadful . . . Have you a cigarette for me?

He had, and lit it for her. They sat shoulder to shoulder in silence, all about them the wood stirring. He lay docile, breathing through his nose, staring up into the yew tree while Imogen went on methodically stroking his furrowed scholar's brow. With the tips of her fingers she caressed his dry sweet even lips. After a while she went on:

– It reminds me of when I was little, I mean a baby in arms, before I could crawl or talk. Being the youngest and most coddled of the four of us, I was occasionally taken into their bed and permitted to lie between the pair of them. This would be on the nights when I cried and couldn't sleep. I recall this as vividly as I will remember your face.

– One night I was lifted up by a pair of hands and came up from between them right out of the bedclothes. I felt so calm and free up there, you can't imagine. Isn't that strange, that I should remember it? Yes, I think it's very strange. The person who held me, who was no longer my protecting father, was trying to decide what he would do with me, something small and wet and feeble with no will of its own, that could only cry and dirty itself and destroy their night's rest, their loving. I didn't know what would happen, – whether my short and insignificant life was about to be snuffed out or not, if he decided to smother me in the pillow, or dash my brains out on the head-rail. I was held up there for a long time, feeling calm and free. Then at long last I felt myself being lowered down again and deposited between the pair of them, quite gently. Well, it's that feeling that comes back to me when I take my air-baths.

– Had you anything on that first night on the avenue? Otto asked. I mean under your raincoat. That crepuscular hour when first I heard your angel footsteps.

– Isn't that what I'm telling you? she said. I hadn't, not a stitch. That was another night of hot impulses.

– Hum, Otto said. Er-hum.

A silence.

– When I was three years old, Otto said, I saw my mother swimming in a huge ocean full of jellyfish with her first lover.

Imogen spoke as if to herself:

– Imagine . . . I got up in such a hurry this morning that I forgot to put on my bra.

– Show me.

– I will *not*.

– Just for me (ardent, rousing himself).

She looked down at him with her eyes half-closed, smiling, then began unbuttoning her blouse with one hand, as if the hand did not belong to her.

– Don't look.

Otto obediently closed his wicked lizard's eye.

– Look now.

He was on his knees with his hands about her bare brave waist, staring masterfully into her eyes. She offered no resistance, a big vein pulsing in her neck; his hands moved over her, she wore flimsy lace knickers, love had taught her that. His fingers found the little filigree chain; he pulled her face down to his.

– *Komm, mach zu*, he breathed into her ear, low and importunate, pulling the chain at the same time, – *streng dich an*.

– You too, she said, – I love you too.

The words were solid and she was swallowing them. She was inclined at an angle against the tree, awaiting outrage. Yew berries, soft and pulpy, fell about them, dropping into the dead leaves and ivy on the ground. Then the tree no longer supported her back and she was on the ground.

Oh Otto Beck, what are you doing to me?

22

She came again to the cottage but would not consent to spend the night there. Some all but basic scruple prevented that. She said she would visit him once or twice a week.

– I am a bourgeois citizen, she said.

It wasn't exactly that. Slow to catch fire, she begged for a little time in which 'to get used to him.' She might with submission grant him her favours ('You are lustier than I . . .') but she was still a little in awe of him, bold Otto Beck, fowler, conscript, prowler, gaolbird, fisher in prohibited waters, apiarist, agriculturist, horticulturist, botanist, gardener, who could speak better English than she and who had at his command apparently limitless regiments of facts, theories and anecdotes, original or otherwise ('Richard Wagner attributed much of the decay of our civilization to the habit of meat-eating'), about periods of history and writers, many of them dead, many more of whom she had never even heard.

– Göttingen, Otto said . . . Kant . . . Fichte . . . Heidelberg . . . Theodor Storm . . . R. E. Raspe . . . The Baron Münchhausen . . . Beyle . . . the Rhine . . . loess . . . lubricity . . . Soxoborussia . . . Narciss and Goldmund . . .

In plain fact the English he spoke was in many respects a foreign language to her, its terms of reference obscure to one who had never bothered to read very much beyond E. Philips Oppenheim, Phillip Gibbs, *'Piccadilly Jim'*, or whatever light reading took her fancy in the study at Springfield.

Otto Beck was a travelled man, had known many places and no doubt women too; a man, moreover, capable of committing violent depredations on the chastity of any female who might chance to take his fancy.

Now that was over, and he was insisting that she spend the

whole night with him, in fact live with him; but she would not. What did she wear in bed – something flimsy? a nightdress? flounces? pyjamas? nothing? She told him.

Troubled now by some unresolved longing, she could not keep away from the lodge. The 'once or twice a week' became a deal more frequent. A few days later she consented to spend the night with him.

Go back then to the timid puritan you were.

She, the puritan, would not touch butter, no, never in her life. She said it made her feel sick. It made for difficulties at boarding-school, and there were times when she went hungry from supper to bed (that was when the nun from the kitchen forgot to put the jam on her plate). Raspberry jam for her alone and all the others looking at her when it wasn't there, staring in silence because speaking was forbidden at supper, yes, and at lunch too. At breakfast, if the jam was forgotten, some of the others would ask and the nun would take her plate away and it would come back with a little jam on it, never very much. Imogen was too shy to ask for it herself. That was the way, always too shy, morbidly so as a girl and blushing at the slightest provocation. 'Getting red,' they said 'look, Langrishe is getting red.'

There was a nun there who could drink like a man. When she raised a full tumbler of water to her lips she wouldn't put it down until it was all gone in one long draught. Madame Monique Claire.

At the long refectory table, in silence, she watched the others eating in silence slices of buttered bread, putting away plates of it, cut into squares and already buttered with yellowish local dairy butter. She imagined that it imbued the other flesh . . . their flesh . . . their almost fully developed bodies imbued with strength and resources denied to her, being finicky and shy and not able to stand up for herself. Forgotten, she ate nothing, just a glass of milk, and so hungry to bed.

She watched the buttered bread going into their mouths. A smear of butter was on their lips and on their fingers. The substance itself was like flesh, puff-paste, the product of cattle, their milk churned up . . . something disagreeable about it . . . herself sometime too, also mammalian . . . marriage, babies, breast-feeding . . . all that was rather disgusting. Like being 'unwell'. She

154

could remember the first time, the embarrassment of it. She was fourteen.

It was the last day of term and they were tidying the classrooms and sorting out books, some to be used again, others re-sold. Stories were read aloud. It happened then. She had to lie down across the seat of her desk because of the pain. The desk was the usual rectangle of wood connected with steel grips to a wooden seat; and down on this she lay on her stomach to try and relieve the pain. There was some relief, but not much. Then she felt the damp sensation. Then the embarrassment in the lav, the show of blood.

At home on holiday she became very sprightly in an attempt to conceal the fact that it had actually happened, and she skipped and whistled in a manner that was quite idiotic, her father perhaps guessing.

She was introduced to the other thing below the terrace at *Deux-Sèvres*. The murmurous greenness of the wood there with the tall conifers going up and the wooden steps going down, the paths covered in moss and twigs, the sun filtering down like under the sea, and Anita the precocious one from Tours with the white blubbery thighs, going on and on – filth and dirt. There was a disused swimming pool there with cracked walls, empty of water. Unutterable misery down there. A few feet of brown leaves, down in the hold.

A name and a day set aside. It was her fate to meet him, be captivated by him, fall for him.

She told herself, One puts wrong constructions on conduct and behaviour when one is entirely ignorant of how the other person feels.

It was so, just so. It was her fate to meet him, be utterly charmed by him, fall for him.

Early morning mist about the house, over the meadow bare of haycocks. All seemed strange at that unaccustomed hour. She had resolved to pitch on; useless to resist; she would go through with it again. The first time had been awful, a *fiasco*.

Flights of swallows darting from the sun. Their tearing cries. Why from the sun? Was it because the insects they fed on flew towards the heat, the warmth, what little warmth there was in the

155

early morning? Their cries. Broken sounds in the air. So sweet. Aubade. Music of blood awaking in young children. Waking when she was a child at Melview and the maids out stretching carpets on the railing and the cattle rising up under the trees. The taste of the soda bread, water drawn from the kitchen tap. A time of courage and hope.

In the plantation life was waking. She approached the lodge. The back gate was closed; moisture clung to the bars. Nothing passed on the road. She knocked on the bedroom window and called his name. After some delay he came to the door wearing an overcoat, his hair on end, his face puffy with sleep, to admit her in. Then he went back to bed. It was 5.30 A.M.

– I've come to make you coffee.

A male lair, male smells, his clothes thrown on a chair, pipe and tobacco pouch by his bed. She went into the kitchen and made his coffee and brought it to him.

– At least I know what you wear in bed, she said.

Presently Otto revived, laid aside his empty cup and, clasping her hips, pulled her down. She gave him a kiss on the mouth, moving her lips on his, softly labiate, the most fluttering and uncertain proofs in the world, which greatly excited him.

Her arms in mute supplication were about his neck. Dread of pain, of piercing, a dread of parting.

Her lips parted. He was impatient as always, his hands from long practice at manual work, rough as holystone. She could not get her breath, her lungs could not take in enough air. Now together like a drowning couple grappling, locked together, surrounded by waves, losing sight of everything, she was smothering in Otto's disorganized sheets. He was pushing himself against her. Her loosened hair fell over him. Tenesmus and groaning and shame, senseless and useless to resist any longer, coiled about him; she must thrust aside whatever bashfulness was in her. She went through with it, afraid that she would choke. She feared she would certainly die, of mortification.

Afterwards Otto lay at peace, looking pleased, coughing behind his hand, staring up at the ceiling; once again he had run his quarry to earth.

She slept the night alongside him, listening to the rain falling on the leaves outside, a full liquid sound, and from thence silently to the ground. She was with him, protecting him as he protected her; the wind was blowing about the lodge; no sound of a living soul.

An iron church bell was ringing in the dark, the big bell from Hammond Lane foundry, its reverberations spreading outwards from the church yard (where it was certainly deafening), the first bell for eight o'clock Mass, celebrated while it was still dark: the sound of a distant bell carried on the wind, mellowed by the distance it had travelled, one Irish mile from its source, the hard strokes of the clapper spread softly outwards . . .

He had a prominent Adam's apple, almost piercing the skin of his neck, moving up and down as he talked. He talked a lot, but there were days when he would hardly open his mouth at all. He had an abstracted manner, bloodless lips, which he had a habit of running his tongue over, foxy, to go with his red hair and slight build and general air of somewhat withdrawn and furtive independence. He had a troubled forehead, a noncommittal expression; the pores of his skin on face and neck (this a source of wonder to her) ingrained with black dirt as though grit had been driven so deeply into the skin that no amount of scrubbing could eradicate it.

His toilet was brief enough, consisting as it did of a pinching-in of the corners of his eyes with a finger and thumb, a dashing of cold water onto his face with both hands, from the water butt, which was in fact their drinking water, – followed by a plaiting down on his hair with both dampened hands. There was a comb in the cottage to be sure, but it resembled more a horse's currycomb than anything in the human line, and this he would apply to his wiry hair on the occasion of an expedition to the city. He had a muddy complexion with some colour on the cheekbones after a good dinner or after drinking a lot, which he did as a rule every evening of his life.

He kept hens. A woman from the back road fed them, looked after him and lit his fire. Imogen had to be away early in the morning. Otto had worked for the Forestry Department in Glencree, but when Imogen first knew him he was giving grinds in mathematics to the clergyman's two acne-faced sons, teaching at the Rectory, and it was upon that slender remuneration that he supported himself.

The hens dirtied all the surroundings, the ash-pit wall, the little outhouses, the kitchen. Their underfeathers and droppings were everywhere. They laid clutches of eggs in the undergrowth which were never found, or disappeared and came back with chickens. Their sad droning cries were a feature of the place. Otto seemed indifferent to them and their dirty ways.

He came on his antique bicycle with provisions, day after day, cursing the clergyman's backward sons. Day after day the woman left, a bit surly, banging the gate. Otto walked through the plantation carrying a towel which he hung on the paling, so that Imogen from her room could see that the coast was clear. The day after she came to the cottage of her own free will, Otto – nothing if not tactful when the occasion demanded it – dismissed the woman from the back road, so as not to compromise Imogen. She went out banging the gate. A fortnight later he excused himself from any more tutorials at the Rectory, saying that he wanted to give all his time to her. He would give all his time to her.

Mornings in the lodge. Ashes of the sunken fire, noises of the hens, Rhode Island Reds and Sussex Whites, Otto's good layers. The door was open. Sunlight streamed in. The droning cries of the hens rooting in the yard. She was struck by the gentleness of his face in repose, a serenity, unguessed-at tenderness. His books on the shelf. A very workmanlike job. Substantial. Professional carpenter's work. His scattered books and papers which she would put into order. German books, a portable typewriter, a virgin ream of Swift Brook Bond, his endless thesis. His worsted breeches up against her. His arms about her waist. Crêpe de chine. Staring straight into her eyes. Master me. (*You will change, you will change.*)

She was obliged to rise first thing and throw open all the windows and doors, for as soon as he woke from sleep Otto Beck would begin calling out for air like Svidrigailov in *Crime and Punishment*. Then she made him breakfast.

– Thrushes whistle and blackbirds sing, Otto said. The blackbirds begin about the first week in February. For a while the singing is very hoarse, as if the bird was concentrating on clearing its throat after a winter of no singing. The male bird sings near the nest, getting a kind of curl (Otto made a motion upwards with his hands, indicating the bird's effort), a grace-note into it eventually. He sings all day throughout the summer, within the intervals of feeding his young. Thrushes begin a bit later.

A blustery morning; overcast; raining on the leaves. Damp in all the rooms. The rain ceases about ten o'clock. The clock stopped. Sun attempting to break clear of clouds. Overcast all day. Blowy.

– Take the word Ailm, Otto said. In Old Irish it meant palm, the tree. In modern Irish it means elm. In Latin, *ulmus*. In Italian, *olmo*. The question is, where did the palm trees come from in ancient Ireland? Phoenician? Like the Phoenix Park? What?

A mystery right enough.

Otto studious, indoors all day, reading, making notes; then silence; a page turned briskly; creaking of his upholstered chair. His quiet breathing. A heavy sigh escaped him, to be followed in a short while by another, more hollow and profound. The book lay on his lap, slips of paper protruding from its pages, Brackenbury's *Campaign in the Crimea*. Hauptmann's *Hannele's Himmelfahrt*. A plate of bread and honey on the table beside him. She had bought a honeycomb from Findlater's because Otto was fond of it.

Otto lowering his chin onto his chest, deciding the fate of nations, turning something over in his mind, presented to her the sparse hair at the crown of his head. He would not hear questions if he did not want to answer them, or thought them beneath his consideration. He talked of 'culturally inferior nations' and of 'culturally insignificant' individuals. Oh, he was hard on people. He had a way of slapping his forehead with the flat of his palm, eyes shut, clicking his tongue, – a combination of mime and sound intended to indicate mortification and high remorse, coupled with wonder at his own folly. How could I have forgotten a thing like that, click, slap. He had elegant hands, long fingers, strong, some hair. A melancholy visage. He cut his own hair, and cut it badly. It grew untidily down to the top of his spine. The index, first and ring fingers of his right hand were stained to the knuckles with nicotine, the thumb blackened at the centre. He smoked a lot, the last thing at night and first thing in the morning, holding his Wild

Woodbines as a labouring man would, between thumb and first finger, the lighted end in the cup of his hand, smoked down to the last inch, sucking, his cheeks sucked in.

She cooked him rice puddings, macaroni puddings with cheese. Prior to that his diet had been spare enough, his meals the meals of the poor – a thin coarse table of potatoes, cabbage, soda bread, eggs always, gammon, tea with lemon. He was not a great meat-eater. It was he who taught her how to drink, gave her a taste for it. Ascetic in many ways himself, he did not stint himself in that respect; but after her arrival there was always something to drink in the house. He lived well enough. Celibacy formed no part of his plan of life; he was the last man in the world to subsist on a platonic attachment. He had his way with her pretty well as he pleased. ('Anything you say, Otto . . . I'll do anything you want.') He persevered so well that one morning love yielded up a kind of sweetish syrup, which flowed unchecked into her mouth; such a sweetness she had never before conceived of.

After that she began to relish his experienced and muscular embraces, the abject slave of her foreign conqueror, even going so far as to dab her nipples with cream from puffy cakes, Monument Creamery meringues; Otto opening his eyes wide at this, a great change in his mistress's former serious ineptitude. She had a stern deportment, pale skin, dark expressive eyes, black hair combed down over her forehead, a high affronted stare, a long upper lip and rather a fleshy nose; a moist modest perfumed body.

Going down to the lodge at night with a flashlight; climbing over the paling, walking across the field. And through the plantation at the back of the cottage. She wore jodhpurs. Looking back at Springfield she saw in the darkness two windows fully lighted by the moon. She was leaving it for longer and longer periods. Another life was beginning for her. The cattle rising up in the field, set for the aftergrass, frightened the life out of her. Skirting a bush that wasn't a bush, it moved, a monster reared up, bellowing 'Master me!'

He was sitting before the fire meditating, sitting in profile to the window on his highbacked chair, a priest in a confessional with averted head and ear cocked at the hour to hear confessions, women's secret sins. She brought with her the scent of her heated body in the red raincoat.

Otto had a drink convenient to his hand, a book on his lap. He laid aside the book and took up the drink.

– I'm tired of disorganized minds, Otto said. Who wants to read such stuff today? Stale old tales no one believes in any longer, full of morals and impossible virtues.

Night after night she came to take her place in his bed, his *âme damnée*. Dark arms. Approaching the bed. The fire blazing.

– My nightie . . . would you pass me my nightie?

– Wouldn't you go without?

– Hush . . . Will you hush.

They slept together in the old iron family bed with its centre sagging down lower than the rusted sides. She bought him a pair of coarse linen pyjamas and consigned his old sleeping shirt, which had seen a lot of service, to the flames.

Cattle coughing in the night. At times troops of horses passing on the road. Always the turf-carts grinding by, coming from the Bog of Allen and bound for Dublin, or coming from Dublin, bound for the Bog of Allen, one after another, the drivers walking by the donkey's head on the journey in, sleeping on sacks on the journey home. All night long, night after night, in winter in driving rain; and she safe in Otto's arms.

One night he was twitching and moaning alongside her, his hands folded across his breast. But when she laid her hand lightly on his, whatever was troubling him ceased to trouble him.

In the long summer evenings at dusk the turf-carts were going by, ramshackle convoys moving in slow motion, like in a dream, their ruby carriage lamps moving in and out of her dream, the little donkeys going past. A time of enchantment began then.

His flesh knows my flesh; he is at peace.

All Otto's past came out of a white cardboard shoebox: dogeared snapshots, mismatched shoe-laces, French chalk, unprinted negatives, old notebooks, old love letters.

Little biscuits, half-chewed and wrapped in a dish-cloth. His odious philosophy: 'Eat and the appetite comes.'

23

They followed the sheep path up through bramble bushes and furze, the thorns catching at Imogen's skirt making it difficult for her to climb. Stray goats and sheep, wandering at will in the dry airlessness about the hornet-infested bushes, had left their dropping on the dusty path. On the summit a cool breeze was blowing. They walked to the far end to see St Patrick's Bed. Nothing very remarkable after all – just a depression in the ground with some stones and nettles, nothing more. They sat in the leeward side in the sun. Otto removed his jacket, staring at the countryside below with a complacent air.

Meadows, wheat and corn fields, the sun shooting fire from the roof of a hayshed, Killadoon in a haze to the north-west and a silver stretch of the river going between the trees. A small square stone-roofed house stood in a field below; St Patrick's House, according to local legend. Above them the high azure, remote white cirrus grazing on heaven.

– This is where they have the motor-cycle races, Imogen said. The Straffan Circuit goes round this hill. From here to Barbarstown cross-roads, from there to Straffan and back by the river. Such a din! The rabbits run mad.

She laid aside her sun-hat and lay back on the burnt grass. Otto said nothing, watching the cattle moving in the shadows of the hedge. In the ditch they had hoped to escape the attentions of the gad-flies, standing restless with their heads down, or shifting about, swishing their tails.

– The holy well, Otto said, – Patrick's well. Most extraordinary. All those ribbons. They look like relics torn from women's drawers.

They had seen it on the way up. A well of spring water surrounded by five rowan trees in a beehive bramble bush the interior of which was adorned with a strange assortment of ribbons, some comparatively new, but many more of them quite rotted away.

– They are, Imogen said, that's the whole idea. It's a kind of penance. One tears off a piece of one's slip and hangs it on the bush.

– I see. You leave something of yourself behind. Your penitential identity. I get the idea.

– Yes, I suppose you could call it that.

She was staring up into the cobalt sky, at remote white cirrus, shielding her eyes against the glare. The breeze was intermittent, coming and going, dry and warm, bringing with it the smells of summer. A threshing-machine droned away in a remote wheatfield.

– Why is it called holy? Otto asked. And why did he choose to sleep up here on the windy summit?

– No, he prayed up here. He slept down there.

– Prayed where?

Imogen did not reply. Something in grey stone behind the foliage. A small doorless one-room stone house with slits for windows, refuge for cattle; St Patrick's House.

– If you mean that cowshed down there, I can tell you that it's twelfth century, no earlier, Otto said with exasperating exactness, whereas your patron saint flourished in the fifth century – correct me if I am mistaken. He could never have lived there.

Imogen raised herself up, pointing.

– Oh look . . . a hawk!

Otto looked up, preparing to refute her (for she couldn't distinguish between a swallow and a swift), but sure enough a brown hawk was hovering over the hill. In the mirage of heat, part of the Hill of Ardrass floated into space.

A hawk; *Habicht*, in suspended motion, hovering.

– A hawk, Otto said, a holy well, a saint's resting-place. We're in the Middle Ages.

The drone of the threshing-machine slackened, faltered, altered pitch, fell off into silence. Presently it began again, a tone or two higher. The hawk dropped, then continued hovering, watching something below. With a deepening pitch and drone the mill of the threshing-machine was grinding up wheat and extruding straw and chaff down its labouring chutes, somewhere quite near after all, behind Odlum's barn.

– The sun comes up, Otto said. The saint is praying on his knees. The sun goes down. Patrick lies sleeping on his bed of nettles. In the morning he walks down dejected to the holy well.

The hawk, giving up, drifted over the brow of the hill. Otto lay back, closing his eyes. She looked down at him without speaking. In the heat she could hear a plaintive bleating, the erratic crackle of bursting seed-pods and the tinkle of the goat bells in the furze. After a while she spoke again:

– Don't the hills look marvellous, all the same? So clear and blue. They look far off, not in the County at all probably, and yet one can see the details so clearly. The blue foothills of the Dublin mountains . . .

– And . . . ? Otto said, staring at the clouds. Time, effacing the fiction of opinion, the move confirms the determination of nature. Ireland: multiple associations: a green road riddled with light.

Turning abruptly now he caught her in his arms and pressed himself ardently against her, kissing with a very *gros baiser*. She held onto his hand.

24

Gin days; greenery everywhere; stiff gins and tonics with lemon floating in the glass. A shape which from its size, mass and density she knew to be Otto's was parading back and forth before her with the regularity and force of an automaton, giving out his harsh views. His words and thoughts floated about the room, pursued by her vacant stares into every corner. He who had been so full of hope not so long before, for his career was going ahead, seeing the London *Fortnightly Review* had accepted an article of his, was now sadly cast down.

When, some days before, a copy of the magazine arrived with his name among twelve other contributors on the orange cover, he had gone out and bought two bottles of London Dry Gin. But then his spirits sank and all his confidence evaporated before a depression that was in part brought on by gin. The magazine, propped up on the mantelpiece, showed fourth in the order of contributors his name and contribution: O. B. Beck, 'Symbolism in Grimm'.

He was staring out the window, plunged in a mood of blackest hypochondria. His career, far from going ahead, was on the contrary at a standstill, if not on the downgrade.

He continued to stare out for a long time at a dreary expanse of drifting cloud and shifting sky. There was no warmth in the air; summer was over; the clouds were passing over Killadoon, over the Council houses on the back road, over the hill of Ardrass, with an air of nothing settled; or rather, with an air of everything settled in nature, but nothing settled in troubled human life.

– Ah well . . . ah well, he said, stirring after a prolonged silence, staring about as though surprised to find himself still in the same room, – even at enormous depths where the water pressure is thousands of pounds to the square inch, determined creatures burrow through the mud.

The article was worthless; he could do better.

Gin days, gin days.

– The first human beings, our first parents, Otto said, Adam and Eve, according to a Kabyl legend of creation, lived under the earth with their fifty sons. And when the time came to build houses the fifty sons started excavating like badgers. There must be some connection here with children's instincts to dig pits and tunnels. My brother and myself went in for it. The urge towards a separation from the parents.

– High time, she said, wagging her head at him, high time you had a bath, mister . . .

So, after dark some days later, Otto was flattening the valerian on the top of the garden wall, edging along the dairy roof, wearing sneakers, and so to the wall of the house, hearing the water running into her bath. The bathroom window was fogged up with steam. He tapped on the glass as per arrangement and she pushed the window up and let him in. She was in her dressing-gown with her hair up. He began to take off his clothes. She put lilac-scented bath salts into the water and they got in together. Living in the lives of others. Her bedroom was next door. He would spend the night with a powdered and scented lady, *patiens luminis atque solis*; letting himself down the Virginia creeper at an unholy hour next morning long before the others were stirring.

Otto made a cardboard puppet theatre with a penknife and razor blade, gum and paste. A warlike stage. He studied it with his pale blue eye. A face from which all play of expression had been deliberately banished, the lines of the mouth set and determined. Watching him she remembered his contempt for faces with 'too much water' in them; the puffy softened features of the spineless ones.

Otto, squinting at the battle array, said:

– Troops advancing to the assault in the Crimea noticed that while the turf over which they were walking smelt of thyme, their opponents, coming from the opposite direction, were smelling of leather . . .

Voices behind the hedge. Two gossiping women from the back road discussing a third party.

– Says I, There's flesh protrudin from the back passage. Says she, *Whaas protrudin?*

He went out at night to get some corn, wading into a wet field of stubble near the back road where a few remaining bundles of corded sheaves were left over near the ditch, and came back grinding it in the palm of his hand. He climbed over the paling behind the cottage and went along the field to a point near the beech tree favoured by the pheasants that came over from Killadoon, and scattered it there in generous handfuls. Next morning he loaded the double-barrel shotgun which Father had lent him, certainly not given him, to 'thin out' the squirrels, and went out early before breakfast, telling her to have coffee ready when he came back. As she was waiting for it to percolate she heard the blunt report of his gun firing from among the trees, and a little while later he came in with a battered pheasant, a hen. He said that he had got his shot in but had not killed it outright. He hung it in the outhouse.

He was going on about place-names and how they changed, how new ones were formed from corruptions of the old names, of French words buried in colloquial Irish speech, common in the nineteenth century but now disappearing. Gams from *jambes* and gossoon from *garçon* and mush (his pipe in his mush) from *bouche*, and of the origin of the name *Celbridge*. Otto knew all about it. From Kildroghet or Kyldroghel, the Church of the Bridge, the *Cill* or church of the bridge.

– In the Inquisitions at the time of James the First, Otto said.

But Imogen wasn't taking half of it in.

– Under English rule the native Irish – of whom you mustn't consider yourself one – were required by law to adopt English customs and English surnames. An Act of Parliament was passed under I think the fourth Edward making this a law within the Pale. Can you feel the indignity of that? Under opprobrium, the dispossessed Irish, having lost their country, their lands and homes, must now lose their own names, their contact with the past, their blood identity. They were offered the choice of calling themselves after a colour or a trade or a science or a town. After that, the census rolls swarmed with Whites and Greens and Browns and Corks and Kinsales and Suttons and Chesters, not to mention Smiths, Carpenters, Cooks and Butlers.

– The Pale, Otto said. The English Pale. The Plantagenets. We're lying in the middle of their bloody fields. This is Pale ground.

He yawned. Imogen looked down into a mouthful of bad teeth. The yawn ended in a groan and tears stood out in the corners of his eyes.

– Dublin, Meath, Kildare, where else? four counties. Offaly, isn't it? he said, wiping his eyes.

Yes, it would be Offaly.

– No, not Offaly – Louth. Dublin, Kildare, Meath, Louth. You are an ignoramus, dear.

– It's true, she admitted. I am an ignoramus. You are far too clever for me. Why you put up with me, I don't know.

Put up with me. Ignoramus.

– My dear, Otto said, smiling his false cat's smile. My dear.

– Don't my dear me, she said, pushing his hand away.

Drills of flowering potatoes. The turned earth, Otto digging potatoes for lunch. The musty fragrant aroma of their pollen-bearing white flowers. The smell of the earth. Otto's spade turning up earth and potatoes. Otto bending, reflecting, throwing the potatoes into a cracked enamel basin. Imogen watched him, hearing the peaceful sound of a man digging in a summer garden. His spade struck something hard. Bending forward. What? Digging the earth out.

She cooked his porridge, his rice; he made German pancakes, from potatoes.

– Archery in ancient China was played traditionally to the beat of music, Otto said. The contestants were allowed four arrows but could only fire at the proper beat of the music.

The Chou Dynasty.

The bridge at Tarmonbarry. A very big bridge across the Shannon there. The boats were in dry dock. It was a very favourite place for Grandad to drive out to from Longford.

Otto, well satisfied with a good meal, lay in the wet grass, loath to stir a hand or foot, smoking his meerschaum, his eyes half-closed, a complacent expression on his face. She came to the paling and leant over it, watching him, Otto supine in the grass.

– Get up, silly . . . you'll catch your death of cold.

A blackbird singing in the plantation after rain, a dripping shrubbery of hazel and ivy, holly, and Otto lying on the damp ground explaining to her that he never contracted colds *except from other people*. The virus, contagion, on account of his good health, you understand.

Indoors all day reading. The frozen silence. The creaking of his chair. Breathing within. You are my weakness.

A rude outside privy. The cottage, now in order, his books on the table, *Niels Lyhne* and the *Works of Ossian* among his papers, pipes and pens. A decent chamber with wood and other necessaries for his firing and proper diet both as to eating and drinking.

The pond in Killadoon in the midday sun. Sunlight pouring down through the leaves. A blaze of lax water. The shadows of the leaves on the grass. A dead black cat under the surface stretched out on the decomposing leaves. Sleepy stagnation. The rotted boat's ribs. The oars.

– Wall? Waldron? Fielding? Flood? . . . some name like that.

– Shannon, Otto said.

Shannon. One cold winter's day Grandad led her across the rickety footbridge at Tarman near where the Comlen River flowed into the Shannon, divided at a place called Ballykenny. Grandad wore a wing collar, a grey tweed suit, black boots; a watch-chain spanned his stomach; he had a waxed moustache that turned up at the ends like the Kaiser's. She, Imogen, was only a little girl, his grandchild, the apple of his eye. Her father and mother stood watching from the bank, waving.

But it was too high and insecure-looking underfoot, where she could see the river running out fast. Her hand was in his, he held her; but she was afraid and had to be taken back.

Imogen, her head on folded arms, with limp strands of long black hair stuck to her forehead, lay sleeping, her mouth crushed out of shape by the bulge of her forearm. She was breathing with difficulty through her nose, presented at such an acute angle to Otto so that he could see into her dark nostrils.

– Blücher, Otto said, the preposterous Blücher. In Germany we laugh at old Blücher.

Otto informed her that he had worked for a farmer in the eastern Tyrol, in freezing Austria, getting up in the dark mornings. 'Their weird and ancient dialect.'

His facial expressions were sometimes quite peculiar: he would stare at her with a slow mad stare that she had never seen on a human face before, and very unsettling to encounter. Then she was a little frightened of him. He did not stop when he should have done. The pale skin, the set of the jaw, on Herr Palindromic Otto, KCEB.

She heard the wind playing about in the trees around the lodge and then the rain falling on the leaves.

I am with him here in bed and protecting him, as he protects me. No sound of a living soul.

He looked at her with his slow mad stare. Jaw clenched, he gave her this freak look. He looked incapable of performing a disinterested good act.

25

Imogen said with her teeth, her jaw, breaking the word in two, a hard 't', she said, The butcher's *meat* and went herself to Young's to select the cuts that were intended presumably for the Springfield table.

Otto was fond of chicken broth. He could see poultry and game only as potential dinners, his eyes on the white breast-meat. And on mine too, she thought.

Yes, on mine too.

I was not myself, yet never have I lived more in my senses ... he entered me in such a way that I forgot to be ashamed ... openly I gave myself to that ardour. I clung with all my poor senses that were threatening to leave me ... inexorable sweetness, embrace of arms, my breath into his; my teeth, my jaws ache with this sweetness of giving; and in that giving too I take ... I partake of him, his body, his past which I know nothing of ... I dwell in him and he in me ... all unloosened I quench my longing in him ...

– Come in, dear. The meal's on the table.

She had a way of scraping out the last morsels from dishes, her face a little flushed, but becomingly so, to fill his plate, which pleased him. But the look on her face, implying that one could always reach a man's heart via his stomach, that did not please him, for it was a lazy way of thinking. Otto, pushing his chair back from the table, crossing his legs, reaching for his tobacco pouch, staring at her.

She had another lazy habit too, removing her shoes without touching them by hand, nipping the heel of the first with the toe of its fellow, nudging it off, then repeating the trick with her stock-inged foot, which did not please him.

Late September days. Days of brown leaves.

A line of uniformed girl students striding out from the Collegiate School two by two, walking on the leaf-strewn path, the leading pair stepping onto the road, then back onto the pavement again, chattering, twenty or more striding along at a good pace, laughing, their elongated shadows flickering by on the wall, bound for Ardrass or Barbarstown Cross, with two severe teachers striding behind them. Then the figure of Otto appeared, cycling towards them, advancing towards their growing interest as he approached nearer, the chatting becoming louder, more disturbed, geese on the run. If Imogen was out walking, she would turn back when she saw them coming.

– Certainly I recall your old man, Otto said, of course. I remember you ... You were all sitting round the lunch table shaking out your table napkins. As I was passing I saw your old man preparing to carve the joint, with a napkin, a tucker, about his neck. The carving-fork was into one side of the roast and the carving knife poised to slice off a prime cut. His mouth was pursed up with concentration. I could feel it was a serious business. Although I could not see you I could feel you all there waiting to be served. Flies were landing on his face, but accoutred as he was he could not brush them off. The maid, what do you call her? ... yes, Biddy, the last of the Langans, she was advancing with a white china gravyboat on a wooden tray. Passing by I saw that through a chink in the dining-room door the day I first came for the key ...

– In life, Otto said, man has choice in life of being either hammer or anvil, as the divine Goethe would have it.

– Oh please, she said.

– From the Dolomites on a fine day, Otto said, you could see from a high mountain-top the outline of the Adriatic coast and the sea. The latter is a lighter and brighter shade of blackish-green as against the land, which is dull black in the far distance.

172

The earth breathed in and out and perspiration started under her clothes. Yea thy pale colours, and yea again thy panting heart!

– . . . A certain mistiness but not cloud over the sea area. If there were any clouds about they would be of the fiercely white cumulus type over the immediate mountain range. I used to lie there with the goats. The swifts and swallows would dive just over my head.

Tender smiles on the women's faces. They sat on the terrace in their summer finery making considered motions with their hands, elegant little gestures, eating cucumber sandwiches, laughing and talking; the men eating their sandwiches from handkerchiefs balanced on their knees.

The tight-stretched net and the sound a well-struck tennis ball makes when it strikes the white canvas. Odours of delphinium, frangipani. The women shedding some of their clothes, their careful ways (even the ones who conveyed the impression of being pinned together). Tender smiles on the women's faces, smiles for the men, their manly exertions; and the tennis balls flying to and fro, to and fro across the net.

Sissy, the lady champion of the court, sweeping the ball on her forehand, running forward to the net. The men in their white flannels, handkerchiefs around their necks, clouting hard returns into the back of the court. The attention of all fully engaged, applause for points won, sets and games won. The heat of the sun quite ruinous to the ladies' complexions as the day wore on, playing havoc with arms and bare backs. At night, bemoaning their foolishness, they would have to apply boric.

Movements and voices from the past. The odour of frangipani, delphinium.

– I have been haunted by a phrase all day, Otto said. Perhaps you could enlighten me as to what it means. *She was a living Rosary . . .*

Otto played Mendelssohn on his Hohner Harmonica, vamping, rolling his shoulders.

Something was shining on the cottage floor, most extraordinary, the size of an onion, a knuckle-bone, glowing in the dark. Otto climbed out of bed and went to it, bending to cover it with his hand. The light went out. He came back to her, a dark shape seen against the window, opened his hand. A phosphorescent ball the size of a double marble lit up his palm and fingers. What was it? A hambone. A week before, Otto had thrown bones down for the cat. A hambone shining in the dark.

Otto appeared before her holding a dead rabbit by its hind legs. He extended it to her at arm's length without a word, staring at it.

It became dark in the room.

His technique of standing too close. He is easing nature at the back door, standing inside in his shirt only. He makes no bones about it. Why should he?, it's natural. It doesn't in any way embarrass me. Why should it? We do not have to speak to each other. He is coming in. We are standing up close against each other. I'm standing in a profusion of undergarments.

– Excuse me, I must attend to nature. (Otto urinating out the back door in the rain, a hearty splashing in the middle of the yard.)

In circumstances such as these the annexing of those territories of her affections which she believed, had once believed, would never go, began.

A late autumn night, with rain, and blowing hard, very blustery.

– Did you know, Otto asked, that one of the heresies of Johannes Scotus Erigena was that the sexual organs would not be resurrected on the Last Day?

A sidelong glance from her mistrustful eye; pursey mouth, pursey lips.

– His students, so the story goes, alarmed by the boldness of his thought, stabbed him to death with their pens.

The rain blowing hard against the window. Dull grey wet days.

– Penises? she said.

At night now bonfires were burning on the hills. All along the Dublin and Wicklow hills the furze was on fire. She could see a glow too in the front field near Otto's lodge. The labourers had built a fire there. A big ash tree had been cut down and was disappearing under the crosscuts and the axe. Nothing would remain soon except the butt in the earth and a scattering of twigs, the shape of its fall indented on the earth for a little while, then that too flattened out. Grass would grow alongside it, saplings rise ... a shrub, a goodsized bush ... In time another tree would grow there out of its obstinate sproutings.

No, that wouldn't happen ... the butt would be smeared with wetted earth so that it could more quickly rot away. Elm and ash, the blackthorn that was unlucky to cut down, all were gone out of the front field. Figures passed in front of the fire, their voices carried across the field. She would have to go by the avenues and be careful.

The fires were still burning all along the hills on the following night, half the hillside seemed to be on fire ... the furze throwing up showers of sparks ... maybe tar barrels had been lit, like when De Valera had first been returned for County Clare.

She had told him that if the fire in the front field was still burning on the following night, that he must come to her, because on the night she had gone to him some young fellows loitering at the back gate had seen her go in.

So, bidden to her bed, he climbed up the ivy on the front of Springfield, shinning up the side of the house like a cat burglar, climbing over the edge of the balcony and passing through her father's empty room, the door and window of which she had left open, and turning right and finding her bedroom door.

– Do not turn left, for the love of God, she said, or you may end up on top of Lily.

They lay in bed together with the Venetian blinds of all three windows up, in a high-ceilinged room facing south, admiring the fires that burned on the hills as though they would go on burning there for ever, celebrating the Eucharistic Congress.

26

The autumn came and went and winter began, damp and cold.
The saturated trunks of the trees turned dark in the rain and the
house appeared through the thinning plantation. An ash tree was
sold and felled near the ring pump. From the house Imogen had
heard it fall.

The loads came across the field, coming onto the back avenue
through the lower gate, the lorry wheels cutting a deeply indented
double track on the sodden ground. As the first half of the chained
trunk came slowly down to the gate Otto was there to open it. He
left it open and entered the cottage.

In the bedroom he drew the curtains and sat on the edge of the
bed trimming his nails, waiting for her to take off her dress. Then
they lay together on the day-bed. With the tips of his fingers he
touched her flank. She turned to him her burning cheeks, her
shining eyes no longer timidly and irresolutely meeting his. He put
his hands under her armpits where he had forbidden her to shave
and pushed her down. She closed her eyes when he spoke low love
words in German which she did not understand. He kissed her
heavy eyelids, the sorrowful folds of skin; his hot breath fanned
her face, whispering to her in German.

– Your limbs, Otto said, they are so white.

It was true: she was a white-skinned woman. The skin starved
for sun and fresh air. There was no natural colour in her face, for
she would not take exercise and ate wretchedly as a natural
consequence.

– Do not close your eyes, he said, they are remarkable.

They were remarkable: when she felt passionate, the pupils
grew correspondingly huge, blacker, purple in their flickering
depths.

– Your tongue, she said.

He whispered in her ear. Something began to throb inside her.

– I love you, Otto dear, she said, lost.

She used his Christian name a lot, although to her he rarely employed that form of address. He was aroused now, removing her underclothes, attempting to find all her person with his ardent lips and hands. In his embraces, she gave him back long kisses with all her heart and guile in them. In the submarine light of the darkened room he was penetrating her. Lost now, indeed lost, she clung to him, held fast in his grip while his narrow head blocked out the light. A little longer. So deeply. So deeply touched. A little longer.

– You are so big . . . so gentle . . . oh so big . . .

Soon she was letting herself go completely, panting:

– Now . . . now . . . God.

Otto groaned. Presently she got up and washed herself in the basin. Then she came back and lay alongside him and lit a cigarette. Otto, coughing politely behind his hand, stared up at the ceiling reaching for his pipe.

– You're only an old goat, she said.

The chained second half of the trunk was driven past the window as they lay there smoking. With difficulty it went out into the road, grinding into gear, bound for the timberyards at Naas. Otto rose to draw aside the curtains.

– There goes another victim of circumstances, he said, staring after the load.

Evening had come down outside. A fine white mist floated through the air. The window was half open. The trees over Killadoon wall were still in full leaf. Otto stared out over the half-length netting, knitting his brows, thinking about something. His pipe smoke glided out the window, low at first, then wisping out rapidly, rising straight up out of sight. A blackbird was choking itself in the wet hedge. From where she lay she could see his head silhouetted against the light. He was mother-naked except for a labourer's cotton vest, which was too short for him. Imogen, smiling to herself, was thinking of the state in which she had first found him, alone in the lodge and living in high squalor. She had to overcome more than her prudery to become intimate with him.

There had been fleas in the bed for one thing; and in his hair. Otto, not in the least perturbed, had offered as a useful precedent the case of the Emperor Julian, who had fleas in his beard. I too, said Otto, I too, permit the little beasts to have the run of me, like animals in a park. But she had soon put a stop to that nonsense. She burnt the sheets, fumigated the whole place, and brought down fresh linen from the house. With his back to her now he asked:

– How much are you getting for the tree, may one ask?

– Two quid, she said. Which isn't bad, considering we get the top as well.

Otto grunted to himself and blew out more smoke. In Killadoon a thin bell began a rapid tolling. Work was over for the day; soon the men would be cycling home down the long tree-lined avenues. Outside in the wood a flock of crows were descending with raucous cries into the trees near Killadoon back lodge. The bell stopped. Imogen rose and began to put on her clothes. It was time for Otto's evening meal.

He turned from the window and collected from his shelf a clean shirt and a fresh collar. She sat on the edge of the bed putting on her stockings.

– Now I know why men look so dreadful without their clothes, she said, staring at him . . . It's because their belongings look like intestines hanging down.

27

Dum bibitur . . . Otto said.

Imogen didn't know a word of Latin. No, not a word.

– Read here, Otto bade her, pointing.

A typescript page in a folio notebook. She read:

'As to the Food of the antient *Irifh*, it will admit of no Difpute that the daily Food of the Common People was in old Times very flender, confifting for the moft part of Milk, Butter, and Herbs; from which Practice the Epitome of *Strabo* gives the Irifh the Epithet of, *Herbis Vefcentes – Herb Eaters* . . .'

– What is it? she said.

– Sir James Ware's *Antiquities of Ireland*. Written originally in Latin, adorned with copper plates, here rendered into pale English. Read on.

'The Herbs (she read) for the moft part were the wild Trefoil or Shamrog, water-cress, Sorrel, & Scurvey-Grass. The ancient and peculiar drink of the Irifh, as also of the Britons, was Ale . . .'

– Henry of Araunches, Poet Laureate to Henry III, wrote a memorable couplet about your Irish tosspots. Which goes, if my memory serves me right:

> *Dum bibitur, nil clarius est dum mingitur, unde*
> *Constat quod multas Faeces in Ventre relinquit.*

I render it into even paler English as

> They drink it thick and piss it wondrous thin;
> What store of dregs must needs remain within?

– Your bottled Guinness, Otto said, it's too thick for my taste, I'll drink it, yes, but give me *Andechser Bier* for preference, or *Dortmunder Union* . . .

Barbarstown House, in ruins. Barbarstown Castle. In residence, Mrs Sims. The Straffan circuit. Stanley Woods.

– Why fail? Otto said. I don't understand it. You have seventy-four rich acres of land, ten of that in tillage. You had a herd of cattle once, a supply of eggs, pullets, a vegetable garden, a fruit garden, an orchard. You did not live riotously; so why had it to fail?

The Collegiate School girls were playing lacrosse, watched by a lone attendant.

Rime of the sky; the low range of blue-shadowed Dublin mountains. The bleating of distant sheep.

The field by the back lodge, a depression in the ground, snowberry bushes, a briar-choked ditch, the pump for the Council houses with straw about it in freezing weather. The cottagers kicking football.

The bridge at Tarmanbarry. Was it Tarman? Some name like that. A big bridge thrown across the Shannon there where the boats lay in dry dock the whole winter. It was a very favourite place for Grandad to drive out to.

A crowd of country people dressed in dark clothes were standing on a hill. A coursing match. The beaters hallooing in the coverts. An unseen line of them advancing through the bracken, making a great commotion.

The greyhounds impatient on the leash. A black and a dappled. The hare breaks from cover, running from the beaters, comes loping towards the dogs. The dogs are slipped. She sees the crowd, and is off. Two greyhounds after her. Doubling back on her tracks. Tear the hare to bits if they catch her.

Coursing matches on Major Brooke's land. The curved white hayshed seen against a battle-grey sky. Otto and she pretending not to know each other, standing apart.

Cries in the cold air. The released greyhounds careering after the hare. A coal black one with a rolling red tongue. The teeth of the dogs in the side of the hare, pulling it apart. Not a sound. The roof of the hayshed over the hill. A pale watery sky.

— I came across this curious doggerel on the fly-leaf of an Irish history book in your fine National Library, Otto said, and took the liberty of copying it out. Here it is
He extended a typed sheet.

> 'IRELAND'
> 'So shalt thou be dear Mother as of old
> God's standard bearer o'er sea and land
> The finger of his hand;
> To point the way unto the gates of gold.
> And when the dark doors of the grave unfold
> And thy sons rise to mount the hight
>   of . . . (illegible) . . .
> Hear from God thy sad and splendid story.'

— The indecipherable line reads something like 'mankindful George', which is even greater nonsense than the rest, and I don't believe it can have been intended. But I must say I like the notion of God having other sons that nobody ever heard about. A curious panegyric at all events.

The hands of the faithful at Celbridge twelve o'clock Mass. The breath of the congregation thick and unpleasant.
The women at their beads. Dry picking of hens' beaks on a broken aluminium basin. The fire has burnt itself out in the open grate.

A song thrush singing in the plantation on December 15th. Singing in the winter. The bare brown branches, a dull brown colour. The baked brown wings of the bird. Not a stir. Miss Hart comes again from the village on Sunday. A wave and set. Blowing on the tongs. Leaving burn marks on newspapers. Gossiping.

— It was like this, Imogen explained. We found we couldn't go on running the place at a loss and pay the men their wages, so all but

Feeney had to be dismissed. Galvin and Flynn drove the remains of the herd to Gavin Lowe's cattle-market in Dublin. That was their last job. Flynn went back to Longford and took a job as yardsman at the Longford Arms Hotel, and Creegan went to work for the Turf Board, so we heard.

First Christmas with Otto. Spent in the lodge.

  – You have a nice nature, Otto said. A nice kind nature.

  – Oh, she said, giving an eldritch laugh, my poor nature's my fool.

Making water at the door, standing inside in his shirt only. The birds alighting on the slate roof as I lie waiting in bed, all their small twig-like feet together. Acorns bombard the roof, scrape along the tiles and fall without much noise into the yard. He is coming to bed. Oh Otto Beck, what have you done to me?

Bare branches of Killadoon trees; elm, beech and larch. A few lost leaves and sodden undergrowth of holly and laurel. The darker trunks of the beech trees after rain. The leaves move where the trunk divides into two arms high up. A squirrel.

  Otto in green corduroys and leather arm patches on his coat, in wellington boots and a cloth cap pulled down over his ears, his coat pockets bulging with cartridges, stood out of sight behind a tree.

  The agile brownish-red squirrel moved in the tree. Otto brought the shotgun to his shoulder, squinting along the barrel. The squirrel went round the trunk out of sight. Otto kept the gun trained on the spot.

  She saw his finger crook about the trigger and the veins on the back of his resolute male hand swell, and covered her ears. A movement and there it was flattened against the trunk. The gunshot echoed hollowly off into the wood. Leaves and broken twigs floated down. She uncovered her ears. Had he missed? Otto rarely missed; something light tumbled down among the leaves.

  Imogen stood over the dead squirrel. Otto approached, whistling through his teeth, the game-bag slung over his shoulder.

* * *

On March 20th at Celbridge Gaelic Athletic Association Park the Army team defeated Naas by one goal six points to no goal one point in the first semi-final of the Celbridge Gold Medal Tournament. The Army stars were Douglas O'Hara, 'Darkie' Ryan, and Brannigan.

– You may talk about your oak forest over St Michan's, Otto said, but in the time of Julius Caesar and until long after all Germany and Samaratia were covered with immense forests. The Hercuprian Forest that began in Belgic Gaul and extended right through Germany and Poland was sixty days' journey in length. But that was nothing unusual in those days, when the hills and plains of Europe were covered in woods, and unwholesome marshes down in the valleys . . .

In the old Inquisitions the names occur: Killdrought, Donycomper, Stacumney. Donoghmore, Killadonanan, now Killadoon, Tristlede-lan alias Castledelan, now Castledillon, Tipparston, now Tipper, Straffan and woody Leixlip; all now the names of parishes.

Stacumney signifies 'the house of Coman', a virgin, thus Toigh Cuimne; the Parish of the same.

Three acres of land called le Telatoran in Water fields . . . a certain place planted with trees, called the Hoolie Stedd, or Hoolie place of Symoneston, a parcel also of the said priory (St Wolstan's) . . .

Castletown, north-west of Celbridge, built in 1772 by William Conolly, Speaker of the Irish House of Commons. A half mile to the north-east lies the old cemetery, medieval Donycomper.

On March 30th at St Coca's Hall, Killcock, the Newtown Dramatic Class presented *Mountain Dew*, a three-act comedy. Doors opened at 7:30; performance commencing at 8:00. Prices of admission: 2s.,1s.

– Killock, Otto said, you know was *Okey* in the twelfth century.

Otto made most determined assaults, determined that she should feel everything too.

– No joking, Imogen said (holding onto the bedrail to keep from falling), the world went round that time. I thought I was going to die.

A wild foray in the blood.

– The massacre of Mullaghmast, Otto said . . . Borodine, Marshal Ney. Beyle. The long white roads. The Russian campaign. The Spanish campaign. Exile (mopping up rich brown gravy with a sop of bread).

– Open the door for a minute and the buggers are in.

Otto staring at the hens that had ventured into the room, but himself making no effort to move.

– I remember arriving in Paris in the evening. I'd been told that Cook's man would look after me. I saw him but there was a swarm of people about him. I went into the hotel in the station, booked a room and went to bed, locking the door. The next morning I made my way across Paris from the Gare du Nord to Montparnasse Station, and still remember the strong smell of coffee right across the city. I sat in the train from eight o'clock in the morning, when it left Paris, until five o'clock in the afternoon, when it reached Parthenay. Madame met me outside the station. Apparently no one was allowed onto the platform, not in those days anyway. She didn't know any English and my French wasn't much better. Parthenay was old-fashioned, built on a hill, with the houses at all levels. I spent two years there and liked it well enough.

(She stood at the table, wearing an apron and kneading dough, cutting out cakes for Otto's tea with the rim of a cup.)

– Husserl was Heidegger's teacher, and his philosophy had a detrimental influence on the latter, who succeeded him in 1928 at Freiburg University. After a while Heidegger would not greet him, much less argue with him, much less agree with him.

– You only love my body, she said looking down, grimacing, drawing the laces of her corset tight.

. . . You made a dead set at me, she said. Admit you did. She had a flower in her buttonhole, begonia, touching it at times with the tips of her fingers, inclining her head to smell its perfume, smiling to herself at her whim, or at him.

* * *

184

On a cold summer morning at Parthenay a young woman sits by an open window composing a letter home. She finishes it. Writes, with much love from your affectionate daughter, signs it with a childish hand. She adds as a pious afterthought, *Laus Dei Semper*, blots it, folds it up. She addresses the envelope to:

> Mr & Mrs R. H. Langrishe,
> Springfield,
> Celbridge,
> Co. Kildare,
> Ireland,

stamps and seals it and puts it away in her pocket. She stands up. She can see part of the terrace below, the box hedges and fish pond where steps lead down, the gravelled walks and the tennis court beyond, the net stretched tight over the recently cut and rolled court with its prominent white guide lines. All is in order, nuns' order.

An exhibition tennis match is scheduled for the afternoon; but she does not care much for tennis. Her face is colourless (cosmetics are not encouraged at Parthenay, *Deux-Sèvres*) and she feels herself to be pale and unattractive. She is homesick.

How many years ago, and was it I?

A group of trees stripped of their few remaining leaves by the wind, silhouetted in the grey light of a cold February afternoon towards the end of the first winter.

– Have you ever noticed how they salute you here? Otto asked. It must date back to the elaborate respect demanded by the old nobs. Peasantry dismounting from their bicycles.

– Salute? Imogen said. That's nothing. Old Mrs Henry who cooked for us used to genuflect. It was more elaborate than a courtesy and certainly very embarrassing. She was ninety if she was a day. One couldn't very well ask her not to – an old woman like that.

– Might break a leg, Otto agreed, nodding his head with a heavy display of German *empressement*.

185

28

Naked in the small cottage bedroom, stretching to draw apart the curtains, opening the window before retiring to bed, her person a little pathetic, a young girl's body. An offering to whom? To Eros?

Otto disentangled the live rabbit from the snare. Applying his heel to the back of its neck, trapping it against the ground, he yanked it violently upwards by the hind legs, breaking its spinal cord. He held it up. The rabbit jerked once or twice, involuntary muscular spasms, then was still.

6th May. First cuckoo.

Otto went fishing in the Liffey at Killadoon. The rod he used was a split bamboo cane, an eleven-foot affair which broke into three parts, kept in a soft fabric case, held with two ties. He made a ritual of oiling it when he came home. Dry-fly fishing was what he went in for. He had fished that part of the river up as far as Straffan bridge. (Straffan, in Irish *Struthán*, a stream, i.e. *rivulus*.)

He did not of course confine himself to the Liffey, but also fished the Rye Water (trout, pike, perch), the Blackwater at Enfield in County Meath, the Barrow trout waters (wet and dry fly) and for salmon and pike near Carlow Town.

He also fished the Cushina, Figile, Slate, all small streams, three tributaries of the upper Barrow near Rathangan trout waters; and the rivers Boherbaun, Bauteogue and Greese – all trout streams.

He began fishing towards the end of April.

She would not accompany him to Killadoon when he went trespassing with his rod and creel. But she did accompany him on some expeditions to the Liffey near Straffan bridge. A fishing expedition was an occasion for her. Otto would decide in the morning, going out to study the sky. After lunch she would prepare the sandwiches, tomatoes, ham, fresh bread. His fishing gear would be laid out on the table and checked, both bicycles pumped. They would leave about three o'clock in the afternoon, arriving in good time for the evening rise at five, stopping at Cissy Salmon's for some bottles of Guinness, pale ale.

Otto used a dry fly in the broader and deeper pools. He took the rod from its case, assembled it, selecting from his fly-case a murderous looking Bloody Butcher, knotted it on the gut, selected his place a little way back from the bank, lit his pipe, made a few preliminary casts.

The rod taken back, brought forward, Otto following it with an expert eye; taken back, brought forward casually, taken back again. Then snapped forward, whippy, the line hissing out with a thin cutting sound in the air. The evening's fishing had begun.

The fish were rising to eat. Soft plopping sound. Bubbles. Lazy winding river. Sandbanks on the far side. Rust-coloured cattle coming down to drink further down. Flies hatching out. The May fly's single day. Taken by the fish, facing upstream, flies carried into their open mouths. Indentations on the surface of the river. Whirlpools and eddies circle out. Break up. Carried away. Shapes re-forming. Constantly. River flowing by.

A bubble glistens. Vanishes. Something white. Trout rising. Rings going down. Dandelions and grass being carried down.

Three small rings of ripples. Then no more. Otto's Bloody Butcher touched between rings, was swept up. Otto cast again. Touches. Same place. Again. Then lower down. Swallows dipping, catching flies. Sandmartins clinging to the sides of the bank opposite. Pitted with their nests. Riddled. Continually on the go. Swifts scouting over the shadowed river, touching the surface of the water with their wings. Smell of the river. The sound of it passing. Peaceful river. Purling. Water purls. A river purls. Kingfishers (a touch of brilliance) fly upstream with undeviating straightness. Waterhens jerking across the current. Their cries. River flags the trout swim among.

Evening. Steam on the surface by the far bank. Cattle come to drink. Horse-flies. Dragon-flies. Carried down. Winding river. Its bends. Overhanging foliage. Ash. Elm. Beech. Ash. A cat on the river wall. Black cat. Washing itself. Complacent. River wall. Endless river. Tireless river.

Summer smells coming through the cottage window. Scent of stock, convolvulus and sweetpea everywhere. Clematis. Sitting in the evening sun. Comfortable declining sensation. Sinking into the earth. Swifts arrive before the swallows (so per Otto). Coming from North Africa. Bats fly at night. Meadows full of white daisies and buttercups. Swallows darting over the hedge. The currant bushes in Springfield garden. Dry fumes of their musty branches. Otto favours blackcurrant jam.

Sunbathing in the vegetable garden behind the cottage. A skin that will not tan. Sweat runs down his face, arms, chest. Thumb and finger marks on the book. The sun climbs laboriously over the trees. Endless summer evenings; evenings unbearably prolonged.

– In the first quarter of the eleventh century (Otto embarking on a lengthy explanation) all Kildare town except one house was destroyed by lightning, and in the following hundred years it was destroyed again eight times by fire. Today nothing would change that. It has that look.

Kildare, Nurney, Athy, Bohereen na Gorr, St Brigid's Park, Tully Road, the National Stud.

– James Rawson in the beginning of the nineteenth century wrote that an unmarried man at twenty-five or a woman at twenty was rarely to be met with in the country parts. Today, *mutatis mutandis*, the contrary might be said to be truer. So times do change.

– Look, she said, look (lying on her back on the day-bed).

For there it was again, quivering on the ceiling, just like on that first day.

– What do you call it?

– It's a reflection, Otto said. From outside.

– I know that, she said, but what does one call it?

– It's what you call spectra of diffraction, Otto said, watching a wasp crawling over the bedside table. I pride myself I still know a little about optics.

The wild briar with its buds in June. Its buds and open flowers together in June.

– Do you recall Maureen Layde?

– I'm not likely to forget her, Imogen said. I remember her only too well. That awful woman with the eye-patch. Why do you ask?

– I met Shannon in town yesterday in a great state of perturbation. He told me she had tried to kill herself and almost did it this time. At all events they had to use a stomach-pump to get about a hundred aspirins out of her.

I'd like to tear, I'd like to tear. – To see do you feel.

– I'm sorry to hear that, Imogen said. How is she now?

– On the mend, Otto said. Don't ask me how she arrives at this state of mind, but apparently it's intended as a reproach to Shannon. He was being . . . indiscreet again.

– I see.

– It wasn't the first attempt. But at least she has the grace to try it on only when there are people about.

Taking a pair of nail scissors Otto cut the wasp in two. It arched its back, darting its sting. He gazed blandly at it. Black and yellow transverse stripes. Narrow-waisted. Blinkered eyes.

– The human eye cannot allow certain shapes, Otto said. Very hard to resist the temptation not to stamp on certain shapes, put an end to them.

Imogen knelt in the yard, leaning over the low ash-pit wall, attempting to vomit up the effects of her intemperance. Her stomach was trying to heave up the load which it couldn't digest and didn't want. It would come halfway, and she, bent double, groaning, her forehead damp, felt the uneasy load stirring in her, coming up halfway and going down again. She forced herself. Her stomach contracted. She opened her mouth wide.

Up it came, lunch and all. She lay back exhausted against the ash-pit wall. She had gone into the yard for fresh air. Otto was sleeping. She had not disturbed him. She held onto the low wall, touching the surface with her outstretched fingers, its rough texture of plaster, cement and stone, cool smooth limestone. In a little while she was sleeping against the wall, her head resting on her arms. You will change. You will change. It was two o'clock in the morning. A mild summer's night.

* * *

189

Clement's gardener, the old gardener from Killadoon estate, stood at the bar in Breen's Hotel, digging with two fingers into his waistcoat pocket, searching for the price of a pint. He drew out a small electric bulb for a bicycle lamp and some coppers. His movements were slow and laboured. He wore a dusty black suit frayed at the edges of his sleeves. A small man with white hair, hobnailed boots, with spittle at the corners of his mouth. Two red-faced labourers pretending to mock him. One asked (pointing to the clock at the rear of the bar), What would her Ladyship say if she knew you were here at six? They laughed, exchanging nods. The old man said: –Six? ... Six? (staring at the clock). Aye. Many's the time I kep her in the gordon until tin at night.

Otto, a man among men, down for the evening paper, downed the rest of his pint.

– For the past week I've suffered because of you, she said. Do I no longer excite you?
    – Trying to butter me up, she said.
    ... Putting words into my mouth I never intended.
    – My aunt in Harrogate, she said.

Sad and heavy the atmosphere. In the airlessness, the heat, no sun. No energy. A new dress. Only nausea, apathy, disillusion.

– Oh, she said, oh please ... but couldn't go on.
    Mean words, delay again. Being mean to me. It's happened before and no doubt will again.

20 May. First corncrake.
    – I am expected to make you pretty speeches? he said.
    He would do all the harm he could, in the time at his disposal. Turning away with indifference, cold.
    Imogen refused to accept any pike, because she said they were dirty fish and she had never heard of anybody preparing them for the table.
    – They are a *dirty* fish.
    – I can assure you on the contrary no, Otto said, in Germany ... *Gespickter Hecht*.

190

– Ach, *Germany*.

Hawkins Street, near Burgh Quay, Dublin.

A meal of cheese soufflé followed by scallops cooked in red wine and Otto smoking a cigar.

St Michan's. The National Gallery in Merrion Square.

– Young Lamb, Otto said, taking his sister Mary to the asylum, hand in hand.

– Have I done something wrong? she said. Tell me what I've done wrong.

– It's only –

– Yes, only what?

– You are a true imbecile, Otto said flatly.

While it was still light . . . after rain in summer . . . ineffable stillness . . . presence, atmosphere . . .

– A woman must have an excuse for going out, she said . . .

Otto blew out his cheeks, saying even more flatly – Ba! Ba!

The fox covert. Acrid smell of the foxes, bitter, scattered bones, rabbit and hen bones, fowl. Plover passing overhead. Dempsey's land. Mournful cries.

By the Liffey in Killadoon in the summer. The walk through the wood. The overgrown path to the water. Silver birches. Their whispering. Nettles. Overgrown path. High grass by the wall. Broken wall. Behind the screen of leaves, laurel and rhododendron, screen of foliage, the murmur of the river. Ceaseless murmur of water. The banks. Fallen tree. Nettles in the field. High grass. River flags. Small trout and gudgeon in the shallows. White façade of a fine big house, its French windows opening on the lawns. Killadoon house.

– *Huchen*, Otto said. It's a certain type of salmon found only in the Danube.

Flat fields on the far side. The Dublin hills. Kingfishers, waterhens. Willows. Alders. Meadowsweets. The way to the water over the broken wall. Stones and gravel at first, then river sand. Yellow sand. A miniature estuary with a tree fallen across it, eaten away by ants, eroded, with a growth of weeds, nettles. The reflections on the surface. Imogen's own curious face. Coming back in the evening through the cool murmurous wood. This was the best time. The peace, she would remember it. The iodine and flags smell of the river on her hands after bathing.

Imogen (a confirmed non-swimmer) in her underclothes, watched her pale body under the brown water. Down in the partial darkness of the stream. Her submerged limbs were moving. She felt the current pushing against her.

– Don't look now.

She removed her underclothes, hung them on the bough, sank again to the full stretch of her arms until the river was up to her chin. Close to her ears she could hear its murmur. Running river, running river, carry me away with you. Sensation of drift, being of water. Quite soon she felt all over her minute sucking mouths, scores of minnows, a touch impersonal, insistent, soft, sucking. She looked down and saw them. Attracted by white flesh, darkly against her, tugging at her. Down below there her white limbs stretched. Touch. Down there being touched.

– Otto . . .

No response.

– Otto! I'm being eaten alive by these damn minnows! Otto sitting near the hamper, examining his fly-case, ground his teeth in fury, ignored her, puffing at his pipe.

Demolish a stray dog or a cat. Their toothless disagreeable little kissing mouths. Kissers. Down sink the white bones. Into smoke of settling mud. Carcass disappears.

– Oh, oh! she cried out, these minnows. Otto, help! I'm being *devoured*! (moving her legs energetically under the water).

They were after her. She felt them touching her all over. Insistent. Gets at your nerves. She wanted to scream. She brought up her legs clear of the water and set up a thunderous splashing.

– God damn you, Otto shouted in a fury. Quiet down there! Quiet! How do you expect me to catch fish?

Branches. Mossy branches. An alder tree. By the water. A screen of saplings. Imogen climbed out onto the branch and sat astride it. Wet moss. Damp seat. I am damp inside. Iodine smell. Murmur of river. A corncrake in the field over towards Temple Mills. Thistles. Killadoon House. Past all the trees. Fields on the other side. Earthen ramparts of the Pale. Not so. The land surrenders up few of its secrets. Echoes of the past. Line of Dublin hills low on the horizon. Why do I think of the Pale whenever I look over there? Why not? Seeing this was one of the principal counties in it.

Otto approaching.

– Did you catch anything?

– A small one, Otto said.

He looked over at her. Sandbank; inlet; saplings, a pool reflecting trees. A white naked woman with long dark tresses astride an alder branch. Sunken in. Water running through.

– Do you know who you looked like up there, fishing? she said.
– You looked just like old Major Storey.

Otto looked at her. Smiling at him.

– Your nipples have come out, he said.

– Oh, *Otto*!

(A stout jolly gentleman in braces, white shirt, no flannels but dark trousers and canvas shoes, with a flaming red face covered in perspiration, ran with contorted features below the high volleyed ball, his tennis racquet held purposefully. The ball fell down out of the blue sky and bounced out of court. The stout man tripped and fell heavily. The ground shook under the weight (270 lbs) of Billy Odlum.

He was there; he saw that. I was there then. And we now.)

A solitary apple tree bearing nine apples grew behind the cottage; a young well-pruned tree. Imogen wanted to make him an apple pie, since Otto was very partial to apple pie, but said she would wait a little longer until the apples were really ripe.

She was away for a week, taking her holiday at Mulranny with her sister Lily. Otto had wanted to go, Imogen providing the money of course, just the pair of them. Imogen said that was impossible. There would be talk. Had he any idea how small Ireland was?

When she came back she found the tree stripped. Not immediately; but after a while; when she came out and found it stripped she laid into him.

– You didn't take any, by any chance?

– Some.

– You might have said so. You might at least have asked me.

– I took one when I was cutting the hedge. When you were away there was nothing to eat. I was hungry, so I took some. I took three. There were eight on it.

– Nine. There were nine.

– One was bad.

Silence.

– Eight or nine, she said, what does it matter now? They're gone. You were underhand about it.

It sounded bitter in her mouth, more so than she had intended.

– Underhand my arse, Otto said, I was hungry.

– Don't be impertinent, she said sharply.

– Am I being impertinent? Otto said urbanely, I was not conscious of it, I assure you.

Silence.

– What happened to the other five, would you mind telling me? she said, they hardly walked off the tree.

Otto said nothing.

– Oh my God how improvident you are! she cried. Will you never learn? Haven't you got any money to feed yourself? Some of your own, even? We don't ask you to pay a penny in rent. Don't I give you enough? Are you never satisfied?

Debris after a summer storm attended by thunder and lightning. Wetted mill walls; the gutters pouring brown rain water. A dead cow near Brennan's shop. Rusty-coloured, a white chest, very common breed. At the protuberant eyes and about the thing half emerged from between its hind legs bluebottle flies were thickly clustered; from its hole a kind of treacle had flowed. The hind legs were thrust wide apart and stood out hard as boards; the bursting sac of skin there, tuberous and disgusting, had half emerged and stood out between the widely-forced apart hind legs. The carcass lay on its side in the water, its neck stretched out. A cow in calf struck by lightning.

One day when Otto was out ferreting, the ferret Nazi refused to come out of the burrow, doing great slaughter inside. Cursing and swearing, Otto was obliged to go home for a spade to dig him out.

He had arranged a net loosely set on some sticks at the mouth of the burrow, and the rabbits escaping the attentions of the ferret were driven into it, weak in the legs with fright. Otto came to one kicking and floundering in the net, very wild, not a sound, disentangled it, broke its neck and laid it down alongside a row of dead rabbits.

He dug a hole some distance on, then another; lying on the ground, he was attempting to find the course of the burrow. When his spade went down he found it. He thrust his arm in with a calm expression, groping about inside. One rabbit evaded his hand, only to be caught in the net. Otto went back and killed it. He pulled out another by its hind legs, killing it as before with a series of chopping blows with the side of his hand on the back of its neck.

After a while he pulled out the ferret, holding him up, reproaching him. A small white disagreeable ferret with blind red eyes.

Otto did some trade in rabbits with Young the butcher.

Placid appearance of the river. Indentations. Fish in it. Hiding themselves in the weeds. The brown river ferns sway out in the current, trout and grilse among them. Salmon. Perch. Cannibal pike. A steam over the surface of the river. Drifting by slowly alongside the far bank.

A thin cutting noise as he casts the lure. Casts again. Line on the water, sinking a little, bellies in the current, sinking down. Oiling keeps it afloat longer. Anything under ten inches thrown back. Trout-tickling at night. Bait. Young frog. Hook through it. Its eyes bulge. Casts it. Splash. The line goes down. Catches something. Hooked this time. Playing with it a little. Leaning back, pipe in his mouth, he pulled it in across the stream, into the shallows. A little brown trout flapping in the shallows, wriggling on the hook. Its labouring gills and suffering eyes. It had swallowed the hook. Otto took from his pocket an instrument for extracting hooks from fish and, forcing open the fish's mouth, retrieved the hook. He cleaned it on the sand, wrapping it in dock leaves he left it in the shade. For our supper.

Later. Another catch. Imogen went over to him. A knifeblade flashed. He had cut the fish open on the grass. Its stomach. Roes. Pathetic mouth. A little trout – female this time. Holding in his cupped hand the helpless larvae, half an inch long, twitching in the palm of his hand, he extended them to her.

– For their first weeks they live on the contents of the yolksac, Otto said.

A *mine* of information.

(His lips found mine, his hands my breasts. How he stared at me with famished eyes! He treats me as if I were meat. His seed burns me. Bonemarrow. The firm pressure of another's body in the cling of the embrace. Gentle and then not gentle any more.)

I'll give you something so you won't be sad, Imogen said.

29

He had been talking about his early student days in Freiburg,
going on about his old life there, the students he had known,
speculating on what had happened to them, his professors. Husserl
had been dismissed from the university to make way for the less
talented Heidegger.

– The Jews in Germany, Otto said, you know they've taken the
names of trees and mountains. They want to hide themselves, the
Rosenblums and Löwenthals. Germany is changing. I am well out
of it. If the National Socialists get into power God alone knows
what will happen.

He went on talking about his student days, much of it known to
her already, his holidays on the Bavarian lakes; and then, out of
the blue, it came out. He had a love affair when he was twenty-
two, already a veteran of the war; the girl was seventeen or so,
completely inexperienced. She had worked as a hairdresser's
assistant. A child had been born, a little boy. He had never seen
him, his son, he never heard what happened to the mother. The
child would be going to school now. Perhaps bearing his name.

She stared at him, hardly able to believe her ears, he had come
out with it in such an offhand way, so callous, as casual as killing
Frenchmen. But later she changed her opinion. The idea touched
her. Somewhere in the world a little Otto was walking about.

– It was the first Rover into Dublin, Imogen said. Father paid
£500 for it. The petrol was delivered to the village in those days in
two-gallon Shell tins. Father bought twenty tins at a time from
Rooney the garage-man. There was no petrol pump in Celbridge
then. The petrol came by lorry from Dublin. The Rover had a
Bosch magneto which was all the go then, and shock absorbers . . .
It had a twelve gallon tank and did I believe twenty-five miles to

the gallon. I remember well its rubber hand-manipulated horn – a mournful old foghorn right up against your ear. We went for holidays to the sea in it, to Bundoran and Greystones.

– I remember too the smell of heated leather when the hood was down.

Later, later. Increasing boredom. Lassitude.

Otto had been speaking about a park in Germany, he thought in Karlsruhe. The trees. The vista. Lombardy poplars. Nurses and perambulators. A line of high buildings overlooking a park. Perhaps it wasn't Karlsruhe at all?, perhaps it was Memmingen, or Pforzheim, or Donaueschingen, or even Titisee, not to mention Schaffhausen, any of those places, supposing they had parks, supposing even there was a park in Karlsruhe, about which he was not absolutely sure, though he had certainly passed through it on his bicycle, en route to the hut in the Dolomites.

Gundelfinger & Weinraub, The Ord Tie Factory, Kahn's Pianos, hot days and leaves falling about the park, the cries of children all day long. As he left, a one-armed veteran of the Great War, sitting near the gate with a suitcase of shoe-laces and razor blades before him, extended the stump of his amputated arm to the passers-by, saying nothing, perhaps struck dumb too. The stump of the arm was three or four inches long, a vein throbbing in the rounded member, which wasn't, strictly speaking, possible. So perhaps he had been maimed from birth?

Otto was for pampering himself, with a kettle on the hob all day for hot toddy and a hot water bottle in the bed (Imogen had gone back to her own), sweating it out of his system, croaking complaints from his bed, propped up on pillows. She had lit a fire in the room, in the small fireplace, a turf fire. His eyes and nose were streaming, the floor littered with used tissues. He was not prepared to move a hand or foot to help himself. A bad patient. Wishing he were dead.

– In the great days of the first century B.C., Otto said, when Sulla rebuilt Rome.

Sleeping away the afternoons, staring out the window, putting whisky into his coffee, perspiring under four or five heavy blankets and an overcoat of Imogen's, only brightening at the prospect of the evening paper. Imogen cycled down to the village for it as soon as she heard the Edenderry bus passing the gate. Otto, a most distinct articulator, catarrh or no catarrh, read out extracts from the *Evening Herald*.

The headless body of a man, believed to have been a passenger on the *Princess Victoria*, had been picked up in the Irish Sea, and brought into Workington, Cumberland, by the SS *Clonlee*.

A reader from Rathgar demanded that Lord Nelson be removed from his high pillar and that he be replaced by 'a revolving illuminated statue of Christ the King', and this would bring innumerable blessings on the Christian city of Dublin. No one could object to an annual subscription to this cause.

– The only capital city in Europe, Otto said, that would tolerate the statues of two recognized adulterers in its main thoroughfare. Two adulterers were too many for one street.

Seven hundred trees had been planted in the grounds of St Ita's College, Dingle, Co. Kerry, when the staff and pupils held their Arbor Day.

Then he was complaining that his teeth were paining him, so Imogen, his slave and doormat, obligingly cycled to the chemist for Albucid Soluble.

– Unscrewed the doorknobs and barred the windows, Otto said. Declared insane. (A scrap of paper thrown on the floor unclenched itself as though it were in pain.)

There was something which he was for trying, which she did not at first permit, nor at any later time relish; but he persisted in it, for he would have his way at all costs in everything, with a kind of voraciousness, of application; and she could not gainsay him, even though mortally ashamed herself at the disgusting repetition; but, dissent or assent, it was all the one to him.

– *Nicht zu geschwind*, Otto breathed into her ear ... *nicht zu geschwind* ...

Not so thick; not so fast.

– Drowned himself in the lake, Otto said, with his jailor-doctor.

– Averhahn, Otto said, ancient cock. The bird of all birds. Nothing sleek about the Averhahn. It's like a turkey, and can hardly fly. It has a short neck and small head and goes with a pumping flight. Before the Ice Age, in Austria.

A narrow bridle path meandering through the wood. The gate, the walnut trees, the vista to the river. Murmuring of the river, shining through the undergrowth in the autumn. Her footsteps in the leaves. Foot-slogging it. Otto a great walker. Walking her off her feet.

The walnuts falling from the tree in Killadoon. Its leaves late to come and last to go.

– Do you know that you grind your teeth at night? Otto said.

Otto had been indiscreet enough, or desperate enough, to buy a bottle of John Jameson Green Label whisky, charging it to the Langrishe account. When the bill was duly presented at Springfield, Helen opened it, offered no comment good or bad and handed it over to Imogen, who was completely nonplussed by this turn of events and could say nothing to save her face.

– God Almighty, she cried, have you no idea of anything. That you can use our name like that? What must they think?

– I don't care what they think, Otto said. They can think what they like as far as I'm concerned.

– *You* don't care, she said. Would you put yourself in my position just for once in a while. Think of *me* for a change.

The orchard. Gnarled black trees in need of pruning. Still branches bare of leaves. Nothing would ever change there. Tangled branches, grey-green lichen and moss, trembling in the bitter north-east winds of spring.

A big black logbook replete with notes. Every page crammed with writing. A bold angular hand of purposeful character, the determined upstrokes and downstrokes running above, below and through the blue guide-lines. Otto's overflow notebook, one of a triumvirate.

The thesis itself was bound in leather and titled in German: '*Das Ossianische Problem und die tatsächlichen Volksmythen und Gebräuche Irlands im Siebzehnten Jahrhundert unter besonderer Berücksichtigung des Werkes Goethes und der Gebrüder Grimm: Eine sozial-philologische-kritische Studie. (Herr Dr Otto Bernhardt Beck, phil. et res. pol. et habil. . . .*'

200

Her eyes read all this without comprehending a single word. Pol. et habil.?

– Gracious, she said, what does it all mean?

Otto translated it for her: *The Ossianic Problem and the Actual Folk Sagas and Customs in 17th Century Ireland, with special reference to the work of Goethe and the Brothers Grimm: A sociological-philological-critical study.*

– My word, she said, full of admiration, that's a mouthful. When will it be finished?

– I have been working on it, off and on, Otto said, for a number of years, ever since my days in the Dolomites in fact. I hope to bring it to a satisfactory conclusion in perhaps four years' time.

– Lord Edward Fitzgerald, Otto said, informed on by the traitor Francis Higgins, proprietor of the *Freeman's Journal* and translator of Mangan, that man of the night. Betrayed in Dublin and shot dead by Major Sirr.

The small painting of the assassination; in the Tate, was it?, he had seen it. The bloodless face. Murdered across his bed.

Imogen had a dream. It was a dream about a hare. Somebody had cut off its legs and head because it was too long for the pot. She asked them, Doesn't it feel pain? The person who had cut it up assured her, No, they feel no pain. He reshaped it completely out of the fur, and made for it a head and little flabby legs. It was a grotesque sight. Growing attached to her it followed her everywhere.

The shadows filing two by two along Killadoon wall. Miss Jameson, Miss Dexter, Miss Johnson. The mistresses pacing behind. Out from the Charter School. Young Protestant ladies, the daughters of parents of insufficient means. Lichen-covered wall. Twig-strewn places. Autumn again. Otto talking about the Hanseatic League . . .

– As true as God, Otto, she said, looking for compliments from you – it's like boring down in a mine.

Imogen came down to the cottage tipsy, and began wandering from room to room picking things up and putting them down again. Otto was in bed, reading. Imogen came and stood over him, smiling to herself, shaking her head. There's only one proper place. Rich smell of whisky from her breath. This comes not in the right place.

– You must read Wasianski's account of Kant's last days, his dotage and death . . .

A cold night in the depths of winter, all the passages sweating. Go and come back; go and come back. Otto's relish for culture.

Wasianski.

– All fairy tales end in violence, Otto said. The north with its long winters is the natural home of the legend and fairy tale. Grimm. The human mind brooding on its wrongs. The cruelty that's at the root of things. There's a baseness in nature, in people . . . The movement of reality towards the myth; the dreamer dreaming.

– When Madame de Pompadour knew she no longer pleased Louis the Fifteenth, she became his pander . . .

Imogen sat before the fire, combing her long black hair down over her eyes. She wore a towel about her neck. With languid strokes she drew the horn comb through her hair, then sat idle, gazing into the grate where wood and grey ash had fallen and was now smouldering away. The room was warm. Otto had stoked the kitchen-range with wood and coal, leaving to one side a barrel of fir cones collected in the wood. She had washed her hair in the big china basin, Otto pouring hot water from the ewer: now she was drying it before the fire.

Where did the palm trees come from in ancient Ireland? Well, who but he would come up with a thing like that? That day at Oakley Park fête when he was going on to Captain Maunsell about the hall-door knocker, damaged by an Insurgent sledge-hammer, according to him, in the Rebellion of 1798.

He sat at the table with his back to her. He had brought out the green baize cloth and set the paraffin lamp upon it by his right hand. Its green shade cast a strong downward light upon his papers, leaving the rest of the room in partial darkness. A pile of German reference books was before him. He was reading one of them, making notes in a thick folio notebook, dipping his penny pen into the inkwell. Otto reading, turning a page, writing again.

Gusts of wind blew against the windows and the fire sent out periodic showers of sparks, but still his pen scratched imperturbably on.

She sat staring into the fire, glancing every so often in his direction. He had a glass of whisky punch within reach and was puffing away at his cherry-wood, deep in thought. Otto reading, turning a page, grunting, going on.

Imogen began again combing her now dry and rippling hair with short firm strokes; the static electricity crackled; the fire was burning up the chimney; Otto's pen moved with unhurried precision along the top line of a fresh page.

– Otto.

He went on writing, puffing pipe smoke.

– Mr Beck.

He came to the end of a line, read what he had written, blotted it, and turned his chair to face her.

– Tell me, she said, don't you sometimes miss Germany?

– Why do you ask?

– Oh, no particular reason. I was just wondering.

He came to the mantelshelf and took from it the wooden piperack with his collection of pipes and various cleaning and polishing implements. She watched him take them down.

– Well, that's not exactly true, she said. I was looking at you just now and thinking that you could go on sitting there for the rest of your life.

– I see, Otto said in a sour way.

When he had collected all his gear together he drew up his work chair, spreading a newspaper on it and arranging his pipes and cleaners on that, reclining himself in the armchair alongside.

– I do not look back, he said, beginning to unscrew the stem of a pipe. *Heimweh* – that's not my way at all. What would be the use of it? For my part, I am contented, as things stand.

With a preoccupied air he began cleaning the nicotine stained inner tube with a piece of newspaper. The others awaited his attention. The Mattner of finest Corsican briar; the cherry-wood; the Bruyere – a French pipe that looked very purposeful in his mouth; the Tanshell from Sardinia; a long-stemmed (malacca?) one with a blackened bowl; his beloved Meerschaum with its pure amber stem and bowl of handcarved soapstone; and a curly German pipe with a vulcanite stem and a wide bowl of knotted ash offset with a bronze finish. He had several other inferior pipes, some of which he smoked now and again, but he rarely cleaned them, whereas the main collection was cleaned and polished with scrupulous regularity. He had beside him an unbroken pack of cleaners, a bottle of methylated spirit, a thin bladed penknife, an adjustable carbon cutter, a Remer cleaner, a chenille wiper, a pipe gadget, and something in a pouch of soft red leather. He moistened a fresh pad of paper with methylated spirit and used it on the stem of the Mattner. She watched him, slowly combing her lustrous dark hair.

– All the same, she persisted, you must, sometimes. You are not a *machine*, are you?

Otto looked up briefly from his work, not deigning to answer, then down again.

– Even I miss France at times, and I wasn't there all that long. I might have gone to Paris. Had I lived there I believe I would have liked it. But I would have been homesick all the same.

He was cleaning the bowl with the adjustable cutter, moving it carefully about, frowning at the grating noise it made.

– Look at my position, he said, tapping out the carbon deposit onto his palm. Here am I (examining the deposit suspiciously), a *battler*, a poor scholar, with free lodging, free fuel, peace and quiet, all my corporal needs attended to (giving her a sly look), so that I can get on with my work. Isn't that so? Why then go back to Germany?

He threw the deposit into the grate, bent forward and picked up the Bruyere, gazing fondly at it. Now the methylated spirit. The ritual never varied.

– Besides, he said, I am not young.

– Oh pouff.

– No, please understand that, Otto said, I am getting on in years. I am thirty-five.

With the tips of her fingers she touched the slack folds of skin about her neck, no longer young, felt the weakly throbbing but persistent Langrishe blood. She was four years his senior, although he didn't know it, for she did not feel obliged to confess her age.

– But if you had the *means* – would you not go back? she said. After all, you are rather cut away from everything here. You have no friends. You see nobody but me, and I am poor enough company.

– Ah, he said, pushing a cleaner carefully through the bowl of his Meerschaum. Hypothetically speaking, if I had *means* – that would be different. I suppose I'd go back to Freiburg University and study under Husserl again. I was a good student. I *am* a good student. Oh nothing would stop me if I had the means. It would give me great satisfaction to attend university lectures again. Higher education in Germany is beyond criticism. Excellent, really excellent.

Now he had begun on the vulcanite mouthpiece of the German pipe. He put it down in order to go to the table and swallow in one draught the remains of the punch. Then he sat down again and began to fill the Tanshell with a plug mixture.

– Better still, he said with a gleam in his eye, to study under Heidegger at Marburg – that would be wonderful. Philosophy. Comparative psychology. Phenomenological investigations. Yes, it would indeed be wonderful.

Greatly excited he put his pipe in his mouth, took a paper spill and lit it with a flourish. He let fall the charred end and stamped on it.

– You are quite right of course, he said (sending up clouds of smoke), I am cut off here. I have no outside contacts of stimulation, none whatsoever. No music. No . . . *Künstlerkolonie*. One feels its absence. In Germany there is the Bauhaus at Dessau; but here – nothing. Even the mattresses are of inferior quality, hard and uncomfortable. In Germany one is at least provided with a decent mattress, with a *Keilkissen* in fact. I miss that if you like.

He lay back at his ease, eyes half-closed, his legs stretched out to the fire, staring at the three pictures over the mantlepiece. *'Jealousy'* and *'Nude with Red Hair'* by Munch, and a primitive original of an unnamed volcano belching fire and smoke, by an unknown hand.

Imogen drew her hair down over one shoulder, and began brushing it slowly, staring at Otto.

– Well, she said at last, apart from the mattresses, what do you miss?

– *Die Schnall'n*, Otto said promptly, and at once regretted it.

– What? she said, perceiving his embarrassment. What?

But he only shook his head, waving his pipe before his face.

– But I am curious, she said.

He mumbled something indistinct.

– I can't hear what you're saying, she said.

– I don't intend you to, he said.

But she was obstinate. She persisted. She would get to the root of it. She wanted to know what did he mean. What did that word mean? Was it something improper? She persisted in asking him the same question over and over again. Exasperated, at last he gave in, saying in a belligerent way:

– Tarts.

– Tarts?

Otto uttered a mighty oath in German.

Imogen began to blush.

– I may not be very astute, she said, but I do think you are being exceedingly rude.

Otto uttered a string of mighty oaths, at the end of which he informed her that *Die Schnall'n* were Munich whores.

– Oh, she said, greatly taken aback, I am obtuse.

Leaning forward Otto removed the middle ring from the kitchen-range with a wristy turn of the poker and fed in a handful of fir cones. The fire, which had burned down, blazed up again. With a generous hand he threw in more fir cones and then a shovelful of coal; after which he replaced the ring noisily, looking quickly at her. She would not look at him.

– You went with street women, she said, and now you make love to me.

He thrust out his chin, expelling smoke from between his teeth. Nothing more remained to be said. But after a short silence she spoke again:

– What age were you when you first went with a – a *loose* woman?

– Believe me, this is a futile line of enquiry.

– But what age were you, all the same?

– Oh, young, Otto said, young (bland, brazening it out). That was more than half a lifetime away. In Munich, during the school holidays.

– Spare me the details.

Otto was silent. But she could not or would not leave well alone.

– Tell me, she said, do you wear one of those things?

Otto stared down at his chest. Medals for valour?

– What things? he said, knowing well enough, but wanted her to say it.

– Oh, you know, she said, loath to be explicit – a device.

– A device? he said. Certainly not. I never have. Somehow – he stopped. (She was always washing herself; it was deceptive.) I somehow assumed that you did, he said, lamely enough.

– Indeed! she said, scandalized.

– I see, he said, I see. That may make things awkward. He went on puffing at his pipe for a time, thinking it over. Then he said:

– Have you missed any periods since, if you don't mind me asking?

– No, I don't mind, she said, embarrassed all the same, her eyes huge. But I don't know either. I miss them anyway, being anaemic. I am not regular.

– H'mm, Otto said.

He had made no attempt to order his embraces so that she would not conceive; that was not his way. He told her now that she must take as many hot baths as she could and dose herself with quinine.

– I will be most annoyed if you find yourself pregnant, he said.

After that she did not bath for a fortnight; and as for quinine, there was none in the house.

One summer day, when she was a young woman, she had watched the sunset beyond the Back Road, the last flares. She was unprepared for this particular sunset: for as she stared at the calmly sinking disc of the sun going down somewhere behind the Hill of Ardrass, it seemed to explode in flames and smoke. She waited for a second explosion, but nothing happened. She had the feeling that something had been violently disrupted; something dreaming had been pulverized.

Blue smoke was rising languidly from the ditch and through the smoke of the tree-butt flung high into the still air by the force of dynamite, its exploded parts were drifting back to earth. Panes of glass were floating through the air, and their razor-sharp edges threatened her.

30

'Dear Otto (Imogen's wobbly and unpractised hand). It is time we made the brake. I have had a promise extracted from me by my Confessor to see you no more. You see, my dearest, I have had to choose between you and conscience and how hard it is to do that. You have meant everything to me except my peace of mind . . .'

This estrangement lasted perhaps a fortnight. At the end of that time he met her in the village and shamed her out of it. She wore a pale tweed suit with a hound's tooth design.

– Have you come from confession? What has he advised you to do now?

– I'm not going to listen to you if you talk like that, she said.

Raising his voice Otto demanded an explanation.

– Does he know me, that he can forbid you to see me? Is it because I am depraving you, is that what he thinks?

– Hush, she said, don't talk that way, not here (here was outside King's shop in the middle of the village; some of the people inside might be listening, were certainly eavesdropping).

Lowering his voice he said . . .

– Did you mean it? Did you really mean that you didn't want to see me again?

– *Ye-ss*, she said, drawling the word.

– You do? Otto said. You mean it?

– No.

Silence.

– There's nothing to drink in the house, Otto said. Can we afford something?

– Wait on the bridge, I'll follow you. I have some things to get.

He waited on the bridge. Below among the reeds a blue crane

stood rooted to the spot, staring into the water. As she came onto the bridge with an expectant look, it flew away.

She propped her bicycle against the kerb and came and stood beside him, touching his arm. A pale face, dark hair.

– Look, a blue crane, he said.

– You look.

On the parapet by his hand, a tightly rolled-up one pound note.

– Get something in Breen's. Say a bottle of JJ.

On the way home she said there was a film she wanted to see in Dublin. A film with Ronald Colman. Would they go?

– Irish piety, Otto said (seldom content to leave well alone), functional as a Boland's loaf.

Shortly after this *contretemps* Otto said he was tired of asking her for money (a lie), and would find work. He would go back if necessary to Enniskerry and work for three months for the Forestry Department.

Demur, demur.

The black and yellow signpost in the village on a windy day, its arms pointing in three different directions, one arm askew. Single decker buses going the roads of Kildare, bound for Edenderry and Birr.

The poor woman Ellen Nolan from Back Weston going begging on the roads with her child.

The scattered baying of the pack.

Dull overcast day. Confined to the house. Beating all the carpets, sweeping all the floors, washing all the dishes, coming down to the cottage in the evening when the rain had stopped with some honeysuckle and two roses from Springfield garden. The vase on the window. The room thick with tobacco smoke. Otto had been working all day, rapping away on his Baby Hermes, bought in Switzerland just after the war for less than £10. Puffing out great clouds of tobacco smoke, full of confidence, an end in sight.

– Why is the Christ child in sixteenth century Flemish and Netherlandish paintings represented as a grotesque? Is it because he is outside the general scheme of things, a sacrifice set apart?

Moths, thick and sticky as fat chestnut buds, fallen dazed from the light that streamed from the cottage window, crawled about on the path, in the dust, and even over the road, dazed. Otto went about stamping on them and cursing in terrible German. Imogen, who had been having a series of illnesses (the sore on her lip wouldn't clear up) watched him. They went in together.

– My next pill at 6 o'clock, remind me, dear.

– Husserl was Martin Heidegger's teacher, Otto said. His philosophy had a determinate influence on Heidegger, who succeeded him at Freiburg University in '28.

Rain falling all day like a hard penance. The windswept hedge; tearing screech of the swifts. Cold early summer evening. Ciphers.

– The Jews in Germany got their names in the 18th and 19th century. The wealthy ones assumed names like Rosenthal, Rosenblum, Mandelzweig, and so on. The poor ones who couldn't pay so much had to be content with essentially Jewish names – Cohn, Levy, Baruch.

Otto fired. The pigeon fell into the field, pumping up clouds of feathers.

– Irishwomen, said Otto with fervour, they are so pure and clean.

– So cold?

– So pure, Otto said, and that's not to be found any more in Germany – that great purity. But here you have it. And also that look in the face, the eyes, and one knows that such women are not corrupted. One knows it (thumping himself on the breast) *here*.

– Ireland is rearing them still, Imogen said, widening her eyes at him.

– A man might sometimes have filthy thoughts about girls. That's natural enough. But when I meet Irish girls and can recognize at once their essential purity, then I am touched, incapable of a base thought.

Imogen said nothing, thinking her own thoughts. You are a rare liar and no mistake, you who not so long ago were observing me through the window with Satan's face, attempting to lure me in. You and your purity. I know your sort. I know you too well, Otto Beck.

– I have a reverence, he said, a great reverence for Irish women.

– What kind of lies are you filling me up with, she said. I should like to know. What kind of lies?

– No lies, Otto declared, thumping his chest as a manifestation of a frank open nature. – No lies.

– Otto, she said. Were you never tempted?

– Was I ever tempted, he said. Tempted to do what?

– To be unfaithful to me, she said.

– Who with? . . . I mean, with whom?

– With the local trulls. Isn't there anyone to fill my place when you're tired of me?

Otto made a face.

– Snotty-nosed short-arsed bitches all of them, he said, you might credit me with a little more taste.

– Not one of them, younger, prettier, lustier than I, ready and willing to take my place in your affections? A pretty one whom you could entice into your bed?

– No, there isn't.

– Liar!

– Why liar?

– I have two eyes in my head, liar. So you go carefully, you and Molly Cushen. I'm not going to tolerate that. I'm not all that magnanimous. What I don't see I don't mind so much, up to a point, but you tread carefully.

– I was thinking about you . . .

– Yes? Thinking what?

– I pictured you off in the Enniskerry woods cutting down trees since eight o'clock this morning. And here you are . . .

– Yes, as you say, here I am.

– Will you ever go, do you think?

– If I can find lodgings. I gave the woman my address. I'll have to go to the Civic Guards first. I must have a work permit.

– Will you be here tomorrow?

– I don't know. It all depends.

– Depends, Imogen said, depends on what for Christ's sake? If you want to go, you go, that's all there's to it.

– No, not quite. I have to find lodging first. And I must have written permission from the Guards . . .

– Written permission, she said in a faint voice, from the *Guards* –

– That nonentity, she said bitterly. That whore.
– You can't call anybody a nonentity.
– Anybody I don't know is a nonentity.
Sitting up in bed, her voice getting shriller and shriller, quarrelling about nothing.
– I hope that nymphomaniac leaves you. That would be good enough for you. That dirty bitch.

They were sitting on the river bank in the evening sun. Her head bent, Imogen plucking at something in the grass. Absent stare. Sulky mouth. Otto glanced at her. She did not look at him.
– What are you thinking? he said.
Silence.
– Well?
She opened her hand, extending to him a shrivelled seed pod.
– I'm thinking of what a boring summer I'm having . . . This is you (extending the withered seed pod) . . . going to seed.
Fields by the river in summer. The trunks of the trees, their heavy foliage, not a stir. The ardent green of the fields and then the milky white and pink of hawthorn; and somewhere there the sunken river Liffey flows, through Kildare's grass green meadows.

Auseinandersetzung.
– Noonan? – Sheehan? . . . a name like that.
– Shannon! Otto shouted. SHANNON!
– Shannon, she said, yes that was the name. Why couldn't I think of it?
A dull day. Damp grass. The river pouring by.
– You're so soft, Otto said, staring before him with a vindictive face. Some soft spineless insect that's been trodden on. I can feel you beginning to curl up at the sides.
Silence. *So schaut's aus . . .* (sighing).
Imogen said in a flat toneless voice:
– We're no good for each other.

Otto took this thrust in silence.

Imogen in Broe's shop overheard an elderly couple gossiping outside. She pricked up her ears. Some scandal. *I shush shush shushsush . . . An' she sez sisch sish sishsish . . . An' says I sosh sosh soshsoshsosh . . . and Oh sez she . . .*

Giving details of her order she moved to a point nearer the door. Provisions for Otto and herself.

– It's a fact, people can never get enough of what's bad for them . . .

A mumbled indistinct reply from the old man. They were both old. The old woman said:

– Kill or cure, Andy . . . this time it's kill or cure.

Is it me? Is it me?

Imogen told him that her Uncle Hercules had given her father a Colt six-shooter with the image of a horse rearing on the butt, and a whip in its mouth. It was a gift. But, even though he had no bullets for it, he had to get rid of it during the Troubles, fearing to be caught with arms in the house.

31

An uncanny dusk. End of an uncanny day. September 6. No
pleasure to swim in the river now. Summer finished. Reading
Peacock's *Gryll Grange*. Dull matter. Dull days. Smell of decaying
foliage. Voices. Dark before nine-thirty. The bed empty when I
reach home. Where is he? The house empty. Helen shut away in
her room. The lodge empty. What is he doing? Saucepan lids on
the kitchen floor. The peas burnt on the ring. The fire gone out.
Heels of loaves on the floor. The hens dirty everywhere.

Long sleeps to escape it all. Fall into bed at nine in the evening
when it's still light, sleeping as though struck dead until noon next
day.

Listless day follows listless day. Heavy atmosphere. Little or no
energy.

Smell of autumn everywhere. Chill in the air. A mist and a red
sky in the evening. A look of winter already.

End of September, and endless winter begins. How I hate it.
The couple laughing in the wood under the drenched trees. Cycle
to Bodenstown. How nothing is ever left, abandoned, but moves
on. Weight of misery. Great desire to be rid of it all. My pain.
Flying moths at night. The half-grown kittens in the kitchen.
Their soundless movements. Clusters of leaves blown by the
breeze. Otto cold, disdainful, pitiless.

The hotpress room, a brass boiler, shelves reaching to the ceiling;
its area and height; a dry warm place. The odour of clean linen,
ironed clothes.

Endless bickering (Imogen thought): I can't help it, can't stop
myself. My vexation with him is reaching its limits, Recriminations
and accusations, reproaches, anything I can throw at him. I can't

stop myself. Sitting up in bed, my voice getting shriller and shriller, arguing about nothing. Heaped-up reproaches – it's great foolishness. Not that it's all one-sided. No. – I won't forget certain unkind inferences. The never-ending drone of his lectures, his bad temper, vindictive nature.

Yes, it's true he is by nature vindictive. He won't forget things, holds them against you. And then, hardest to bear, his indolence. The days when he works, what are they to the days he doesn't do a stroke? He goes out on his bicycle allegedly collecting material but what sort of work is that? His fondness for explaining the unknown by the still less known, *ignotum per ignotius,* he says, a cloud of words, what's that but a cloud of words, self-indulgence and nothing more? It's a pleasure for him to cycle and to talk. And all the time his nose stuck in a book, that's a pleasure for him too. I'm sick and tired of all this. I have very little money, a fact that he doesn't seem to be able to appreciate, and will not lift a hand himself to earn any. I'm tired; I'm forty . . . getting on. And where's this getting me? Nowhere.

Above all to be warm. She resented his too forceful approaches, casting aside sheets and blankets, freezing her. She developed a series of colds, had begun to turn away from him, refuse herself. Is that me? In winter, love cooling.

– I want my sleep, Otto . . . just let me sleep.

Just to sleep. Just to be warm.

Imogen lay listlessly on the day-bed, staring at the ceiling, listening to the noises in the wood. Otto was away somewhere killing rabbits.

He had had a dream. The wind had been blowing all night, making a great commotion in the trees. In the morning he said I had a dream . . . a dream about myself as a child. Gouging my father's eyes out. Am I the child on his back, reaching into his face? My fingers find his eye-sockets. Are they just holes in a wall of flesh and bone? Is he my father? Am I his son? That was a strange dream to have.

She fell asleep; and only woke up when the gate slammed to; Otto was back, from wherever he had been.

* * *

He established his intellectual superiority. Namely that she accept the role that had been given her: that of being unable to contribute anything. He indicated pretty plainly enough that her accomplishments were inadequate. He put questions to her that he knew she could not answer. Then his intolerable sharp pedagoguing. What? *What?*, as though she were a hopelessly backward student. In that reasoning she began to feel no better than a whore; all she was good for was to be made love to. So her hold on the relationship was very frail, and becoming frailer. The compensations of physical pleasures were not enough; far from enough. It was all over.

Ending, ending.

– That monotonous condition of the soul, Otto said, halfway between fulfilment and futility, which comes with living in the country.

Futility, futility.

– Among bats, Otto said, which have connection in the autumn, the sperms can remain dormant in the uterus throughout the whole of winter and impregnate the ova in the spring.

Ended.

Two springs, two summers, three autumns and two winters. That was all; and now all over.

32

Can I help it if I'm feeling sick? . . .

He was most unreasonable, so selfish himself and such a bad patient, yet had no time for others when they in turn fell ill. No, because there was no leavening of charity in him. None at all. Or very little anyway.

– Well, now can I?

She was lying on the couch in the parlour with not a vestige of colour on her cheeks. She had begun to show her age – a certain broadening of shape, a heaviness of limb, loose folds of skin under her eyes and at her neck. And if her mouth still retained its cupid form, as indeed it did, the effect was marred by the suggestion of a moustache above.

What could have upset her stomach? Something had disagreed with her. A surfeit of fruit? But whatever she had eaten he had eaten, and yet he was well. Could it have been the stewed apples of the night before? Had they been perhaps a little sour?

On recent occasions she had complained of feeling tired, being run down. Well, that was one thing. But now she was feeling definitely ill. She did not feel well at all. He offered little enough consolation, just stood there with his hands in his pockets alternately staring out the window and eyeing the clock. It was mid-morning, a bright day in early October, and he resented being indoors. He had an assignation. He was wearing his *lederhosen*, green stockings with black tops, a white open-neck shirt, had shaved with particular care and cut his own hair as best he could.

– Such a lovely day, she said in a doleful voice.

He said nothing. She heaved a heavy sigh, staring out the window, looked quickly over at him and then down at her feet. He moved away and began to fill a pipe with two Wild Woodbines which he took from an empty tea canister and broke open standing by the mantelpiece, giving the matter his full attention, with his back to her.

– Could you at least look at me? she said, her voice rising.

He turned to face her, excessively composed, drawing down his brows and moving the lighted match over the tobacco, avoiding her eyes.

Would he do something for her? Would he fetch her a bottle of cordial from the village? It would relieve her. A bottle of Solo. Would he do that for her, if it wasn't asking too much. She had ptomaine poisoning.

Otto threw the spent match away, puffing out great clouds of smoke.

– All right, he said.

He entered Dunne's shop. Some villagers were there buying groceries and the Sunday newspapers. Mr Dunne himself was serving behind the bread counter – distributing loaves of day-old Boland's bread and an occasional double or triple layered slab-cake. The served customers shuffled out, saluting Otto by inclining their heads at an angle as if they had cricks in their necks, then jerking them up to the vertical again – a familiar rural form of mindless salutation for one's co-equals, but never for one's superiors. One yokel remained leaning over the counter. Mr Dunne, a small rotund man with a sandy moustache, glanced towards Otto.

– Now you mane to tell me, (feeling his chest with plump unringed fingers, a man of substance), – mane to tell us that you've never heard of the cela-brated outlaw Robin Hood?

The villager turned the upper part of his body slowly about and gaped over his shoulder with a very inflamed eye at Otto.

– Solo Orange, Otto said, pointing abruptly at the shelf.

Mr Dunne's daughter served him, wrapping the bottle in a slovenly way in newspaper. Otto paid and left the shop, groaning to himself. He clipped his parcel onto the heavily-sprung rear carrier, tied it secure, mounted his Raleigh (Imogen's present) and cycled home.

He put away his bicycle in the outhouse which stank of hens. As he came out of the shed with the bottle in his hand he heard her calling from the garden:

– Otto . . . I'm here.

He went into the kitchen, unwrapping the bottle, poured out a liberal dose into a tumbler, added some cold water from the kettle, took down a packet of cigarettes from the shelf and carried them out to her.

The invalid was recuperating in the sun, sitting in a deckchair reading the newspaper which had been delivered in his absence. Otto handed her the drink and cigarettes.

– You are so good to me, she said, looking down under her eyelashes.

He watched her swallowing. She made a noise. Her manner of eating oranges had always irritated him, for she made a sucking noise getting the juice and swallowing the shreds, which she gulped down. More recently her manner of dealing with spaghetti had begun to irritate him. Now her manner of swallowing Solo Orange irritated him. She had applied too much powder; her colouring was not good – saffron. She set down the tumbler half-empty on the grass.

– Ah, she said, I feel better already . . .

She offered him some pages of the newspaper. He sat on a rock some distance away. She took up the paper again.

She had mean ways. For instance, that ridiculous quarrel they had had in the National Gallery. A lover's tiff. What stupidity. The paper bag and the cakes. An equally divided assortment on a formal bench beside the Correggio. Crumbs on the polished floor. She was dressed in brown. Without thinking he had consumed two of the same kind, staring at the painting. What tantrums she had flown into! She had lost her temper completely and called him 'an ignorant buff' and accused him of never thinking of her, and had got up and left, her ears red, going slowly down the winding stairs. A flushed middle-aged woman with bowed shoulders, behaving ridiculously like a young girl. An estrangement in the depths of winter, in Dublin, long ago.

A strange woman had come up to him and asked:

– And what do you think of our Uccello? The *Madonna and Child*.

Another time, when they were to go to Dalkey Island, she had insisted on first visiting her hair-dresser. She had passed up the stairs of a place in Anne Street to have it set, calling back to him that he could do what he liked but that she was determined to have her hair cut, because she 'looked a fright'. The spectacle of her legs and tight corseted rump ascending with unbecoming haste had not pleased him. He walked about in St Stephen's Green for an hour by the pond, the breeze whipping up little waves and all the foliage straining one way so that the pale underparts of the leaves were exposed, the sky changing, autumn beginning. A couple with their heads together sat in the pavilion by the water, holding each other's hands. After a time they parted, the young man leaving the Green in the direction of Kildare Street. The young woman walked by alone.

He had gone back to find her waiting, her hair crimped and stiff, cut and set in a way he detested. And they had not gone to Dalkey Island.

Turning a page now, she looked across at him.

– What have you done to your hair? she said, as if she could read his thoughts.

– I cut it myself, to save a bit.

– You do look a proper guy, she said, and buried her nose in the paper again.

He had cut it, using her handmirror and scissors, shaved, wore his best shoes and a clean shirt, to please Molly Cushen.

– I'll leave you for the day, he said. You need the rest. I have an appointment with some people.

She finished the drink and began studying the empty glass in her hand.

– Try and get some sleep, he said. You'll feel better for it after.

She stood up. Staring into the trees, she said:

– Let me say this. If you leave me now, you needn't come back.

As he found he had nothing to say to that, she took up the glass and the scattered pages of the newspaper and retreated slowly indoors.

Sitting bowed in the parlour chair with a pair of nail scissors in her hand, she did not offer to look up when he entered, but asked straight off:

– What will you have for lunch? There's chicken broth if you like that (he was particularly fond of it) ... that is, if you still intend staying.

– I told you, he said, I have an appointment.

She was silent, not looking at him. At last she said again:

– If you go off now, you needn't come back. You have made use of me. How selfish you are, only thinking of your own pleasure and never once considering my feelings! After all, you could have gone to your friends during the week. Oh no, that wouldn't do. And now, just because I'm sick a day you want to leave me. That's not fair, Otto.

– You reproach me with having made use of you, he said, but haven't you made use of me often enough?

Restless and perturbed she left her chair and moved to the window, staring out.

– Be that as it may. I'll tell you now, that if you go, if you leave me now, you needn't come back, and I mean that.

Still looking out the window she began to tap the glass with the handle of the scissors. He saw the weak reflection of her face there.

– You can get your meals elsewhere, she said without turning.

Snick-snick, went the scissors. *Snick-snick*. A mean sound.

– You need never come back, she said, flat and final.

How tired I am of these antics. I'm tired of him. Every bed I wake up in is the wrong one. When I wake up in his bed I'm thinking it's my own old bed. When I wake up in mine sometimes I'm hoping it's his, but sometimes not. When I wake up on the settee it's the wrong one still. I must be getting old.

– I have an appointment, he said, as I believe I have already told you. With some friends.

– You are not a good liar, I am afraid, she said in a pitying tone.

This remark he let pass in silence.

– Nor am I an entire fool, she said, please believe that. You have no friends here that I know of. None at all, except perhaps that Derek Barton, and he's in London, as you know and as I know. I don't believe your appointment. You're going to see that one. That common little thing you're after.

Silence.

222

– I have an appointment, with friends, some fishing friends.

A more prolonged silence.

– If you go now, she said, speaking slowly without turning, you need not come back. I have no friends myself, and all because of you and your selfishness. I gave you everything, all my time, everything. You didn't want me to see people or go out anywhere, so I saw nobody and never went out, and consequently I lost any of the friends I had. When you could be, you were rude to them. If I went now, if I even – if I were to –

She began to weep hopelessly into her handkerchief.

– Oh this is hopeless, he said, and left the room.

He entered the bedroom. The bed they had lain in, slept in, had not made love in, was as they had left it. He threw the clothes up in a rough way and tucked the sheets in, punching the pillows. He stooped under the bed and pulled out his haversack and packed it, rolling up two spare shirts and putting them into it with his tennis shoes, his Honer harmonica and shaving gear, then he took his manuscript out of its folder, rolled it into a compact scroll, took out one of the shirts and fastened it about the scroll, knotting the sleeves together, and thrust this in with the rest. He went back into the parlour holding the haversack behind his back. She wasn't there. He entered the kitchen. She was there, had powdered her face, was dusting the top of the kitchen range.

– Will you not go to bed? he said.

She looked at him, relenting a little.

– Ah no. I'd be better doing things.

He watched her. When she moved away he threw the haversack behind a chair. She turned to face him.

– Unless you tidy up at once, she said, everything gets out of control in a small house like this.

She had gone to auctions here and there, bidding for pieces of furniture, two comfortable armchairs, a table for him to work at, necessities for his comfort. She liked to have things in order about her.

– Would you brush the floor for me? she said. I don't ask you to do much about the house.

He brushed the parlour and then the kitchen floor, swept the henshit into the yard, then came back and put the brush away. She watched him out of the corner of her eye. She had begun to tidy things away, folding the *Sunday Times* together with its pages in order, punching the cushions.

– Would you ever set the fire now? . . . so that it will be ready.

He left the room without answering, pulling his haversack after him and throwing it into the yard. The airless room; to be shut away with an invalid; no; he closed the door behind him and sat on the back step staring at the backs of his hands.

After a while he rose and stood in the yard. The sun was over the chimney-pot from which smoke was now ascending in a weary spiral into the still air. She had lit the fire. It was time to go. He looked and saw behind the net curtain her shadowy form, her white arm uplifted, and heard her fingernails tapping on the glass.

– Are you not gone yet? her voice said, muffled.

He did not answer.

– *Otto!*

– No, he said, watching her.

He had set the fire. It was burning now. She had her paper. He had collected his bag. She hadn't noticed. The position of the sun behind the chimney told him it was time to go. It was Sunday, October 4th. He had shaved himself with particular care for Molly Cushen, wore his best for her, was glad that the sun shone that day, because of her.

The door opened and she stood there, staring at him.

– Can't you make up your mind? she said, – as usual.

– No, he said, watching her.

– Will I make it up for you? she said, bitter as vinegar.

They stood staring at each other for a moment or two in silence.

– All right, he said.

She continued to stare at him, then turned on her heel and went back into the kitchen. He thought that now perhaps she would do something violent. He heard her drag something from the table and run to the door with it and took a step forward but he was already too late; she was there in the doorway and the contents of a basin of dishwater came at him in a spreading sheet and struck the ground at his feet, drenching his shoes and stockings to the knee. Then something, passing over his head as he bent to inspect the damage, hit the wall behind him and fell with a great clattering to the ground. She had thrown the basin as well, for good measure.

– Ah here, he said, take it easy will you?

– Take it easy, she wailed, I'm taking it easy. I'll . . . I'll . . . and was speechless, panting with rage.

– All right, Otto said.

She glared at him. From the step she watched him brushing himself, bending, brushing with solicitude. The good stockings were ruined, the carefully polished shoes soaked.

Am I ending it? Can I be ending it? (She had seen it, the bag obscenely crumpled in the yard.) *All this is unreal. It's not real.* (He was brushing himself with his hand, looking rather pathetic.) *We are like figures come loose out of a frieze. This will end. We'll pick up the threads again, tomorrow. Yes, tomorrow.*

He looked up then and cursed her, employing a very offensive term of abuse, first in German and then, to make it quite plain, in English.

– Charming, I must say, she said with a pinched look. Charming.

– Let me say this before I go, Otto said. I have always thought your notion of life in general, and your own life here in particular, what you consider proper, is so dreary that it's hardly worth the effort to live it. What have you to say?

– You wouldn't like it, she said.

– So say it now, he said, and get it over. This farce has gone on long enough.

– Very well then, she said, curt as though addressing a servant. Get going . . . and don't come sneaking back like last time. Because you're not needed here.

It's real. I'm ending it. It's ending now. In a minute or two, there it is: the mistake of a lifetime.

– All right, he said. Now I know. I leave now.

He picked up his haversack and entered the outhouse. Inside, he hung the bag over his shoulder and bending, proceeded to put on his cycling clips. Then he began to push open the door with the front wheel of his Raleigh.

The next moment she was there, pushing the door from the outside with all her strength. From his side he pushed, and from her side she pushed, and to such effect that the door was closing on him; it was closing, so she wanted him to stay. He exerted all his strength, holding both handles, using his shoulders, and forced the door open again with the wheel; it was opening, so he wanted to go. She let him force her out of the way and the door swung wide; she turned then and ran into the house.

As he mounted, taking his time, he heard her hurry through the parlour and into the bedroom. Now she knows, he told himself, complacent, now I am going, and for good. He mounted and began to cycle at a leisurely pace out of the yard, whistling by the whitewashed side wall, *'Muss i' denn, muss i' denn zum Städele hinaus . . .'*, past the clematis, and so to the gate, which stood half open. As he passed through he caught the spear at the top and swung it back violently and it slammed shut.

Now, he thought, now she will know what it feels like for a woman to be left. (*Did she tap on the window, even discreetly? Did she watch me go? If she tapped on the window, even discreetly, she did not want me to go. If she watched me go she knew I would not come back.*)

Pedalling slowly on the Dublin road with not a care in the world (he could send later for his Baby Hermes and the rest), Otto was whistling. He glanced casually at the gap in the hedge and saw something that froze his blood. The black maw of the open window, glinting sun on the glass above, and something else besides. The muzzle of a shotgun was trained directly at him from below the innocent fringe of the sash. Groaning he saw it, too late already, and bore down with all his might on the pedals.

Distraught, Imogen ran through the rooms, consumed by a desire to rend and destroy, to inflict pain, to tear or smash something and as violently as possible, but never for one moment intending to take the gun. That was not in her head at all – to take it, or load it, much less aim and discharge it. She went frantically into the bedroom, saw how contemptuously he had thrown together the bed; and there it was, like fate, propped up in the corner, with the game-pouch bulging with red cartridges: Father's double-barrel shotgun. It was in the corner with the game-bag; she had only to reach out and take it. So she took it, broke open the breech, and kneeling thrust her hand into one end of the pouch, pulled out a cartridge with its red case and brass percussion cap, slid it into the breech opening, ramming it home. She pushed the shotgun through the six or so inches of open window, cradled the stock against her cheek, forced back the hammer claw with her thumb as she had seen him do it. It clicked ready to fire. She held it close to her, trembling, taking a sight along the barrel, smelling now the sobering odour of its varnish and fine metal. She searched the break in the hedge for a glimpse of Killadoon wall, his white shirt.

Behind the hedge he was cycling, with not a care in the world, whistling. '*Muss i' denn muss i' denn zum Städele . . .*'

She brought her finger to the wicked curved tongue of the trigger, closed her eyes, thinking wildly, I'll put a stop to your fun, mister; and squeezed it slowly into her.

The gun, louder than she could ever have imagined, roared and thundered in the bedroom. The charge emptied itself into the hedge. A lick of flame on the heart; blue smoke, a whiff of cordite. She had murdered him through the hedge. She squeezed, squeezing all her rancour and hurt feelings to herself.

There it was, in a split second, the mistake of a lifetime. The thick obscene feel of it and the kick, the sensation of the stock cushioned in her arms, the recoil . . . she heard and felt nothing more. The fingers of her left hand spread themselves along the hot barrel. Had she given him time enough, waited long enough and allowed sufficient time for him to get out of harm's way? Or had she killed him? She would give her life to take it back again, not to injure him.

Trembling worse and worse, shaken and groaning (she was being torn bodily apart), her heart twisted in a vice. She had killed him. She closed her eyes then and life went away. The gun clattered on the stones outside.

But beyond the hedge, out of range, Otto, given a new lease of life, cycled at top speed, bearing down on the pedals, towards Temple Mills and Molly Cushen's arms.

33

Time passed. The pale white privet flowers vanished from the hedges. By mid-October only the blackberries remained. By then the swallows had gone too. Before the end of the month the bush bearing privet berries had begun to fade and wither after the blossoms. Over Castletown front gate the rain streamed down the eroding forms of the sphinxes, down their simple faces, tautened ribs, down the gate columns embellished with bas-relief targe and drooping garland of ivy. The leaves on the lime trees had turned the colour of copper. Water streamed down the walls of Christ's Church within the estate grounds, down the spears of the gate. She stood there, facing the open gate, looking along the avenue of limes darkening in the rain.

November:

Stri-stro-stroh
Der Sommerdag is Do ...

He had sung that foolish old song, learnt as a child. German children, holding aloft long pretzels, had sung it before him, marching in procession through the streets of Starnberg.

Weeping gates.

Children with satchels on their backs, dressed already for winter, passed in under the dripping arch of the convent gate on their way to school. Second Infants; Sister Rumold. They had learnt the penny Catechism, chanting behind the school wall, God-is-the-Creator-and-sovereign-Lord-of-Heaven-and-Earth-and-of-all-things. From the road before Brady's corner she saw the spire of the obelisk risen against a grey November sky and knew that winter had begun. Otto was gone. One grey drab lifeless day followed another.

In December on Castletown drive the water formed in a long irregular puddle between the grass verge and the down-slope of the avenue. In the distance the limes seemed to draw together. Dark places had rotted into the drenched boles where yet more water had collected in rotten cavities and holes. Somewhere in herself too pain had lodged itself. Clenching her teeth she tried to control it, but could not. No. For at night now she wept, long and bitterly, for her condition, hours at a stretch, – she could not control it. Only a week previously she had made a painful discovery. It was while taking a bath before going to bed.

She ran a good hot bath, as hot as she could bear, and climbed into it. She lay in it for a long time, loath to leave it, staring up at the white celluloid picture which had come from Melview and had been with her since she was a child. Two Mabel Lucie Attwell infants in a bath, rosy of cheek, tubby of limb, one with a yellow tuft of hair, a chubby leg up, balancing a sponge. And below that a motto for deportment which she could not see from where she lay.

Her stomach was submerged, hot steam drifted about her, fogging up the window. Something something daughter. She would stay where she was a little longer, she felt so relaxed at last, and then pull out the plug . . .

She caught it between her toes and pulled. The water began to flow away. The adornments of her nature came into view. At one time she had been rather ashamed of it all. Something something you never oughter. Never leave the bathroom wet. White stomach. Nor leave the soap still in the water. Curly hair. *Flocci*. The hairs of her lower stomach, darkly curling out, blackened wettish grass, at first submerged, now fully exposed. The hairs began to stretch out. Grass, thrawneens after rain, the water level sinks to nothing . . . sunken now . . . withdrawn . . . has shrivelled away to nothing. Water draining away rapidly now, gurgling down the drain . . . and what remains? I remain, I, Imogen Langrishe, loved and left by Otto Beck . . . inundated ground, uncurling hair (. . . the grasses began to stretch themselves, free in the warm air), with slack loosened stomach muscles . . . now to receive to enjoy . . . (her

229

heart gave a strong flutter). Her stomach was a mound, a hillock, a rounded white hill, grass grew at the foot, always a bit of a bulge, although Otto had liked bulges on women (and did she imagine it or were her breasts . . . ?) . . . He had not liked her to wear a belt or a corset . . . but my *seat*, Otto, it should be flat! . . . don't grudge what God has given you, Otto said . . . Nor leave the bathroom wet, nor leave the soap still in the water . . .

Her stomach was now fully exposed. Water in the cup of her navel. A drop rolled down. It was time to get out. The bathroom was well heated. But there was something about her stomach . . . too full . . . and not a heavy meal before bed by any means . . . something flowed under her . . . daughter wet . . . never leave the soap still in . . . daughter daughter . . . it moved, undulated, a muscle . . . feeling of nausea fright, – with shock she was right up against it . . . another second now and she would be confronted with it . . . why to lose all taste for cigarettes? . . . didn't they say that was one of the . . . the symptoms? All those weeks . . . *months* now . . . feeling miserable beyond words, worn out, grieving for herself because he had gone and so callously . . . just sending back for the rest of his belongings . . . and the men driving off with the packing-cases on a dray and the gate being closed. Miserable beyond words, and feeling that she was now over forty and recalling what Otto had once said about the August of a woman's life, probably a quotation like most of his sayings, to the effect that a woman of forty was no longer anything to anyone save to the men who had loved her in her youth, – probably intended as a backhander, although he never knew her age. All that time and she had never once thought of the one obvious thing, (not that she was forty and that no one would want her, because Otto had wanted her, for how many times had she said, you only love my body), the one obvious stroke of misfortune that would finally finish her off in the eyes of the locals, namely, that she was in the family way, no possible doubt of it now. She looked down in horror at her stomach. That had put the lid on it. In a little while she climbed slowly out of the bath, holding her burden with one hand.

And then to wake up next day and to know it. Seized with restlessness and horror she had dressed and gone out. And then the day after. And the day after that. And how to hide it. Putting on weight. Impossible to hide it. Distracted and not knowing what to do.

She began to drink heavily. All those days, weeks, finally months. Days, but none as bad as the first. The terrible first day, walking by herself near Oakley Park. Dark bramble bushes in scurvy fields. A pasturage of nettles and thistles near the road, and standing quite near, seen as soon as she rounded a bush, a young boy standing there holding a shell cupped to his ear, his head to one side, his eyes closed, raggedly dressed, standing there among the nettles in the weak December sun, backed by a great disturbance of clouds piling up over the hills, which seemed to have drawn closer, the blue Dublin hills. Music had suddenly blared out of the square Georgian house and he removed the shell from his ear and saw her and then she had heard the shouts of children, and turning saw others engaged in a disorganized game of football, their coats doing service as goalposts, playing football in Oakley Park land where they had no right to be, where she had no right to be.

34

The child is dead. Stillborn. I will not think of it. It's gone to join
the angels in *Limbus Patrum* . . . or rather the other place, that
nebulous region, where neither the damned nor the saved go,
deported into Limbo. I'll think of the terrace and below it the
wood, the greenness, canopy of tall beech trees and conifers, steps
leading down, three hundred or maybe even five hundred . . . far
down at all events. I wanted to go all the way down and kill it, stop
it living in me. I must have been mad that day. The path was
covered in leaves. It was like under the sea. Sun filtering down.
The swimming-pool there at the bottom which had not been used
for years, empty of water, just a few feet of brown leaves. I was
walking there. That was England. I will not think of it.

I will think of it, that most terrible time for me. I didn't feel life,
didn't feel it moving at all for a week. The baby had ceased to
move, waiting to see what I would do, walking down those steps
trying to kill it. I hadn't killed it because it had already ceased to
move, it was already without life, and I not knowing whether it was
dead or not inside me. Had I a dead baby there? Was I carrying a
dead child? Because its blood was different to mine I made it
suffer. It was getting no food, was dying, I didn't know. How could
I know all that unless it was told to me? I imagined that he would
come back because he would want to see his child, yet how could
he know? I could not get in touch with him. That thing dug up in
the garden by Otto, put in bed by me and crowned with a laurel
wreath and christened in derision 'the Comforter', it resembled in
a way the drawings I did of men on the clapboard walls of the
summerhouse at Melview, prodigies of bad perspective and faulty
anatomy, all seen in profile, just the head and shoulders of avatars,

if that's the word, avatars – freaks of nature anyway. His child, I thought too that it would be deformed in some way . . . that head and shoulders of a man, the cement mould dug up out of the ground by Otto's spade, its blank eye sockets, heavy presence, dismembered being. His child would be heavy too, impossibly so. Then the child dead and no reason for him ever to come back. My dead child no longer in existence. Three months before I knew. I couldn't tell for sure until that time in the bath. That day I felt so miserable, wretched beyond words. Later it was different. Erotic feelings in the night time and in the day time. I thought, gradually my shape will change and I will disappear from them. A feeling of secrecy and triumph. I began to notice children for the first time. The schoolchildren creeping along by the wall to the convent at Celbridge, satchels on their backs, snot on their sleeves, stones where their hearts should be.

Three months of knowing . . . the drawstring didn't hold, muscle didn't hold . . . child came half out . . . had to be pushed back and muscle sewn up . . . it rotted in there . . . germs killed it . . . exposure to the air. After the thing, the cervix, had been sewn up . . . it didn't come away in a piece . . . decaying matter . . . six months old . . . what size, I asked him, what size? Oh *that* size, the doctor said, holding out his clasped hands. My stillborn child of that size, his child, turned over inside me and choked itself. The stitches undone . . . whole thing came away . . . flood of dead matter . . . he wouldn't let me see it . . . he said it was a little girl . . . he thought I never knew how it died . . . I knew well enough how it died. The dead child no longer in existence. I came back here, as I had to come back, not recovered. I told them a cock and bull story to the effect that I had German measles, a rash on unspecified parts of me. That seemed to satisfy them. German measles. Not showing on my face, hands, legs. I don't think sly-puss believed me, wouldn't be surprised if she had her eye on him herself, I don't care particularly. I don't care about anything now. Then to go away. To England, to Harrogate in York-shire, to all those steps going down and the unutterable misery of knowing then that it was all finished.

I am walking here in Killadoon estate where I have no right to be, but it's quiet here, and I am out of the way. The mound with bushes growing on it, it's supposed to be a cold storage plant from the old times ... I see its barred window and the blackness beyond. Nearing the herd's cottage now ... that gate ... the cattle-trap, if that's what it's called. I walk to one side. Wet field after wet field. It has rained. I walk on the avenue towards the back gate ... Brazill's house is on the left, then Hollingsworth's.

I hear the sound of a football, thuds, strife. I feel so ... Over the hedge I see them. The young men from the Council houses are kicking a football – one in a blue-and-white Celbridge jersey. I hear the thump of boot on ball and there the sodden orb is rising, going over the trees, and falling slowly, shedding drops of water. A boot connects with it and again it blunders up into the air.

– Get up to your man!
– Burst the goalie!
– Get into him, Josey!

I am there, watching, unescorted. I am walking by. They know me by sight but will not look at me. *The* Miss Imogen of Springfield, the scandalous one, she is walking by. Do they know? They know everything. The knowing girls calling out, jeering voices behind the hedge, 'Who were you with last night, Mister?' Going off laughing on the road, calling back. Otto (my backyard date) smiling. He was too free with them; confidences, indiscretions, I dare say, at night in Breen's with the men, drinking whisky, perhaps discussing me, he was quite capable of that, would say anything when he was drunk.

Now the wood closes around me, wet decaying vegetation, the look of things on a day of scarce sun and travelling showers. Damp undergrowth, wet trees, the deeply rutted way where carts have gone before me, my feet sucking and squelching on the sodden ground. This winter will never end. I don't want it to end. My feet have taken me to here. Before me this still pond of stagnant greenish slime, with reflections of bare trees, a still forest motionless in its silent depths. Matter floats on the surface, bubbles rise, not a sound. The wear and tear of long ago, the illusion too, that others can participate in one's life shattered for good and all. Moss, fungus, smells of the wood enter my lungs, fill me. There, the sound of a rotten branch parting from some tree. And in the silence that follows, far off, gunshots echo in Killadoon.

III
1938

'... water and thornes, with bogges or rotten plashie ground on either side.'

Sir James Perrott
The Chronicle of Ireland
1584–1608

35

The hearse stood at the gate, emptied of its bier and flowers. Shouldering the coffin the pallbearers bore it slowly along the centre lane between the cypress trees and the headstones. Their footsteps, not in time, shuffled over the loose gravel. The entire cortege passed on into Donycomper cemetery.

I am among them, Imogen thought.

They advanced along the main path, elderly pallbearers making heavy weather of their burden. High on their shoulders the varnished coffin, known to her down to its minutest details. The slowly advancing procession moved along between the lanes of trees. Erected by Patrick Mahon, Coneyburrow, Celbridge. In honour of his mother. May God have mercy. In loving memory Patrick Kevany. Died November 1928. Jesus Mercy.

They arrived at the open grave. Now they had to get it down somehow. Two of the undertaker's mutes hurried forward to lend a hand. And between them, feet struggling for a purchase on the very edge, they managed to lower the coffin safely into the ropes laid ready.

There in an untidy circle were assembled a crowd of people whom Imogen had never seen in her life before. The convent children stood looking up at their elders and betters and then down in wonder at the hole before them, into which a dead person was about to go. Some of the little girls held bunches of flowers.

She saw the coifs and bloodless faces of Holy Faith nuns back among the trees. Sister Digna was there. The white mute faces were watching her, Imogen Langrishe, the eccentric lapsed convert daughter of lapsed convert parents, (since deceased).

She stood there before the open grave with a wreath in her gloved hand, by Lily attired in decorous black, waiting for the priest to arrive and say a last prayer over her remains. He had been delayed in the village and was coming on his bicycle. The news arrived just ahead of him. He had arrived; he was at the gate.

The priest, a blond big-boned rustic man in surplice and stole, stood by the coffin-head with all the stormy sky reflected in his face, speaking the words of his office, asserting his will against them, raising and lowering his heavy eyebrows, pumping up something portentous from within himself. Then his heavy head, rather hopeless, bent near-sighted over the close print, and coughing at times behind his hand, he read out the Office for the Dead. He read badly.

He stood there heavy, inflexible, holding the breviary in his raw hands, his heels in the clay of the recently dug grave; bringing his broad fingers together, he raised the breviary to his chest and began with involuted hands to intone a prayer in a resonant baritone voice for the repose of the departed soul of Helen Langrishe. Then he opened the book at a marked page and began to read aloud again in Latin, turning the worn pages, declaiming alone. Moistening his index finger and thumb, he turned a page and went on reading aloud. Seeking inspiration, he raised his eyes heavenwards, revealing a strong blue-shadowed male neck shaved to the quick. When he summoned his gaze back to the printed page it did indeed seem that an improved light had been shed upon the text, for he read with more force and assurance, and with a marked acceleration of delivery. Behind him the local gentry and their ladies stood a little apart. The ladies and gentlemen of the Kildare Hunt. Imogen thought that she recognized the choleric features of Lady Brooke, of Pickering Forest.

The villagers, not wishing to miss anything, had assembled in force. The low cemetery wall was lined with their faces. Here and there children were being lifted up to gain a better view. She thought she recognized faces from her childhood. The bodies might have thickened and coarsened, but the character of the faces had not altered much. Across the road a flock of crows were wheeling and cawing over the trees.

And I, – I look down into the grave, into a hole in the earth once reserved for Mamma and the others and now got ready for her and I hear a stream running by and far away near Hazelhatch, the sound of a train passing over the tracks of the Great Southern & Western Railway, and I think, *All right, all right* (my feet frozen in the clammy yellow leaves and in the clay) *everything I breathe of this polluted air is my life, but not for her down there presently . . .*

At that moment they came forward.

Two little urchins came with stiff school-trained decorum to lay their bouquets of violets on the bank of clay alongside ours. They bent together and left them there among the other wreaths. As they passed, going back, I felt a cold something touch my flesh between glove and coat sleeve and through my veil I saw a little waif's face staring up at me. Then she turned away and was gone. My hands were frozen in their woollen mittens, my feet chilled to the bone. I looked up and saw a mass of sluggish cloud being carried down the wind towards Rathcoffey. The air was chilly, typical March weather. I was veiled and in deep mourning; some of the others wore diamond-shaped pieces of crêpe stitched to the upper arm of their coats, out of respect for the dead. I felt no different; certainly I felt no great sorrow for her in my heart. As I looked down into the grave with the sides all pleated with laurel and little white flowers and the bottom covered in fresh green grass, it dropped away before my eyes until the pit was bottomless and all I could see was this dark awful hole in the earth opening up and out of the darkness down there a dank wind blowing, I could feel it on my hands, and I was back again frightened under Killadoon wall, in the middle of the hole.

I saw a frog hopping about below in the grave. It was jumping against one of the sides, attempting to gain a hold and hopping back again. I took a step forward until I stood on the edge of the grave and looked down. Well, it was only a frog that had fallen in, its protrudent glazed eyes looking in stark amazement at all the greenery around it, the festivity, then filming over, as if it had had enough.

I was in the middle of the hole. It was an opening at the base of the wall separating Mangan's field and Killadoon estate. Some of the stones had been removed, presenting an entrance of sorts with scant headroom above. The stones were not of regular proportion but offered now smooth now jagged surfaces that were sharp and difficult to negotiate. Some of the earth had been tunnelled out,

239

perhaps by the dogs, so I crawled down into flints and dust . . . The smell of the field I had just left, the close dry smell of the smell of the hole . . . then the scents of the summer wood, the marine whiffs of its undergrowth . . . the trees in leaf permitting only a filtered sunlight down . . . there everything is green and shadowy by the quietly flowing river . . .

I went through the hole with increasing difficulty . . . in dread of the mass of stone over me . . . attempting it alone I was held fast, not being able to move forward or back, caught between two spurs of stone . . .

Lying there in the dark among the woodlice and other ground insects, in my mouth the taste of fallen mortar and weeds, I heard the wind in the wood and the noises that begin there at night, a prey to curious fancies.

A face had drawn close to mine in the dark for I could feel its heated breath on my hands.

When I came to my senses darkness had fallen. I had fought to free myself as though I were struggling for my life, and had only succeeded in getting inextricably caught between two spurs of limestone that pinched my sides and would not let me turn one way or the other. I did not know where I was at first; but presently I did, and all the terror rushed back to me. Lying there in the dark among the woodlice and the ground insects, in my mouth the taste of fallen mortar and the weeds, I heard the wind playing in the wood, and the noises that begin there at night, and I fell a prey to curious and disturbing fancies. I imagined a creature's face had drawn close to me in the dark: I swear I could feel the heated breath on my hand where the fingers had ventured out through the wall, though the rest of me could not follow. And then that went away, and other terrors took its place. I thought a great abyss fell away on the other side of the wall from which the wind was coming, and my hand grew heavy as lead, protruding there where it should have drawn back. And then all the trees had gone and there was a level plain on the other side and this wind was feeding on my hand, drawing me out into places where I should not go, but all the time the pressure on the small of my back persisted, as though hands were pressing me down, among the mortar and the dust and the weeds out of which I would never escape.

A long time seemed to elapse before I saw lights bobbing through the wood which had closed around me again. They came nearer and I heard voices; it was the men from the estate coming with carriage lamps to find me. Emily, having first led them to the river, had told them where they might find me. They found me there and had to dig me out, and brought me back, safe home.

Later, in my religious phase, when I read of the apostle Thomas putting his finger in Jesus' side I remembered my old childish terror and felt that he must have felt something like it too, putting his doubtful finger into God's fire. But in those days I had very fancy notions, later to be superseded by a certain complacency of outlook, for good or ill. But there in Donycomper it all rushed back to me.

They lifted up the coffin then, and I moved back as they began to head it in. The big oblong elm box went in the entire length of the grave, going down bigger than you would ever suppose necessary. And then I felt my face going stiff inside my veil, for I realized, as they did too, that it would not fit. They had dug the grave wide enough and deep enough, though not long enough. They tried to force it down. It resisted and seemed to grow bigger. Then I gave up and looked away. The sky, with cloud formations shifting about, seemed calm as ever, with an air of nothing settled; rain was on the way. I was expecting something, one of the mutes to come forward and stamp in the coffin, or the lid to fly off, something unthinkable. Nothing of the sort happened, for when I looked again they had lifted it out, both of them sweating profusely, and now its polished ends and sides were smeared and soiled with clay and grave-mould, and our wreaths had fallen sideways from it. They set it lopsided on the bank of earth and hurried away for shovels. A splash of rain fell penetrating the veil on my face and I began to cry. I wept for shame because I could not endure this humiliation any longer. Not any longer.

In a short while they came back with long roadmenders' shovels and one of them got down into the grave. I was waiting for him to tread on the frog but he pretended not to notice or else did not see, at all events he left it alone. They began to work on the grave,

241

one above and one below, the shovelfuls of earth falling fast, but not as fast as my tears nor as loud as poor Lily's wailing. And throughout all this the priest was leading the crowd in the singing of a hymn – a lamentable choral work for a mixed choir of untried voices, men, women and children, the voices blown about in the wind that was now rising, bringing the rain. To Jesus, heart all bur-burning.

At last it was done; made all ready for her. They had lengthened it sufficiently to receive her and came out with awful faces as if in a bad temper and took the coffin up again. The rain started to come down heavily as they lowered it in. I knew the cold feel of it against my face and hands as this bottomless pit began slowly closing before me. I had raised my veil and the tears running down my face were falling into the grave. The rain, falling at an angle, scarcely touched the coffin, but my hot tears fell directly upon it, and I fancied they made a hollow sound. I stood there surrounded by a crowd of imbeciles and their suddenly raised umbrellas, while all around me more and more silk was being hoisted up. The priest was protected under one. The rain now sweeping across the graveyard made on the stretched black silk a continuous but varying volume of sound that was almost like applause. The mourners stood under their cover while the rain poured down. All of them were flying backward in their heavy thoughts, confusing incidents that concerned themselves only with other incidents that concerned themselves and the deceased, hopelessly entangled with dread thoughts of their own last end. They were grateful for the rain, somehow it made things easier, united them all under it; for many were embarrassed, you could give them that at least; nobody knew anybody else there or where they came from, seeing the principal mourners came from outside the County, old tennis partners and relics from the heydays in Springfield House. A little later the rain would abate and then cease; then it would be time for the last act of the farce to begin; I mean the condolences for the bereaved.

Then the fiasco in Latin was finished at last and the book shut. The priest flung a handful of earth onto the coffin and the grave-diggers spat on their hands and began to push earth over it. Scraping their shovels sideways and letting it fall in, they covered it to a depth of perhaps two feet, then stood resting on their handles. The funeral to all intents and purposes was now over.

I stood over the hole for the last time and knew that she was down there, gone from us, down in the bottom of the world. All the dead things that were piled there one upon the other since Donycomper began, parting their stiff ranks a little, allowed her in. And is it not strange, most strange, that a life which can be so positive, so placed, going on for years, seemingly endless, can one day go; and, which is strangest of all, leave little or no trace? She had passed below us, going into eternity. Even as I looked some earth collapsed into the grave. Gaining speed as it fell, it rattled over the sunken coffin. My heart missed a beat then, why not, seeing it's the last sound our heart recognizes, responds to, even if it is dead, the echo of a life that still persists in spite of all, before it loses every contact with the living and their grand ways. Yes, the earth, a small portion of which had been disturbed to make room for Helen, was subsiding into place once more, and nothing would ever change again.

Through a gap in the cypress trees the wind blew coldly out of a murky sky and more earth collapsed into the open grave. *Le vent chant dans le cordage.* Nothing was ever still in the world. I felt miserable beyond words and wished I were elsewhere. Now a great pulling off of gloves began as they came around us, and I saw faces that I never saw in my life before or ever wish to see again, offering me their warm sympathy and, worse still, their warm hands. *All right*, I thought, *all right now; let it be.* And they came around me.

– I have many pleasant recollections of her . . . one said in an affected sing-song way.

A little man with a small head, dressed in a heavy overcoat with buttons all the way down, holding my hand with a manly grip that I neither relished nor attempted to return. He was pleased with himself, he had said the sincere thing, employed the unforgettable phrase that touches the heart, and he would be remembered for it. A fool of a man.

– All of the best! a voice said in a loud heartfelt tone, though presumably in error.

– Who is that? I asked Lily. Do we know him?

– Why certainly we do, Lily said, it's the kind Dr Broadbent.

Then began a truly endless shaking of hands. I hate the touch of hands. The priest himself had offered me his moist palm, the benison of his anointed touch, and I had to accept it. And offered me as well the sincerity of his watery brown eyes, which I was obliged to look into. He said something under his breath to me. It might have been *I'll remember her in my prayers*. Or *I'll remember you in my prayers*. He went after the others who were passing through the gate. He seemed tired. At all events it was with an air of constraint and weariness that he went away.

It turned out to be only a shower after all, for they were all folding their umbrellas, passing by on the opposite side of the wall, shaking out the last drops as they went. The villagers were calling out to each other that it was clearing up, thanks be to God. The gravediggers began working again, filling in the grave now. I went away. True enough, it was clearing – though the sky, swept clear of clouds and discoloured in places, as if broken by the storm, still seemed on the point of shedding a few further tears.

36

'ANSCHLUSS!
FINAL DOWNFALL OF AUSTRIA
GERMAN TROOPS POUR IN'

'Innsbruck Occupied. War-planes land at Linz.
'Since 5.30 this morning units of the German Army have been marching across the frontiers of German-Austria.

German bombing squadrons are flying over Vienna. Hitler will arrive at Linz this afternoon. Tomorrow he is expected in Vienna.'

'The small portion of what remains of the mighty Empire of the Hapsburgs has passed under the sign of the Swastika. Today it enters on a new phase of its existence as a Nazi state, and part of the German Reich . . .'
'The first German troops arrived in Vienna on the night of the day that Dr Schuschnigg, the last Austrian Chancellor, should have held his plebiscite on March 13. They were accompanied by the dreaded SS guards whose chief, the head of the Gestapo, Herr Himmler, were sent to Vienna by airplane on Saturday, March 12, to make sure that none of Herr Hitler's intended victims escaped. That same evening it was announced that Austria had become part of Greater Germany . . .'

Imogen sat subdued in Helen's room, reading the *Saturday Herald* of the preceding day. She laid it aside and picked up Wednesday's paper, March 16.

'MAJOR FEY, "STRONG MAN"
OF AUSTRIA, FOUND SHOT
DEAD.'

'Suicide in Vienna flat. Wife and son also die from gun wounds. Other prominent Austrians kill themselves.'
'Latest moves in Europe. Two Dictators speak today.'

and further down the page:

'Major Fey founded the Heimwehr after the war. He was with Dr Dolfuss when the latter was assassinated in the Nazi revolt of 1934, and later held a Cabinet post under Dr Schuschnigg. It was stated that he would never tolerate Nazi influence in Austria.'
'Also found dead this morning was Professor Gustav Bayer, aged 69, of the University of Innsbruck, who is reported to have first poisoned his daughter and then himself.'

At the foot of the page in a Reuter's block, she read:

'DR SCHUSCHNIGG'

'Vienna, Wednesday.
Nothing is known in official circles here of the reported marriage of Dr Schuschnigg and the Countess Vera Fugger. Although improbable, it is impossible to confirm or deny the report. – Reuter.'

Imogen laid aside the paper and stood up. What did it mean? That another senseless war was about to begin? She went to the makeshift altar and collected some of the Mass cards and brought them over to Helen's bed and laid herself down on it. They had been placed on the lid of the coffin and handed out to Lily and herself when the Requiem Mass was over. She had not opened any of them. She opened one of them now.

A dove setting off between flower petals on an oval of silver. A silver Madonna with a blue inner surround. 'O Mary conceived without sin pray for us who have recourse to thee.' A stylish cross. 'Sincere sympathy (Gothic script).' The names Mr & Mrs Dempsey written in pen.

Inner leaf. The Lamb in a surround of flame. 'The Holy Sacrifice of the Mass will be offered for the repose of the soul of Miss Helen Langrishe. R.I.P.' Picture. A bearded priest saying Mass, taken at the Consecration, his hands upraised, holding up the blessed Host. The altar-boy holding up his chasuble, about to ring the bell.

Other facing leaf. The Lamb again. More flowers. 'With sincere sympathy from (in pen) C. A. Maxwell.' Celebrant: Rev. Fr D. Binchey, PP.

Back leaf. 'Grant we beseech thee O Lord that the soul of thy servant be purified by the sacrifice and receive both pardon and eternal rest.' Very ornate.

She picked up another card and examined it. It was in white, with a thin black cross above the line 'Requiescat in Pace.' Inner leaf: a blank white page with the name of the Celebrant after that title at the foot. Facing page: 'As a sincere expression of deepest sympathy the Holy Sacrifice of the Mass will be offered for the happy repose of . . . Miss Helen Langrishe' (written in pen) . . . 'from . . . Mr & Mrs T. Farrell' (written in pen).

They had sat in the front of the church during the Requiem Mass. Mass over, all had converged on the coffin which was resting on trestles at the back of the church, near an alcove separated from the rest of the church by a grillwork gate. Behind this, rising up twelve feet or so, a dark mass of winged figures that might have been the ornate steeple of another church erupting through the floor. The cards were handed out to them, the sisters of the deceased, then the coffin was placed on a trolley and wheeled out to the waiting hearse which was parked in the church yard. The undertaker's men placed the coffin in and the hearse drove out at a funereal pace, the procession falling in behind for the walk to Donycomper. Imogen dipped her hand in the holy water font with 'Pray for Sean Cummins' cut into it, and went out first.

And then the funeral.

Imogen lay resting on Helen's bed, reading the entertainment section of the evening paper, four days old. *Dr Syn*, with George Arliss, was still playing at the Grand Central. *The Edge of the World* ('Selected as one of the best pictures of the year'), starring Niall MacGinnis and Belle Chrystall, was coming to the Pillar Picture House. March of Time, 3rd year. *It's Love I'm After* was still showing at the Savoy. Leslie Howard, Bette Davis. A photograph of the German cameraman Karl Freund holding up a reel of film to the light. Noted for the great attention he pays to detail . . . will be remembered for his brilliant work filming *The Good Earth*. Naas Rugby Dinner & Dance. St Patrick's night (March 17th), Lawlor's Ballroom. Admission 10s. (including tax). The white face of the veteran actor George Arliss stared at her from his black box. *Dr*

Syn. Imogen laid aside the paper and lay staring up at the ceiling where there was a cluster of circular discolorations, full circles or parts of circles spreading out haphazardly.

Helen had gone out for the last time a year ago to Donycomper, almost a year, for the last time, and after that hardly ever stirred from the house. A year of wasting away and illness. And now dead. Helen dead. She would half-lie, half-sit mostly, silent on a chair for periods, sighing, always sighing and restless, but could not sit for long. And so it was being seated all day or lying down on brittle bones, and no one to listen to or talk to, and solitude insupportable to a mind which is not easy. She wouldn't listen to anyone towards the end, had no strength left in her legs, with great effort shuffled about the house. She said she couldn't stand the sound of people walking about over her head. So she was spending more and more time upstairs, and latterly all the time.

Imogen could hardly bring herself to look at her dead sister – she had shrunken so, with a white rose in her mouth and cotton wool up her nose; the eyelids, closed for good, were superhumanly heavy, and the complexion of the corpse was bad – cold grey spongy skin.

Her eyes, when she was alive, one did not notice, nor her face nor its habitual expression. One noticed her eyes not because they were beautiful, for they were not, but because of the expression that dwelt in them – a fitful and anxious brightness.

Her heavy eyelids; a queer complexion; spongy skin; cotton wool up her nose. Helen wearing her bad old hat, turning away with indifference, cold. Hanging onto life, aged greatly in a year of worry and uncertainty. Hepatitis – and then, to cap it all, a stroke. No longer walking out. A stiff figure going by the tennis court, by frozen worm-casts.

– Hepatitis . . . it's a kind of chronic jaundice the doctor said. She said, 'When I look into the mirror now, I see an old, old woman, last week I had such a terrible pain.' She had become very morbid in herself, turning away from life, seeing only the bad things in it, God knows there are enough of them. Her stiff manner with me when I brought barley sugar from the village for her, because she could smell my breath, sitting up on her chair close to the window, looking out at the hills where there was snow, only opening her mouth to tell me that the milk bill was up to £9 or to say, we live uncomfortably . . . I'll die uncomfortably.

On the makeshift altar the candle flame sinking when she took the sacrament. I saw the perspiration on her powdered face. She had difficulty in swallowing. Her mouth open to receive, her neck stretched. She received the Host on her tongue, and then found difficulty swallowing, perspiration on her forehead, the priest's bulk over her.

Hanging on, obstinate. The illness made her very stooped. When she wore her wretched old fox fur she was poor Robinson Crusoe coming from the other side of the island with a kid for the pot. Her outfits were a sight to see.

And then no longer going out. The need to exercise, the compulsion to move, to put one foot in front of the other, to get up an appetite – all that was over. Wintry air in the room. Retiring into herself. Palely in the light which is already a twilight. She lay awake in bed. Many troubles (her finger-drill). Many things troubled her. Tremor in the wasted temples behind which burned an intense heat, when I asked her would I get the priest.

I am alone. Helen's dead. I remember her life, her peevish expression, austere bodice, don't-come-near-me eyes and difficult ways. Walking over the stiffened grass of the tennis court, walking by hard worm-casts.

Orphrey, white lace; the linen on the altar; the small feeble light before the crucifix. I heard the almost soundless crackle of its powdery wings. The perspiration started out on her face, but she managed to swallow. The moth was burning in the candle flame.

Her hands were locked, all of her locked . . . no more, no more Helen. The priest gave Extreme Unction. Sometimes life comes back, if God sees fit, considers it to be expedient. But on this occasion He had not seen fit. The priest washed his hands and went away. Helen seemed to be recovering; only to sink again, and died quite peacefully a week later.

Tu-quoque. We must all come to it.

It was dark, almost so, but for a candle butt that was going out on the mantelshelf. In the corners of the room the shadows wavered.

Yellowness of perfumed laburnum cascades over the gate; lilac, violets, Love-lies-bleeding, menace of a name and a presence. White smoke waving on a fine summer's day. A causeway of flowers. The wind in the beech again. *Le vent chant dans la cordage.* Trying to calm myself. Impossible to wait. A shower. The branches smoke!

That dirty ceiling. Far off by Hazelhatch the whistle of a train. This fear that gets into me; not that I will be wiped out, but that all will be wiped out – it'll pass, maybe. Sometime. But it begins now.

The rare Northern Lights were seen in the night sky over Vienna. All day long squadrons of heavy bombing planes flew low over the stricken city, going in to land at Aspern Airport. Himmler was landing.

That name – *Seyss-Inquart!*

Premonition of one's end.

(Tired out by the events of the day, Imogen felt herself sinking, drifting away as darkness was entering the room. It was cold. She covered herself with the eiderdown. The papers and Mass cards slid to the floor. In a short while she was sleeping; all in one piece, in a religious attitude, like a saint in a niche.)

37

Imogen awoke early. A church bell was ringing in the dark, the rope pulled by someone half asleep. She waited for half an hour, until some light had come into the sky, and then rose up. It was blowing hard.

Passing downstairs, letting herself out the back door, she crossed the yard and went through the stable passageway leading into the rockgarden, past the privy where Father had kept his petrol cans.

Shrubs and grass hid the pathways. The iron funnel of the cesspit chimney rose up clear of its mock maidenhair fern, which, grown top-heavy, had fallen of its own accord and was now beaten down flat by the winter's snow and rain. The summerhouse had all but collapsed after the snow. Its roof had fallen in at an angle and broken glass covered the floor; only the side windows remained intact. Imogen walked about for a while there.

She quit the rockery by the wooden door facing the bleach-green and turning left walked thirty paces or so, entering the front yard from that side. Her hens were picking about in the yard near the garage, where the Rover was down to its hubcaps, covered in henshit and feathers. They came running to her from every quarter, their wings out. It was an unprecedented hour for her to appear. She drove them off and with no particular purpose in mind entered the harness-room.

Broken sacks of wheat on the floor and against the walls, rotted harness equipment hanging there, rusted bridles and bits; a carpenter's bench crowded with forlorn things long out of use, files, horseshoes, a hammer, parts of a bicycle and a patched-up inner tube, a yellow box of French chalk. A short flight of wooden steps led to the hay loft above. On one wall hung a row of keys with buff labels attached. She took one down. Written on it in indelible pencil was, 'Rear Lodge'.

Taking a short cut through the side shrubbery she passed under the branches of the great beech tree, walking slowly. A little way on a pyrocantha bush grew, on fire with transparent red berries. She broke off a sprig and went on.

The back gate was closed. The lodge door was locked. It was difficult to effect an entry, for dirt and lumber had been piled against the door. She forced the door to give a little and edged her way in.

Such filth and disorder in the old rooms, a smell of poverty, disuse, rotting wainscoting and dirty beds. Wind echoing in the deserted cottage. The torn parlour wallpaper hung from the mildewed walls and on the floor matchboxes and scores of razor blades strewn about. Sets of old newspapers had been piled on the couch, *Heralds, Mails* and *Irish Fields*; their rank odour filled the room. The couch had broken asunder in places, exposing its rough horsehair and burst springs. The window curtains, blowing in on the draught, were disintegrating on the rails. Spiderwebs trailed from the corners of the ceiling and hung from the pictures. Articles had been shifted about in the room, and it looked as if someone had been living there.

She went back to the door and closed it; then went into the bedroom. Grey wintry air in the old deserted room. Someone had been there, no doubt of that. The mattress had been pulled from the bed and there was a bad smell.

Imogen crossed the parlour and went into the kitchen, and what she saw convinced her that someone had been living in the cottage, or was still living there. A few sacks of chaff had been pushed into one corner; there were pots and pans that might have belonged to a tinker – they certainly weren't hers; and on the floor a thick layer of grease, showing the marks of boots. She walked over this in distaste and stood at the window, staring out. The ash-pit was overflowing. A tyreless and chainless bicycle with a drenched saddle was foundering in a great pile of sodden newspapers, sacks and straw. Mice crawled over the junk. Tattered articles of clothing – beggar's rags – blew on the bushes. The potato drills had been flattened out and the rockery to all intents and purposes had

252

disappeared. Before her in the yard, face up and sodden through, a pair of poor man's black trousers lay with rusted tin fly buttons. She pushed the door open with her foot and stood there looking out, thinking. After a while she went back, this time to the room where formerly Otto had stored his books and papers.

A scene of even greater squalor there confronted her. The intruder had slept there, away from the road, facing the plantation where the feeble glimmer of his candle would not betray him. The mattress was on the floor. All about it his candles had dripped grease on the boards. A tinkerman, perhaps, had slept there, coming in from the back way.

Imogen, troubled, went back into the parlour and stood before the empty fire, looked up at the pictures draped with spiderwebs, under the wild naked woman with red hair and the volcano erupting lava into a nameless sea rimmed by stubby black trees. He had come when she was miserable and lost, telling his tall tales, putting his invincible mailed fist on woman's weakness.

When she heard a sound behind her she turned quickly. No, nothing. Grey light. The wind on the door. Nothing at all. She went to the window facing the avenue and stood there with her back to the windowsill. Tenuous air, bare fields, the beginning of a typical winter's day.

She turned her face to the window again, to a soft diffusion of winter light. The beginning of a mild March day. On the shadowed windowsill a few dead flies remained, leftovers. Hide away here, let the days pass and hope that things will change. Clouds were slowly passing across the window. Yes, that – or nothing at all. How the wind blows today!

Fiction in Paladin

In the Shadow of the Wind   £2.95   ☐
Anne Hébert
Winner of the Prix Femina
'A bewitching and savage novel . . . there is constant magic in it'
Le Matin

'Beautifully written with great simplicity and originality . . . an
unusual and haunting novel'
London Standard

Love is a Durable Fire   £2.95   ☐
Brian Burland
'Burland has the power to evoke time and place with total authority
. . . compelling . . . the stuff of which real literature is made'
Irish Times

To order direct from the publisher just tick the titles you want
and fill in the order form.

All these books are available at your local bookshop or newsagent, or can be ordered direct from the publisher.

To order direct from the publishers just tick the titles you want and fill in the form below.

Name _____

Address _____

_____

Send to:
Paladin Cash Sales
PO Box 11, Falmouth, Cornwall TR10 9EN.

Please enclose remittance to the value of the cover price plus:

UK 55p for the first book, 22p for the second book plus 14p per copy for each additional book ordered to a maximum charge of £1.75.

BFPO and Eire 55p for the first book, 22p for the second book plus 14p per copy for the next 7 books, thereafter 8p per book.

Overseas £1.25 for the first book and 31p for each additional book.

Paladin Books reserve the right to show new retail prices on covers, which may differ from those previously advertised in the text or elsewhere.